BRIAN BECKER

UNPARDONABLE

ISBN 978-1-54399-344-8 eBook 978-1-54399-345-5

In Memory of My Father, Benton Lee Becker

AUTHOR'S NOTE

I'm indebted to Adam Becker, Grace Chung Becker, Jeffrey Becker, Joanne Becker, Kira Becker, Robin Becker, Scott Becker, Eric Blum, Jon Cockes, Tom Coipuram, Gregg Goldfarb, Richard Haber, and Scott Smiley for their review, and to Michelle Horn for her editorial assistance.

This is a fiction work of alternative history. The Steuben family is entirely fictional, although they experience certain historical events that did occur, and scenes take place in certain facilities that were operational at the place and time stated in the story. The Peckertski family is based on the household of my paternal grandparents, whose name was actually simplified to "Becker" at Ellis Island several decades before they appear in this story.

Most of the other characters are people who lived and worked during these time periods. These represent a mix of "historical" figures whose actions and thoughts were contemporaneously well documented and other individuals that were known to live and work in certain places and times. The historical figures' spoken words are either taken verbatim from a known speech or I make my best interpretation of what they would say or do under the different circumstances laid out in the story.

The addresses and occupations of the other characters are historically accurate, but further details on them (actions, words, children's names, etc.) are typically the fiction of this story.

I'm heavily indebted to the many fine historical works and references that others have compiled. I include a full list of such sources at the conclusion of the book.

PROLOGUE

FALL 1937

With his Springfield Model 1861 rifle cocked and loaded, the assassin waited nervously behind a patch of oak trees beyond the old horse trail. Soon, he spotted his target—a tall, thin, black-haired man in his mid-fifties riding quickly uphill on a chestnut brown horse. The target's speed made for a much tougher shot, affording the assassin with only a single opportunity. He set, aimed, and fired.

But the rider maintained too fast of a pace for the assassin, and the bullet disappeared into the trees. The sound of applause competed with the sound of the assassin's rifle as he dropped it to the ground.

The spectators offered a standing ovation to the actors that had reenacted this famous scene outside Abraham Lincoln's summer cottage, as the target and the assassin took their respective bows.

The crowds gathered daily for the Lincoln Assassination Attempt on the grounds of the Old Soldiers' Home in Washington, DC. A retirement home for veterans from the Great War, the Spanish-American War, and Indian conflicts, this extensive facility with its rolling hills and mature trees had served as President Lincoln's summer home decades before in the

1860s. This free reenactment had become a very popular attraction among cost-conscious Depression-era families.

Seventy-six-year-old Benton Steuben frequently watched the early afternoon showing of the reenactment. Still a stocky and strong man with curly white hair, age had softened the intensity of Benton's facial features to present a more grandfatherly and approachable look. Only a small child at the time of the real assassination attempt during President Lincoln's first term, Benton would often entertain crowds after the show with stories about Washington, DC during that time period. Financially sound in his retirement, Benton always refused tips. But, he never refused requests for stories, and he always answered the questions fielded by any children.

The Lincoln cottage area used to stage the reenactment only constituted two of the 250 acres in Old Soldiers' Home. While originally designed for the veterans, the neighborhood children would use much of the remaining 248 acres for its trails, hills, and grassy fields to sled in the winter, ride bikes in the summer, and play baseball and football year-round. Eight-year-old Stanley and five-year-old Wally Peckertski spent more time playing at Old Soldiers' Home than any of the neighborhood kids after finishing their school days at the red brick school building on Decatur Street known as Barnard Elementary School.

One day in October 1937, after finishing the last story with a crowd of spectators, Benton Steuben walked the grounds of Old Soldiers' Home where he saw an older boy teaching a younger boy the finer points of football tackling. Both boys wore knickers, as they used their school book bags to mark the sidelines. First, the older boy with jet-black hair tackled the brown curly-haired younger one. Demonstrating that practice makes perfect, he took down the smaller boy ten straight times. Both were still smiling after, but three of their four knees were now bleeding.

Before going home to treat their wounds, the boys changed places where the younger boy tried to tackle the older boy. The younger boy made the tackle the first three times as his shirt ripped and his face bloodied, but finally the older boy used his superior strength to burst through on the fourth try. So excited to break the tackle, the boy kept accelerating well past the book bag sidelines. The younger boy looked up, and saw the older boy running at full speed without looking forward, and heading straight into an older man.

Benton Steuben felt a thud and noticed the young Stanley flat on the ground. Soon, guards and doctors from the medical facility ran to the scene to try to help.

"Please leave me room to look at him!" The young doctor quickly but efficiently examined Stanley, who remained on the ground unconscious.

After what seemed like much longer than a few seconds, Stanley's black eyes fluttered open.

Everyone breathed a sigh of relief to find that Stanley had sustained no injuries.

Once Stanley fully regained consciousness and stood up, Wally laughed. "Stanley, you fell just like you ran into a brick wall."

Recovered from the fall, Stanley regained his manners and approached the older man, "I'm very sorry for running into you, Mr. ..."

Offering a wide smile, the man focused his warm eyes on Stanley. "Steuben. Benton Steuben. And there's no need to apologize, young man. It's the most excitement I've had in a long time. I guess I'm just getting old—I saw you coming towards me, but I just couldn't react fast enough to get out of your way. Now that you know my name, maybe you two football players can tell me your names." Benton offered Stanley a hearty handshake.

"Well, I don't know. My parents always told us not to talk to strangers, so we probably shouldn't," Stanley said, while shaking Benton's hand.

"I understand that, but I think the guards and doctors here will need to get your names anyway so that they can tell your parents that you're OK," Benton smiled.

Wally was relieved to see his older brother unharmed, and he liked listening to Mr. Steuben. He blurted out with a trace of a lisp, "Yes, I'm Wally." He gestured toward his brother. "My brother Stanley tackled me pretty hard out there. I tried my best to stop him, but I just missed that last tackle."

While shaking Wally's hand, Benton looked at the brothers and said, "Well, my father used to tell me that a little bullying is a good thing. It toughens you up. I know I didn't like it when I was a kid, but I still remember that my older brother used to push me around and wrestle with me all of the time. I think my father was right. It's still a lot better than ending up like our neighbor, Harold Simpson. He stayed away from us boys as a kid. I don't know if that is why, as a grownup, he's been scared of his own shadow. He has to ask his wife permission to do anything. I'm pretty sure Stanley would have sent poor Harold to the hospital if he ran into him instead of me."

As the two brothers walked slowly around the grounds of Old Soldiers' Home laughing with Benton, Wally's ears perked up. "When did your older brother stop pushing you around, Mr. Steuben?"

"Well, my brother Nathan stopped pushing me around after I got old enough to push him back harder and win some of those wrestling matches. But, we never stopped competing against each other. Races. Wrestling. Baseball. Billiards. Darts. Push-ups. You name it. I never met a more competitive person than my big brother. He always said that he would rather compete and lose than to not compete at all," Benton said.

Stanley stood transfixed—this is not the kind of thing most old men would say. Mostly, he had heard old people tell him how different it was back in the "old days" before cars and electricity, but Benton Steuben just sounded like one of their friends from the neighborhood. By now, he felt it safe to speak with Benton Steuben as they approached the living quarters of the veterans. "I know what you mean. My brothers and I compete for everything from food to clothes to chores. Anyway, do you live here? Were you in one of the wars?"

Soon enough, Stanley and Wally began to find out a little about Benton Steuben. He lived a few blocks away in a row house at 4319 2nd Street NW. It had been built twenty years ago, and he had moved in seven years ago. Benton's spent every Wednesday afternoon at the Old Soldiers' Home, first watching the reenactment, and then catching up with some of his friends.

Stanley thought that Benton must have been a football player since he was so strong. But Benton had to disappoint Stanley on this point and told him there really wasn't much football being played when he was a young man in the 1860s and 1870s. Baseball had become popular, but Benton never was a serious player. At that news, Wally felt some disappointment as well.

The brothers left Old Soldiers' Home excited that evening, though, when Benton told them he had collected a lot of old baseball relics over the last sixty years. He wasn't sure how valuable they were, but he promised to bring them there for the boys to see the following Wednesday if they could take a break during their football training.

Visitors to the Old Soldiers' Home the following Wednesday could easily locate Benton Steuben. One could not help but notice that Benton was the only adult man on the grounds not wearing a hat. At a green picnic table in front of Scott Hall, Benton sat at the highest elevation in the area, in front of one of the city's tallest buildings as if he wanted the superior vantage point to anyone who might approach him.

Benton had been sorting through a pile of ancient baseball cards, pictures, programs, pins, caps, and shirts for fifteen minutes. His new friends soon came into view, racing toward him as if they had waited all week to see him. They arrived at his table, breathless, and shook Benton's hand.

"Boys, I forgot to mention that while I never played outside of my neighborhood, my brother was a pretty famous ballplayer. You may remember that my last name is Steuben and I told you that my brother's name was Nathan. If you are baseball fans, you have probably heard of him?" Benton said.

The boys' jaws dropped. Nathan Steuben had played for nearly twenty years in the National League and then managed for fifteen more years. A lifetime .300 hitter with more than 2,500 hits, newspaper reporters like Terri Coffin Jones speculated that he might be elected into the Baseball Hall of Fame's 1938 class next year, along with one of his ex-teammates, Charlie "Old Hoss" Radbourn. None of the "old-time" players from the 1800s had received the requisite number of votes to be elected in the first two classes, but baseball writers expected several to be voted in before the facility opened two years from now in Cooperstown, New York.

Benton smiled as he watched the boys leafing through his dusty baseball treasures. "So, I brought some pictures and old programs from when Nathan played and managed. I wanted to keep a few pictures and stories about Nathan for myself, but you boys may keep the rest of these materials. I think you will recognize my brother and some of his teammates. Please be careful to take good care of them since they are almost as old as I am. I've brought them in these leather folders to help you."

"Thank you!" rolled off the tongues of a distracted pair of boys. Their eyes wide open, the Peckertski boys sorted through all of the materials, recognizing famous players and managers from the past twenty years of nineteenth-century baseball: George Wright, Cap Anson, Willie Keeler, and Buck Ewing. They knew they had a treasure trove that would make all of their friends jealous. The boys began to place the pictures and cards into different piles for each team.

Before they knew it, the boys realized their parents would soon expect them home for dinner. They would first meet their brother, Melvin, who had recently matriculated as a freshman to the overcrowded Theodore Roosevelt High School.

"We have to leave, Mr. Steuben, to meet our brother, Melvin, at the streetcar turnaround," Stanley said while pointing towards the busy confluence of streets where the streetcar line ended down the hill.

"OK. It was good to see you boys again. Enjoy the baseball pictures and come visit me whenever you want." Benton gathered up the rest of his memorabilia and walked back to Scott Hall to visit with his old friends.

Stanley and Wally could not stop gushing over the baseball materials Benton had given them. Melvin and their parents would hear of nothing else over dinner the next few nights.

When Benton ran into the boys the following week, they gave him a hug and relayed a message from their mother.

"First, our mom said we have to be careful not to talk to strangers. She also told Stanley not to run into the strangers either. But when we told her more, she said you must be a very nice man. She wanted to thank you for giving us all of the baseball pictures, and she wanted to invite you over for dinner on Friday night. Our dad agreed with her like always. Are you married? Because Mom said your wife can come too. We live at 130 Webster Street," Wally said, without taking a breath.

"Stanley, I can see why you let Wally talk. He seems like he would be comfortable telling story after story in front of any audience. But, thank you. I guess you live almost in my backyard—with that alley behind us. I thought I recognized you when I saw you that first day. Neighborhood boys seem to always be playing football, baseball, or kick the can in that alley. And, so far, you haven't broken any of my windows. My neighbors have not been quite so lucky," Benton replied with a smirk.

Feeling a bit guilty over the broken windows, Stanley replied, "Yes, Wally talks more than everyone in our family combined. We will make sure to stay away from your windows though, Mr. Steuben."

With a small frown that only the highly-trained eye could see, Benton continued, "I would love to join you on Friday night. I am not married, so please tell your parents thank you and I will see you on Friday."

Later that afternoon, they agreed to meet at the Peckertskis' home at 7 PM on Friday.

Benton arrived at a crowded apartment with three active boys. The narrow apartment faced the complex's front yard and backed up to an alley. Certainly, Mrs. Peckertski had her hands full. While Mrs. Peckertski began preparing dinner in the kitchen, the boys introduced Benton to their brother, Melvin. The serious-looking, skinny, fourteen-year-old scratched his head while reviewing his math homework from the algebra book on his desk.

"This is the hardest class I've ever taken. I can barely understand what this book is saying. I can't see why I care how many cups of hot chocolate Johnny should buy in this problem or how fast the population of New York has grown in the other problem," Melvin said in a voice cracking from the effects of puberty.

Benton chuckled. "I sure can't help you with that. The Steuben math gene never got passed on to me. Geography was always my favorite. But, now with 38 states, studying geography is a lot harder for you to memorize the maps and state capitals than when I was going to school."

While the boys laughed with Benton, their parents came into the room. With a smile that put everyone in the room quickly at ease, the thirty-four-year-old head of the house politely offered his hand to his older guest. "Charles Peckertski and my wife, Gussie. May I take your coat and hat, Mr. Steuben?"

Taking off his light brown jacket after shaking hands, Benton replied, "It is my pleasure to meet you, Mr. Peckertski. Thank you for taking my jacket, but as your boys will tell you, I don't wear a hat. Maybe, that's why I've been able to keep my hair all of these seventy-six years."

Gussie Peckertski laughed. "I never liked hats anyway. Welcome to Webster Street, Mr. Steuben. We're so happy you could join us for our Friday dinner." Mrs. Peckertski, at an even five feet tall, looked up to meet Benton's eyes.

"Thank you for the kind invitation, and congratulations," Benton said. "When is your baby due, Mrs. Peckertski?"

"In February of next year," Mrs. Peckertski replied, smiling with her hands on her stomach.

Benton enjoyed the relaxed nature of the Peckertski home with its comfortable dining chairs, soft cushion couches, and containers of colorful hard candy. "The pleasure is all mine. I love wine, so I decided to bring these over for dinner with your boys graciously offering to carry the bottles," Benton offered.

"That's very generous of you. We'll probably need it, as our boys have a habit of skimming the cream from the top of the milk bottles sometime between when they are delivered and when they get placed in the ice box. Watery milk is no substitute for a good bottle of wine. Let's open the first bottle right now," Charles Peckertski said with a smile, as he brought his full five-foot-eight frame up to the counter to open the first bottle.

"I'm still in shock that my boys would actually help you carry the wine bottles. Whenever I see them after getting off the streetcar at the turn-around with my hands full of groceries, they act as if they have never seen me before. They're too busy trying to extract tips from the little old ladies struggling with their heavy bags," Gussie Peckertski moaned, as she readjusted her apron on her way back to the kitchen.

"Well, Mom, we do make some money with that, though. I need to start saving for that big mansion I plan to buy when I grow up," Wally said without a hint of sarcasm.

"Not to mention the weekly streetcar tickets we pick up on Friday night from the commuters that we turn around and sell to the tourists on the weekends. We have found lots of ways to make money from the streetcars," Stanley added.

A loud but gentle voice from the kitchen replied to her young boys, "Yes, I remember reading in the newspaper the other day that the two of you would soon take over John D. Rockefeller's spot as the world's richest man now that he has passed away."

Over dinner, Benton learned that the Peckertskis had married in 1922 in Elkton, Maryland, and that Gussie had grown up in Baltimore. Charles, born in Russia, worked as a life insurance salesman in Washington. Both growing up in large families of five children, the Peckertskis started their own family shortly after moving to Washington DC with the birth of Melvin in 1923. They had, however, just recently moved to the apartment on Webster Street.

Melvin was their oldest, and an "Irish twin" daughter followed. Sadly, she passed away when she was only six. Taken from them while Gussie was away one weekend in 1930 visiting her mother in Baltimore, Gussie had never really gotten over that loss. But, she didn't have time to mourn with three active boys to bring up. Now with a fourth child on the way, the Peckertskis hoped for a girl. Gussie's childless brother and sister-in-law who lived just over the Mason-Dixon line in Waynesboro, Pennsylvania even offered to take the child to live with them if the Peckertskis had another boy.

After several minutes of talking about their own family, Charles asked, "Mr. Steuben, why don't you tell us a bit about yourself?"

Benton thought for a while as he finished his first cup of wine, "Well, I've always been happy to talk about my family and old stories about

Washington, DC. They do make me very proud. I've always shied away from talking about myself, but maybe it's about time. I'm a pretty old man with many years of stories, so we may need a few more bottles of wine, though.

It all started in a small town in western Prussia almost one hundred years ago …"

CHAPTER 1

DECEMBER 15, 1845: KUES COURIER HIRES NEW COPY BOY

Fifteen-year-old Jonas Schteubrein had reached the age where he needed to earn a living. His home of Bernkastel, a medieval west Prussian wine-making village of one thousand people, was blessed with beautiful buildings dating back hundreds of years, but job variety was in short supply.

Jonas's father had spent decades transporting local wine and other products up and down the Moselle River. Jonas's older brothers also procured good positions with local ships. His older sister married a manager of a local vineyard. But, Jonas's interests drifted elsewhere.

Jonas could not stop reading. As a youngster, he would read anything. By adolescence, Jonas only read nonfiction. The Schteubreins went through more candles than most of their neighbors, as Jonas would devour articles about news and politics late into the evenings. The 1830s and 1840s gave him ample opportunities with revolutions, weakened monarchies, and growth in the "New World" across the Atlantic. What Jonas read contrasted sharply with the daily interests of the provincial citizens in his hometown, who rarely concerned themselves with news from outside of the local area.

With encouragement from his father to strive to be the best at whatever profession he chose, at age fifteen, Jonas earned a position with *The Kues Courier* newspaper in the town of Kues directly across the river. The next morning, his family smiled proudly at the headline that announced Jonas as the latest employee of this long-running enterprise.

Riding the ferry across the Moselle to work from the home where his family and ancestors had lived for more than two hundred years, Jonas could look off into the distance and see other towns on the river's banks. The Moselle River Valley not only represented the geographic boundaries of his vision, but also the geographic boundaries of the news covered by *The Kues Courier*.

Like others starting out in the newspaper industry, the first job for Jonas at the Courier was as a copy boy. With ink all over his hands and clothes, Jonas aspired to become a reporter and maybe even an editor in time. He marveled at the speed with which the reporters transformed various bits of information into a readable story. As Jonas began picking up their tricks, his superiors rewarded him with more and more responsibility.

Advancement came slowly. With Prussia being a traditional society focused on rewarding older and more established employees, Jonas quickly observed that the newspaper industry, in particular, had its centuries-old traditions. As Jonas's older colleagues never failed to remind him, the world's first newspaper had been printed in the same region—for the Holy Roman Empire. While his newspaper covered news that was far more mundane than the rise and fall of the Holy Roman Empire, these long-standing traditions still required Jonas to wait until he was eighteen before he would be considered for a reporter position. So, he waited and bided his time.

Revolutions throughout Europe made their way to Bernkastel, and Jonas joined the local militia in 1848 when he was approaching the age of eighteen. Weeks of drills, songs, and never-ending drinking toasts turned out to be for naught, as the Bernkastel militia saw no action. Soon, the "Spring of Nations" came to a conclusion with changes throughout Europe, but little noticeable change in Bernkastel and Kues.

Upon his return to work in December, the tall, lanky eighteen-year-old Jonas beamed, as he received the promotion to reporter. Excited at the great timing, Jonas began researching stories of the revolutions in France, Italy, and Denmark. Devoting many hours of his time, he learned about Louis-Napoleon in France, Lajos Kossuth in Hungary, and Karl Marx in nearby Belgium. Jonas turned in his first piece on Denmark to his editor one night and went home excited. Though the story never ran because it was beyond the scope of what the newspaper readers wanted, Jonas's editor was impressed. A story assignment regarding the local grape harvest, however, turned out to be Jonas's reward.

Not content to write mediocre stories of only local interest, Jonas searched for ways to extend the reach of his stories. An interview with a local boat captain would focus on the foreign foods the captain tasted in Italy, France, and England. An announcement of a wedding at the local landmark, Landshut Castle, would lead to a history lesson of the centuries-old castle and the kings and queens that had lived there, with only a quick reference to the guests at the wedding and the colors of the dresses being worn by the women. But, his editors strictly enforced the rules that forbid his stories to focus on major international political events outside of the area. This restriction continued to frustrate the young reporter.

One evening after a long day of work, twenty-year-old Jonas brought some clothes for repair to a local seamstress near his home. The elderly seamstress had stepped out, so Jonas conducted his business with the young assistant, Katia Erin. A tall eighteen-year-old blonde with a good head for numbers, Katia knew of Jonas from his articles in the newspaper. Before Jonas realized it, they had been talking for fifteen minutes, and the elderly seamstress had returned.

From that time forward, Jonas seemed to have more and more tailoring needs. Whether it was his own clothes or those of his parents or siblings, he would volunteer to drop off or pick up from the seamstress shop multiple times each week. He always managed to show up at the shop while the elderly seamstress was away. Soon, these trips turned into a courtship with Katia. It didn't take long for the young couple to realize they wanted to be married.

After receiving both parents' blessings, the young couple wed. In March 1851, they hiked up with their friends and family to the ruins of Landshut Castle. As the readers of Jonas's stories knew well by that time, this Bernkastel landmark had been built in the thirteenth century and served as a scenic venue for their special day. With a panoramic view of the Moselle Valley before them, Jonas and Katia Schteubrein took their wedding vows.

The Schteubreins moved into a small home with two rooms near Katia's store and enjoyed the routines of married life as newlyweds. Two years into their marriage, they welcomed baby Sandra into the world.

The Schteubreins knew that they wanted their children to experience a larger world, and that would not be possible in the small, provincial towns of Bernkastel and Kues. So, it would only be a matter of time before they moved away. Jonas had learned so much about the New World across the Atlantic from his readings that the couple quickly focused their attention on emigrating there. Their friends—Arthur and Hazel Jensen—had moved to New York several years earlier and they offered an open invitation to the Schteubreins to stay with them. Once Jonas mentioned his interest in opening a store selling newspapers and other small items, the Jensens suggested settling in a smaller town like Washington, DC where they would face less competition with lower operating costs.

The young couple hatched their plans. They felt confident that they could both secure jobs in hotels, restaurants, or on ships in Washington to make ends meet, but they ultimately wanted to activate their more entrepreneurial plan to open their own store. They recognized the difficulties with the language barrier, but they were confident they could make a life for themselves and their children with hard work. Jonas found that the residential community of Washington had begun in the Georgetown area and that the main river known as the Potomac flowed past Georgetown. So, the couple targeted Georgetown as the place to live and set up shop in the Washington area.

The Schteubreins diligently kept their spending down and had saved enough to emigrate by early 1855. Moving thousands of miles from a home their families had known for centuries proved to be particularly difficult and emotional. Jonas and Katia fully expected to never see Bernkastel and Kues again.

With heavy hearts, Jonas, Katia, and Sandra left Bernkastel for their three-part journey to America. First, they embarked on a small steam ship on the Moselle River that would take them—via the Rhine River—to Rotterdam.

In Rotterdam, they faced a three-day delay of their ship.

While the impatient Jonas and Katia complained of the extra costs and wasted time from their delay, these three days on land in Rotterdam became a blessing in disguise. The young family took the time to explore this city of ninety thousand people that dwarfed their home in Bernkastel and Kues. Using those days to walk, eat well, and rest soundly differentiated the Schteubreins from many on the steamship who quickly fell ill from the ship's movements and the heavy pounding of the waves. Jonas and Katia took Sandra out on the deck for most of the trip where they enjoyed the fresh air. Sandra spent her time playing with her dolls and walking in the clogs that her parents had purchased in Rotterdam. By the time they neared New York City, however, all three travelers looked fatigued.

The United States had recently opened an immigration center on the southern tip of New York in Battery Park. Previously, a promenade, beer garden, exhibition, theater, and opera house, the facility known as Castle Gardens had hosted such famous acts as "The Swedish Nightingale" Jenny Lind and Lola Montez performing her "tarantula dance." But, just two weeks before the Schteubreins arrived, the facility transformed into the Emigrant Landing Depot. The Schteubrein family spent its first hours in America being processed at the depot. The parents' modest command of English greatly assisted in this process, as many other immigrants waited for hours to be seen by an official who spoke their native tongues. The waiting persisted throughout every stage of the operation, but a friendly clerk suggested to Jonas that he take an American last name to speed up their processing. With the clerk's assistance, Jonas and Katia agreed to change the family name from Schteubrein to Steuben.

With leg two of the journey complete, the newly-named Steuben family left the depot and strolled into the heart of New York City. Still shocked by the size of Rotterdam, New York with seven hundred thousand people made their heads spin. To Katia and Jonas, it seemed like the particular area where they stayed was the most densely populated spot on the planet. Their Bernkastel friends—Arthur and Hazel Jensen—had settled on the Lower East Side of Manhattan Island three years earlier on Ludlow Street between Broome and Delancey Streets.

After three days, the Steubens left New York and ten hours later arrived at the Baltimore and Ohio Railroad Depot in Washington, DC. After setting back their watches 12 minutes to Washington time, they made their way across Washington City and over the Rock Creek to Georgetown, where they moved into a boarding house.

For two months, the Steubens explored Washington. Jonas worked at the Saw Pit Landing restaurant—the original name for the Georgetown area—and other odd jobs where he could find work. The Steubens immediately felt a comfort with Washington—which was approximately only one-tenth the size of New York. They found some areas like Georgetown with concentrated settlement, but nothing like New York's Lower East Side. After some discussion, they both agreed that Georgetown with its small-town feel, proximity to the river, and ease of reaching Washington City would serve as the optimal location for their store and new home.

CHAPTER 2

FEBRUARY 12, 1856: STEUBEN'S ORDINARY OPENS

Katia and Jonas toiled many hours to prepare Steuben's Ordinary for its grand opening day of February 12, 1856. Purchasing inventory, cleaning the space, and advertising to the neighborhood taxed all of the physical strength and language skills of the young couple. With a mix of local, foreign language and out of town papers; they presented a thorough and crowded newspaper aisle display. For the final touch before opening the front door, they placed the article in *The Washington Constitution* announcing their grand opening in the display window.

Weather was a major concern for the young couple scheduling their opening. January 1856 had recorded amongst the lowest temperatures in the city's history. Fortunately, the temperature spiked around the time of the opening, and business was strong the first few weeks. Nonetheless, like any new business, the ability to keep a positive cash flow remained a major concern for several years.

When the store opened in 1856, the Steubens heard many customers talking of the upcoming presidential election. A new political party known as the Republicans would submit its first presidential candidate, John C.

Fremont, trying to draw upon his fame as a Western explorer nicknamed "The Pathfinder."

Katia and Jonas had yet to develop their own feelings on the 1856 election, but they quickly received some lessons on national politics by scanning their many newspapers. Finding the various publications reporting apparently contradictory stories about the same political event, the Steubens saw similar discussions play out amongst arguing customers in their store.

After starving for such discussion for years in Bernkastel and Kues, Jonas and Katia now thoroughly enjoyed every minute of the animated conversations. Customers would debate each other in the store, and often those debates turned violent. Jonas soon became adept at stopping those conversations before the store—or the customers—got damaged.

Charles Sumner, a Republican Senator from Massachusetts, frequented Steuben's Ordinary in its early days. The middle-aged Senator with the well-known large part on the right side of his wavy black hair was good-natured and evangelically devoted to the cause of emancipation. While Sumner resided on F Street between 14th and 15th Streets across from the Treasury Department in Washington City, he often visited the markets in Georgetown. He lectured Jonas one day, "Mr. Steuben, the Democratic Party has become nothing more than an excuse for the enslavement of Africans. No greater moral outrage exists today."

Jonas remembered that conversation in May of 1856 when he learned of the horrible fate that had befallen Senator Sumner. While in the Senate chamber, a (Democrat) South Carolina congressman beat Senator Sumner with a heavy wooden cane. In an ironic twist of fate, Sumner survived and remained a loyal Steuben's Ordinary customer for many years, while his young attacker died—of natural causes—shortly thereafter at age thirty-seven.

Jonas and Katia found out that violent and vitriolic behavior in the halls of Congress was unfortunately fairly common, and could harm

Democrats as well as Republicans. Another customer, Democrat Thomas Hart Benton of Missouri—coincidentally the father-in-law of John C. Fremont—ended up on the receiving each of such treatment.

Still spiteful at his state for voting him out of office first as a senator and then as a congressman, the septuagenarian explained to the Steubens how he ran into political trouble. "A few years back, Senator Calhoun from South Carolina attempted to get voting uniformity on Democrats in Congress to forbid any legislation that would interfere with slavery in our new territories out West. Calhoun and I did not exactly see eye to eye, and our disagreements got pretty heated. Even Vice President Fillmore shouted at me on the issue, across the Senate floor. When Fillmore became President, he didn't forget our shouting matches."

"Didn't your citizens in Missouri own slaves?" Katia asked.

"Yes, and I did too. Still, sometimes you have to stand up for what is right, even if your constituents disagree and may vote you out of office. With this peculiar institution of slavery, its time has passed," Senator Benton replied, as he stared intently at Katia down his long, angular nose.

"That must have made you very unpopular. Especially with your Southern colleagues," Jonas said.

"I was a very unpopular man. The Senate tried to ram through that Compromise of 1850 that Calhoun had devised with Senators Clay from Kentucky and Webster from Massachusetts. But, it generated a lot of resentment. Mississippi Senator Henry Foote and I took opposite sides on this issue, and he took the dispute personally. He even aimed a gun at me in the halls of Congress, but several others wrestled him to the floor before he could pull the trigger," Senator Benton continued.

"That's awful. I hope that brought you some sympathy with your citizens back home?" Katia asked.

"By that time, the state of Missouri had seen enough of Thomas Hart Benton. They concocted some legislation to bar me from a sixth term in the Senate. I won one term as a Representative in Congress after that, but they voted me out again. I'm an old widower having spent three-quarters of a century on this earth, but I'm hoping to get back to Congress in 1858. Maybe you would consider hanging one of these banners for me on your window?" Senator Benton smiled as he handed Jonas a banner that read in large block letters, "Benton for Congress."

"It would be our pleasure. You showed a lot of character standing up for what you believed in, Senator Benton. Please visit our store again." Jonas waved as he began to hang the banner outside of Steuben's Ordinary.

"A principled and courageous man in politics. Who knew that such men existed? This may become the first of many banners to hang at Steuben's Ordinary. Benton for Congress," Katia said to Jonas, as they stepped outside to admire the new banner.

Steuben's Ordinary struggled in those early years, but the young Steuben family was up to the task. In early 1858, they added a son, Nathan, to their family. A routine developed throughout the day, which allowed for some free time for both Jonas and Katia.

Katia's favorite part of every day came after the close of business once the family had finished their dinner. She would read Sandra and Nathan a variety of stories. Stocked with all of the Brothers Grimm fairy tales, Katia would put the children to sleep while reading a different story each night. Wanting to strengthen her own English skills, she began to supplement her German fairy tales with articles in the newspapers and journals that they sold in the store. The children waited every night to hear a new story from the newspapers.

Jonas soon began to join the family at story time to listen himself. One night, he decided to surprise the children by bringing in a large glass jar of grape juice with some cups for the kids. However, he slipped on Sandra's old clog purchased in Rotterdam, and the glass jar came crashing to the ground.

Jonas didn't miss a beat, though. "Nathan, why did you spill that grape juice? You're lucky that I'm going to clean it all up for you."

The children and Katia looked at each other with amusement. Then, they began to chuckle as Jonas scurried off to find some towels. He returned as if nothing had happened, but "Nathan's spilling of the grape juice" would be retold as a running joke in the family well into the 20th century.

After the grape juice night, Jonas decided to be less heroic and only bring himself to the story session. With his full days at the store, though, Jonas usually fell asleep on one of the chairs in the kids' room. Katia didn't mind. Sandra would usually get up quietly to place a blanket on her snoring father, as Nathan laughed at each loud snore.

The Steubens' three-room apartment consisted of the children's room, the parents' room, and a cooking and dining room. With such a small space, it was easy for Katia to gently wake Jonas up at the end of her story, and they would walk over to the bed in the next room.

By 1859, Sandra had begun attending school. Zoned into the First District, the Steubens sent Sandra to the Primary No. 2 School on the corner of 19th Street and Pennsylvania Avenue in Washington City at Wilson's Hall. If Sandra kept up her studies, she would advance to Secondary No. 3 in a few years, also located on that same corner.

Katia and Nathan would walk Sandra the fifteen blocks to school in the morning and pick her up around 3 PM. They would wait for Sandra in front of the Seven Buildings, which were named for seven luxury residential three-floor brick row houses built in the 1790s. Not quite as luxurious as these homes were in their heyday, Sandra reported that these buildings had housed President James and First Lady Dolly Madison after the British set the President's House ablaze during the War of 1812.

"Maybe so, but they just look like rundown old buildings to me," Nathan retorted.

"You're probably right. But, when President Madison lived there, it was the center of Washington. They used to call the corner house the House of 1,000 Lights. Some of the old houses in this neighborhood still look pretty fancy. President Monroe lived right down the block here at 2017 Pennsylvania Avenue in this large home with 13 windows facing the street. You wouldn't call that one rundown or old," Sandra replied.

Nathan just rolled his eyes and smiled. Nathan viewed these walks as the highlight of his day. First, he got to spend time with his favorite person in the world, Sandra. Second, he could see all of the sights and sounds of the city from the merchants to the politicians to the large buildings. He and Katia would usually stop at the West Market, just a couple of blocks from the school. Nathan's eyes widened the most when they walked along the grandest street of them all, Pennsylvania Avenue. When the weather cooperated, Katia would walk a few extra blocks with Nathan in the mornings to see the imposing President's House and to play in Lafayette Square.

Katia, of course, loved to visit the parks and the beautiful historic homes. Her ability to interest Nathan in those adventures was limited. A park with children and animals held some of his attention, but historic homes like the famous Octagon where the Treaty of Ghent ending the War of 1812 had been signed usually put young Nathan to sleep.

CHAPTER 3

FEBRUARY 5, 1861: CONFEDERACY FORMED WITH SEVEN STATES

Still shivering from his morning walk, Jonas Steuben skimmed the pages of the *Alexandria Gazette* and placed the newspapers at the window display in his small store. Located on the corner of Congress and Water Streets in Georgetown, Steuben's Ordinary was situated two blocks north of the Potomac River separating Washington from Virginia, and six blocks west of the bridges into Washington City.

On a main corner of Georgetown, the small store welcomed customers arriving by foot, horse, or boat. Steuben's Ordinary had its "regulars" from local businessmen like John Marbury, the president of Potomac Insurance Company, and the Rittenhouse brothers from the Bank of Commerce. But its location and its reputation for stocking newspapers from around the country ensured that many business travelers would meet Jonas in his store.

True to Jonas's dream back in Bernkastel, Steuben's Ordinary stocked a particularly large offering of multiple newspapers printed in Richmond, Washington, Baltimore, New York, and smaller surrounding towns. Most were English-language papers, but they also carried German newspapers.

Beginning with the limited supply of literary and scientific magazines at that time—including *Harper's* and *Scientific American*—Jonas and Katia supplemented newspapers with these additional publications.

The newspaper headlines that many had feared for several months now brought in a particularly large crowd that morning. South Carolina, Mississippi, Florida, Alabama, Georgia, Louisiana, and Texas had left the United States.

Knowing how unpopular Lincoln and Republicans were in the South—none of the states of the Confederacy even included the Republican Party on their ballots as a choice—Jonas saw trouble brewing after Lincoln was elected. When he read the February 5, 1861, newspapers, he knew that this trouble had boiled over. The United States of America had suddenly and formally become un-united.

Raised voices engaged in heated political disputes using language that the ministers at the Christ Church, the Congress Street Methodist Protestant Church, and the Mt. Zion United Methodist Church in the neighborhood surrounding the store surely would not approve of. The presence of children in the store tempered such discussion, but the Steuben children heard more than their share of heated exchanges.

"Dad, will we be able to keep the store if there is war? What about if all of the Confederates leave Georgetown and we lose all of our customers?" a distressed Sandra asked Jonas.

"Honey, don't worry. I'll work a second or third job if I need to. You and your brothers will always be taken care of. That is what fathers do. But, let's hope for the best," Jonas replied calmly.

While the conversation calmed Sandra, Jonas realized this military presence far exceeded anything he had experienced in 1848 with the Bernkastel militia. He knew that his family's safety and economic survival would task his energies and abilities if a war broke out, as so many were predicting.

Jonas had become not only an active reader of political activity, but he had also joined the nascent Republican Party. Jonas's decision to become active in politics began in 1858 where he read the details of each of the Lincoln Douglas debates for the Illinois Senate. He found himself siding consistently with Lincoln, not only on policy grounds, but also from Jonas' fascination with Lincoln's famous stories, anecdotes, and analogies, like "A house divided against itself cannot stand." They reminded him of the Brothers Grimm, as he found himself nodding and chuckling when reading these speeches.

Already a fan of Lincoln, Jonas timed a business trip to New York to coincide with a speech Lincoln had scheduled at the Cooper Union engineering college in February 1860. Jonas and his old friend, Arthur Jensen, arrived early to make sure they would get seats. Amazed at the size of the auditorium, which accommodated more people than the entire population of Bernkastel and Kues combined—1,500 seats—Jonas sat transfixed. One passage he would never forget concerned the southern states:

The question recurs, what will satisfy them [the Southern States]? Simply this: We must not only let them alone, but we must somehow convince them that we do let them alone...

Lincoln had delivered perhaps his greatest speech to date, and Jonas devoted much of his free time and extra money over the next nine months to assisting Lincoln in getting nominated for President and then elected as the first Republican President. He and Katia would store away the obsolete banner of the late Thomas Hart Benton while advertising an "Honest Abe for President" banner at Steuben's Ordinary during that election cycle.

A tough four-way election ended with Lincoln winning by a comfortable margin, as Breckinridge, Bell, and Douglas split the Democrat and Southern vote. After the victory, Jonas and Katia attended several Lincoln victory parties in November and awaited Lincoln's arrival in March to take office as the next President.

The Steubens enjoyed a more important arrival during this time. Katia gave birth to their third child in early January 1861. Back in the comfort of their apartment, the Steubens cleared away old papers and other materials to make way for their new baby boy. As Jonas moved some clothes from the closet, he and Katia came face to face with the old banner "Benton for Congress." Sadly, Senator Benton had passed away before the 1858 elections in November, but he remained close to the Steubens' hearts.

"Benton. That would be a strong name for our son. Naming him after a courageous politician during these dangerous political times seems only fitting," Katia said.

"Yes, my little Benton Steuben, you have entered a very unstable world," Jonas said, as he placed his baby son down to sleep.

Baby Benton distracted the Steubens for a few weeks, but the Union dissolved when Benton was only one month old. The news headlines of the newly formed Confederacy competed for attention with the Steubens' new baby. Katia and Jonas both knew that Lincoln would be inaugurated in four weeks, and he would face a fork in the road. Whether he would choose to oppose or accept the Confederacy as a separate country was anyone's guess.

Looking out the windows and walking along the streets of Georgetown, the Steubens saw that citizens had already chosen sides for secession and war. With so much uncertainty over the timing of the war and which states would make up each side, it was too early to display flags or other patriotic symbols just yet. But, enterprising citizens had already started trying to profit from the impending war. Real estate agents descended like locusts on suspected Confederate sympathizers who might soon be looking to sell their property. Another aspiring entrepreneur began compiling a list of wealthy citizens willing to pay a substitute—allegedly as much as $300—to take their place on the frontlines of the war. Matching up to that group, another list contained the names of poor individuals willing to join the fight for such payment.

Walking through a four-deep throng of people outside, a new customer that Jonas and Katia had never seen before entered their store. With a serious but friendly look, the well-groomed man of about 30 looked like he could be a military officer or a policeman with his formal mannerisms. Displaying his heavy Scottish accent, the blonde-haired man reached out his hand to Jonas, "Good morning, sir and ma'm. My name is David Trent. I recently moved to Georgetown from the city of Chicago, Illinois."

While Jonas shook the somewhat taller stranger's hand, Katia smiled, "Mr. Trent, we welcome you to Steuben's Ordinary. We hail from Prussia, but we have now operated this store for five years. We are Jonas and Katia Steuben."

Looking around the store, David replied, "Mr. and Mrs. Steuben, you have a lot to be proud of. This is a fine establishment. I hope to catch up on my Chicago newspapers here."

Jonas took baby Benton from Katia so that she could re-arrange the shelves, "We welcome your business and your company, Mr. Trent, as time allows for you. As you can see, we have our hands full here as well. Benton here is our baby, and Nathan is his older brother. Sandra remains at school presently."

David stared at baby Benton while he reached out his hand to shake with Nathan, "He sure seems like a good baby just looking around intently and not crying at all. You must be good parents. Also, please call me David."

Katia thought for a moment and said, "Please call us by our names as well David. I can't quite understand it, though, Benton stopped crying as soon as you walked in. He has remained focused on you since then. Would you like to hold him for a minute?"

David was a bit uncomfortable due to his lack of experience with babies, but he wanted to be polite, "Certainly, I would love to, Katia."

As Jonas placed baby Benton in David's arms, the infant remained calm. Soon, David Trent learned how to hold the baby properly and rocked him gently, "Well, maybe this isn't as hard as I thought. I have never been married and my family remains in Scotland, so I don't have much experience with the little ones. My work as a Pinkerton detective also does not give me any exposure to babies."

Still marveling at Benton's calm in David's arms, Jonas replied, "An investigative detective must be a fascinating field. Secession and the threats of war must keep you awfully busy."

Passing Benton backed to Katia, David replied, "Yes, too busy these days. In fact, I am going to be late if I keep holding Benton. If only he could help me with my work, that would be another story. But, I truly hope we can avoid a long and deadly war. Great to meet you, Jonas, Katia, Nathan, and Benton. I look forward to meeting Sandra another day."

As David left the store, Benton began to cry again.

CHAPTER 4

MARCH 4, 1861: LINCOLN'S TRAIN SNEAKS INTO WASHINGTON AFTER THREATS IN BALTIMORE

The *National Republican's* headlines sadly came as no surprise to citizens of Washington, DC living through that long winter period between Lincoln's election and inauguration. In the month since the Confederacy had formed, tensions rose sharply across the country. The residents of Washington, which was surrounded by slave states that had not yet joined the Confederacy, experienced this firsthand on a daily basis. The Lincoln-supporting Steubens especially felt the tension in Georgetown where Confederate sympathizers lived on every block. Citizens labeled the stores as either "Confederate" or "American," based on the allegiances of their owners. More than a few fights and other forms of violence had erupted.

Steuben's Ordinary had been spared any attacks and property damage, but Jonas and Katia kept a much closer eye on their establishment than they had in the past. They feared that Confederate sympathizers would boycott or even plunder their store. With three young children to feed and protect in a country thousands of miles from their families, they followed the political news on Abraham Lincoln and the Confederacy very closely.

The newspapers provided all of the details concerning President-elect Lincoln. Baltimore gangs, led by the Plug Uglies, who had previously been involved in a number of riots, had been lying in wait for Lincoln's train. Some deft maneuvering and disguises while walking across Baltimore to avoid certain areas and train stations kept the Lincoln family safe. President Lincoln would be indebted for life to the engineers and detectives Allan Pinkerton, Timothy Webster, and Kate Warne that executed this plan.

Katia woke up early on the morning of March 4, delighted to see the newspaper headlines. Abraham Lincoln had arrived safely in Washington and would be inaugurated at noon. Rain had been falling for several hours (there was hope it would clear later that day), but Katia roused her entire family to witness the inauguration.

Sandra was surprised when they decided to take the whole family down to the U.S. Capitol Building to see the new president. She thought baby Benton would ruin the whole day. "Won't he just cry and sleep the whole time?"

Katia would not change her mind, though. "We came to America, to see these great events of history. Mark my word. Your children will read about what a great man Abraham Lincoln was. Seventy years from now, Benton will tell his grandchildren that he attended Lincoln's inauguration on the rainy day. I wouldn't deny that opportunity to our baby. With a few extra blankets, we can make him nice and cozy."

So it was that Jonas and Katia bundled their family into their carriage wearing their best clothing to befit this important day. Jonas drove the horse to the hitching post just a few blocks from the Capitol next to the St. Charles Hotel. By this time, hotel guests had already started crowding the long second-floor balcony as they fought for good views of the Capitol. With a checkered history of housing dignitaries, surviving the British invasion of 1814, and operating as a slave-market holding pen, the

St. Charles Hotel would serve a different role on this day. Not only would it serve as the Steubens' hitching post, but it would also host a lavish party for Lincoln supporters.

Looking diagonally across the street corner from the hotel, Jonas spotted the McClees & Beck Photo Studio at 308 Pennsylvania Avenue. He recognized the name from the many Indian pictures seen in the photo booklets in Steuben's Ordinary. Jonas decided to splurge. The Steubens would sit for a family photograph on the morning of Lincoln's inauguration. Five large photographs dated March 4, 1861, would cost a small fortune—ten dollars.

James McClees faced a long line of customers in one room, so Dorsey Beck would take the Steubens' picture. This turned out to be a fortunate occurrence, as Beck and his wife, Rezin, had frequented Steuben's Ordinary on their day trips to Georgetown. The Steuben children knew the Becks well, which made it somewhat easier for Mr. Beck to coax Benton and Nathan into remaining still for more than a second or two.

The cameras and the lighting fascinated Sandra and Nathan, but baby Benton would not remain still long enough to take a clear picture. Finally, after several failed attempts, the Steubens had five good photographs—one for each member of the family. "This first picture will remain on our wall at home. Our store will display the second picture. When you're grown-ups, you can display your own photograph in your own home to remember this day, where the weight of the world is on President Lincoln," Jonas said to his still distracted children.

After their adventure in the photo studio, the Steubens walked outside, and Nathan could hardly believe his eyes. He thought that he glimpsed Abraham Lincoln in his procession to the Capitol, but so many cavalry officers and infantrymen obscured his vision that he could not be sure.

Sandra was quick to impress the family with all of the facts she had learned at school. The eight-year-old's voice carried none of the German accents heard from her parents. "Mr. Lincoln will be sworn in by Chief

Justice Roger Taney. He is from Maryland and was a close friend of Francis Scott Key. But, the Chief Justice did not support Mr. Lincoln."

Nathan asked, "Who is that old guy next to Mr. Lincoln?"

Sandra knew the answer immediately. "Chief Justice Taney is the oldest on stage, but I think you're pointing to President Buchanan. He is almost seventy years old, but you are right that he looks older. He is the only one of our fifteen presidents never to have been married. They say his fiancé died many years ago and he always had a broken heart after that. One of his nieces lived with him here while he was President to help with dinners and parties."

Katia tried to test Sandra once more. "That Abraham Lincoln sure is tall. Who is that other tall fellow just behind him? He looks very familiar."

Sandra continued to impress. "Hannibal Hamlin from Maine. He is to be the Vice President. They say he is 6 foot 3—almost as tall as Mr. Lincoln. We have seen Senator Hamlin when we walk by the Washington House where he lives. A lot of Senators and Congressmen live there. See, Mr. Lincoln just walked on the stage …"

Jonas recognized him right away from the prior year's Cooper Union speech. Pictures in the newspaper did not prepare the others for his height. Adding to the effect with his large black stove pipe hat, Lincoln resembled a giant. Athletically built, the fifty-two-year-old Lincoln, in the prime of his life, stood in stark contrast to his old predecessor, James Buchanan, and the ancient Chief Justice, Roger Taney. Many reporters for the northern papers that day remarked on Taney's and Buchanan's physical appearances representing the old, ineffective policies, while Lincoln's strong, healthy look signaled a new era.

The Steubens would not have to wait long, as the ceremony followed a strict timetable. Just as the black ball dropped on the roof of the National Observatory on the corner of E and 23rd Streets as it did at noon every day, Abraham Lincoln took the oath of office. Then, President Lincoln revealed his plans for the United States with regard to the Confederacy:

My fellow Americans. Old country lawyers like me have a habit of getting to the point very quickly, and I will provide you that courtesy today.

The seven Southern states of the Confederacy weigh heavily on everyone's mind in America. I have tried not to consider their secession as a personal affront to me or to the great Republican Party, but I must recognize several clear facts.

First, while our ticket proudly received nearly 2 million of your votes around this great country, we did not receive a single vote in the seven states of the Confederacy. In fact, all of those states felt their political differences significant enough to warrant leaving Vice President Hamlin and myself off of their ballots.

Second, the Confederate secession began shortly after election officials confirmed our ticket as having won.

These actions were a direct protest to this result.

While these acts do not cause me personal fear, they do alert me to the magnitude of the differences between the states of the Confederacy and the rest of our United States. The leaders in these states have found our political differences so extreme, that they have chosen to leave our union that has existed for four score and five years. They are even unwilling to use the political tools of democracy to consider other options. Rather, they have simply chosen to abandon the United States, and their friends.

I say "friends" because many of us count amongst our closest friends men and women whose states have chosen to leave our country. Even the Confederacy's own Vice President, Alexander Stephens, remains a long-time friend of mine.

I considered whether and how the United States should resist the formation of the Confederacy through military, economic, and political means. Recognizing that the Confederacy does not possess the manufacturing capability, or the population of the United States provided me with optimism. Our strength would ultimately prove decisive in any military dispute.

Such a military approach, however, would quite frankly mean war on this hallowed land. Many of you have lived long enough to remember our last war with its atrocities. The United States fought much of that war away from our large cities and even in Mexico itself. Yet, we still feel its effects today, as students learn to "remember the Alamo" when honoring some of the many fallen heroes of the Mexican War.

Sandra nodded and smiled at this, as she remembered her lessons on Davy Crockett, Jim Bowie, William Travis, and the other American heroes that the Mexicans killed at the Alamo.

Lincoln continued, "Some of you are even old enough to remember the British burning down this city and the President's House during the War of 1812."

After delivering this line, Lincoln placed his arm on the shoulder of the Commanding General of the Army, Winfield Scott. A young soldier and hero from the War of 1812, the elderly and overweight General Scott had more recently been honored as the namesake of the recently completed Scott Hall at the Old Soldiers' Home.

My military advisors offer a very mixed set of opinions when I probe further on this option of war. The more optimistic believe a war begun in the summer would have the troops home victorious, to celebrate Christmas. Others believe many years and hundreds of thousands of lives would be lost before an American victory.

While I believe the United States would certainly achieve a military victory, I ask you what would victory mean? To force back into this country men and states that do not want to be here at the cost of perhaps half a million lives? Surely, such a forced re-entry of the Confederate states would not stop further political strife and differences.

I struggled with these thoughts as I witnessed the hatred on the faces of gangs in Baltimore and even here in our nation's capital. I also considered our own beginnings in 1776 when thirteen colonies voluntarily took their leave of Great Britain.

The reasons for the current tensions do not escalate to our struggles for representation as colonists in the prior century, but the United States does not intend to operate as a totalitarian government. As President, I will not pursue policies that require states to remain in our union under all circumstances.

These thoughts and many others led me to this decision. We will recognize the Confederacy and begin to negotiate how we will divide our current assets and to co-exist peacefully on this continent for many generations.

At this pronouncement, Katia heard many loud "boos" from the audience, as the police in their tall black stovepipe hats and shining silver badges—along with less conspicuous Pinkerton detectives—tightened their circle around President Lincoln. But Lincoln continued:

Slavery represents the largest issue that precipitated secession. I campaigned that I would not initiate legislation to outlaw slavery in states where it existed, and I intend to uphold that promise for all of the states remaining here in the United States. Thus, slavery will not be abolished in Arkansas, Delaware, Kentucky, Maryland, North Carolina, Tennessee, Virginia, or even here in the District of Columbia by legislation that I initiate.

The speech would continue for several more minutes, but Lincoln's main themes had been addressed. Jonas could not wait to discuss this speech with the one person whose opinion he valued the most in the world: his wife, Katia. Jonas feared that Lincoln's decision would avoid immediate war with the Confederacy, but he was far from confident that all hostilities could be ended so quickly.

Whether Steuben's Ordinary could survive during this time would largely depend on Virginia. If Lincoln could manage to keep the state of Virginia in the United States, Jonas held out much more optimism for economic success. But, he realized that many of his loyal customers would move over the river to Alexandria if Virginia joined the Confederacy. In such an event, Jonas doubted the store could survive while waiting for new citizens to move to Georgetown.

Before he could think about the implications of Lincoln's speech, Jonas had to navigate his family home safely, as many of the more radical Republicans and intoxicated elements of the crowd were not happy with the speech. They longed for—or at least thought they longed for—immediate war against the Southern traitors.

The Steubens passed a number of unsavory crowds on their way home. Down Pennsylvania Avenue between 6th and 7th Streets, a crowd formed near Matthew Brady's photography studio threatening to light it on fire. As the Steubens advanced a few blocks further west, several dozen men cleared space for a fist-fight between Pennsylvania's Galusha Grow and North Carolina's Lawrence Branch. The tall, heavily-bearded congressman from Pennsylvania and the clean-shaven congressman from North Carolina had traded insults on the floor of the House, and had unsuccessfully attempted to stage a duel several months earlier. The chaos that ensued after the inaugural address made it easy for their fight to escape the police's attention or concern.

Although they couldn't fully keep up with the large crowds, Washington City maintained a strong police and military presence that day who were helpful guiding the dignitaries around and thwarting any significant violence. Following the directions of two policemen on horseback, the Steubens walked through the lawn of the President's House as it began to rain. Despite all of the excitement and rain outside, baby Benton managed to fall soundly asleep as Sandra thought she spotted President Lincoln in an upstairs bedroom window.

Sandra proved to be an unlikely leader of the Steubens' long ride home avoiding the mobs. Once they neared 17th Street, she guided them in and out of alleys of the neighborhood where she and her classmates would normally roam during their school days. Once the Steubens had reached Rock Creek, the crowds dissipated.

The evening editions of the local newspapers had been delivered to Steuben's Ordinary shortly after the family arrived home. Besides voicing outrage at Lincoln's stance, they provided Jonas and Katia with details of the violence engulfing the city. Fortunately, the President and the Lincoln family escaped harm, as President Lincoln was quoted in the *Evening Star*, "Shuffling through those crowds reminded me of my time as a boatman on the Mississippi swerving around ships of all sizes coming in all directions. But, that portion of the inauguration day experience did not please the rest of my family quite as much."

A much less historically significant conversation happened on Water Street once Benton, Nathan, and Sandra had fallen off to sleep. Jonas and Katia had chosen to move from their sleepy Prussian town to a major city experiencing some of the larger events of the day. But they hadn't quite expected the economic and social tensions they would experience living in a city torn apart by nationalists of two different countries. How the United States responded to the Confederacy could make or break Steuben's Ordinary and Jonas and Katia's dream of life in America.

Katia called from the kitchen table, "I can't believe how much violence we saw in Washington City today. I am glad that things are calmer here in Georgetown. I suspect our new Pinkerton friend, David Trent, didn't sleep much today investigating those crowds."

Jonas joined Katia at the kitchen table. "Yes. I hope David had a chance to listen to Lincoln's speech, though. Just reading those words in the newspaper does not capture President Lincoln's command of the stage and of the audience. He knew exactly which words to emphasize and the right times to shift gears or pause. I saw that at Cooper Union last year, and his command of an audience has only improved since then."

Katia nodded, "Yes, he spoke in a way that both educated and non-educated people could understand. The United States is in good hands."

Jonas glanced up from his pile of newspapers on the table, "I now understand why President Lincoln chose not to fight at this time. Fighting an enemy and then accommodating that enemy to rejoin your country would not be an easy task."

Katia added. "Yes, he balanced the cost to a potential war with hundreds of thousands of lives against the benefit of bringing back seven states that don't want to be here to begin with."

Jonas nodded and then asked the question that had been on his mind all day. "What I don't understand is now that Mr. Lincoln has the votes to immediately outlaw slavery, why wouldn't he do that? He calls himself an abolitionist, after all. More than 1,700 slaves live right here in Washington DC. I thought that showed weakness."

Katia thought for a while and then said, "Mr. Lincoln is a very smart and analytical man. He abided by his own campaign promise that HE would not start legal approaches to abolish slavery. This makes him a man of his word that can be trusted, and it also possibly keeps the remaining 'slave states' in our country. Remember, he made a point to name all seven slave states. Also, he didn't mention that CONGRESS might introduce laws abolishing or restricting slavery. Finally, he knows that pressure from our trading partners will probably force slavery's abolition sooner rather than later."

"Katia, I see that your intelligence extends well beyond your beauty and your strength with figures to now also include American politics. I would never have come up with that analysis. But, he must balance appeasing the abolitionists as well as the remaining slave states. President Lincoln has clearly chosen a path. I hope that he possesses enough strength to see it through."

Katia and Jonas returned to their bedroom and went to sleep. They would wake up the next day for the first time in American history with a Republican President in office.

CHAPTER 5

APRIL 1, 1862: LINCOLN AND VIRGINIA DELEGATION LEAD CONGRESS TO RENEW CONSTRUCTION OF THE WASHINGTON MONUMENT

The Steubens sat around the rectangular cherry wood breakfast table and smiled at the headlines of the *Daily National Intelligencer*. Jonas said, "Lincoln is a genius. I knew Congress would make this a close vote, but now Virginia will certainly remain in the Union. Virginians cannot help but have pride in the world's tallest man-made structure as a monument to their favorite son. Thousands of citizens in Arlington and Alexandria will be able to see it clearly across the river every day."

"It sounds so tall. 555 feet. The doctor measured me last week, and I am less than four feet tall," Nathan added.

"I want to watch them build it. Those workers must be brave to climb so high. The newspaper here says that it will show the progress every day so that we can track it on a chart at home," Sandra added.

Katia smiled, "I am sure we will take many trips over there to see the construction. Once it's done, they will let us walk to the top and look out the windows. It is hard to imagine being up that high, but I can hardly wait."

After breakfast, customers packed Steuben's Ordinary to read about the Washington Monument from newspaper accounts around the country. Jonas and Katia could barely keep up with the crowds.

Virginia Senator John Floyd arrived early at Steuben's Ordinary that day, "A proud day for the Old Dominion to be sure and for the United States as well. President Lincoln has been a much better friend to our state than I ever expected. I still remember his speech at the Richmond Convention and his kind words at President Tyler's funeral. Last year, he promoted our own Bobby Lee to head the army. And now the Washington Monument! Mrs. Steuben, to celebrate, would you mind displaying the Virginia state flag next to this new American flag with its 27 stars?"

"Of course, Senator. You have remained a great customer of Steuben's Ordinary and we appreciate your assistance keeping Virginia in the United States. I don't know how our enterprise could have survived if Virginia left the Union. With all of the changes, though, perhaps we should all become flag manufacturers. We must have a dozen different flags in storage—even this 28-star flag from last year that still represented Arkansas," Katia joked with the balding, middle-aged Senator.

"I think we politicians will continue to keep the flag makers in business. My colleagues from North Carolina and Tennessee worry about Congress trying to pass a restrictive law on slavery. If it does pass with serious regulations, you may be seeing another star or two disappear from your flag, Mrs. Steuben," Floyd said.

"I certainly hope not, but I defer to your expertise, Senator. I would rather see the flag change by adding instead of subtracting stars. Maybe some of our western territories like Nevada and Nebraska," Katia replied.

Floyd smiled as he left the store, "We will do our best. Good afternoon, Mrs. Steuben."

Steuben's Ordinary remained a healthy operation after six years, throughout the changes in the Steuben family and with the country. Sandra doted on her little brother, Nathan. He tended to embarrass her, but she enjoyed being the big sister. On certain days, they would walk home with their friends—Mandy and Harry Burrough—and spend a few hours at their house. The Burroughs—Thomas and Eunice—had become close friends of both Jonas and Katia after they arrived from Ireland in the late 1850s.

Katia often spent hours with Eunice during and after school hours. They both relished their roles as mothers, and Eunice also shared Katia's passion for reading and discussing current events. A Republican like Katia, Eunice closely followed the latest news from the President's House and the Capitol.

President Lincoln and the First Lady often took afternoon carriage rides that passed in front of the Burroughs' apartment on the corner of D and 27th Streets NW on the Washington City side of Rock Creek Park. With the bridges to Georgetown essentially in their backyards, the Burroughs could also watch the boats on Rock Creek travel up as far as P Street. Jonas always liked to visit the Burroughs due to its location around the corner from the 27th Street brewery of Clement Colineau and Joseph Davison.

On one occasion when the little boys were playing near the Burroughs' house, the presidential entourage stopped abruptly when Harry Burrough and Nathan Steuben stepped directly in front of the carriage. The unplanned stop did not cause any injuries, but the two mothers felt mortified to have the president meet their children—who were, of course, clad with mud from head to toe—under these circumstances. However, the good-natured President Lincoln enjoyed a long laugh and smiled warmly after riding past. Even the typically dour Mary Todd Lincoln perked up at the site of the muddy little boys.

Katia and Eunice marveled at the many opportunities their children enjoyed at that time in comparison to the lives they had left behind in Europe. Sandra and Mary would learn about their president, senators, congressman, and other government officials in the morning and then they might see them all in person walking home from school. Washington had changed a lot in the past few years, but it still very much remained a small town.

The children could also witness firsthand the completion of the extensions to the old Capitol building. Citizens could marvel at its height from anywhere in the city, but many chose to walk right up to the construction site to get a closer look. On their last trip to see the construction, Katia noticed that the street signs of Georgia, Louisiana, and South Carolina Avenues had been changed to Washington, Adams, and Jefferson Avenues. She jokingly noted to Eunice, "I guess secession created a bonanza not only for flag manufacturers, but also for street sign manufacturers."

Sandra performed well in all of her subjects at school, but math was always her specialty. Something about it just "clicked," so that she would understand math concepts well before teachers fully explained the concepts in class to students who would learn by repetition and memorization. Sandra wanted to understand and learn the underlying concepts instead of just applying a formula. According to Primary No. 2's principal, Adeline Lowe, about one in a thousand people were born with that "math gene" that Sandra possessed. For everyone else, math could be taught, but never fully understood at a high level.

Many believed the math gene could be traced back from heredity, but not always from parents or direct relations. Jonas and Katia mastered computations and algebra, and Katia had a particular ability to compute figures quickly, but neither of them had a true math gene. They found it both a proud and frustrating moment when they knew that they would never again be able to assist their nine-year-old daughter with mathematics.

Nathan and Harry's interests expanded elsewhere. They loved wading on the banks of the Potomac or in Rock Creek, where they could throw rocks, play in the mud, and search for gold coins. The markets—especially West Market—were another favorite. The boys could taste the different foods, stare at the rich people with their fancy clothes, and (usually) run into some of their friends from school.

Katia often found it difficult to believe all of the scientific and other advances that were impacting their lives after growing up in a town where most buildings were hundreds of years old. She still marveled at the clear photographs that appeared in the journals she sold every day. The railroad routes also made it easy for her suppliers and customers to move around the country.

Even boat transportation had improved dramatically, and Katia often ferried quickly and easily from Georgetown to Alexandria weekly to buy and sell products for Steuben's Ordinary. Soon, a horse-drawn streetcar service would be starting, and Jonas had chosen to become a minority partner in this new venture known as The Washington and Georgetown Railroad.

Katia worried about Jonas's investment. Small shopkeepers would rarely have an opportunity to invest in a large business like this in Europe. Europeans felt that citizens needed to be patient to participate in such large commercial ventures—often waiting for decades or generations.

Jonas listened to Katia's concerns, but he had observed a different climate in America. "In Europe, people are cautious and patient. But, in America, impatience is a virtue." With this philosophy—and a view of the business plan—Jonas joined the venture with Katia's belated blessing.

Jonas enjoyed the many advantages of his family's situation and delighted in his children. Sandra spent several hours a week helping in the store.

Nathan's tendency to get dirty and to "get into trouble" on his walks with Katia didn't concern Jonas. Rather, he told Katia, "You should worry about a five-year-old boy that does not get into trouble. I'm sure President Lincoln got into his fair share of trouble, just like Nathan when he was a child. You don't want a milquetoast like the Simpsons' son, Harold. He might seem well behaved, but he will face a difficult life when he grows up. This country opens its arms to everyone, but the strong rise to the top."

"You're right, Jonas. But, I still plan to do my best to make sure your boys have some manners before they leave our home."

Jonas accepted at least some semblance of manners for his boys. Benton had ceased his evening crying while sleeping through the night. But, Jonas had recently found himself chasing the now-walking baby Benton around the store and through the streets and waterfronts of Georgetown. Jonas enjoyed the chases the first few times, but Benton's need to explore every nook and cranny of Georgetown as if searching for clues ultimately left his father exhausted by the end of most days.

The Steubens' lives still remained tied to the fortunes of their store's improving fortunes. Katia had tallied the figures for the day, "We collected $8.35 from newspapers and magazines, $10.65 from books, $19.92 in home products, and $20.15 in food."

Jonas smiled, "All in all, a good day. If Abe Lincoln keeps the country stable for the next few years, I have high hopes."

CHAPTER 6

NOVEMBER 9, 1864: LINCOLN LANDSLIDE OVER JOHNSON

Thomas Burrough walked through Steuben's Ordinary holding the *Washington Star* out for all to see. "Andrew Johnson made a fine showing, but no one could have beaten Abraham Lincoln and William Seward this year."

Sandra had been following the voting closely in school and in the newspapers, "Mr. Burrough, you are right that Senator Johnson was fairly close to President Lincoln in terms of the total votes. But, the Electoral College gave Lincoln the landslide. Johnson only won Tennessee, Maryland, and Delaware. He probably also would have won North Carolina if they hadn't left us last year."

Burrough looked back astonished at the perky eleven-year-old, "Sandra, I have heard of your math prowess and you demonstrated it here again as I look carefully at the map and the electoral vote tallies. So, I will defer to your expertise, and simply offer three cheers for President Lincoln."

The entire store echoed, "Hip, hip, hooray."

Thomas Burrough did not overstate Sandra's math skills. She had now matriculated to Secondary No. 3. Her lightning-quick reflexes in math were the talk of the school, as the teachers could present oral "math games" to her at any speed. By the time she turned eleven in 1864, she had mastered Sherwin's Algebra and then began Legendre's Geometry and Trigonometry. Of course, she also performed all of the bookkeeping for Steuben's Ordinary.

But, Sandra's math skills and the cheers for President Lincoln only delayed the inevitable debates among the customers at Steuben's Ordinary. Soon, William Godey's powerful voice rose above the crowd. Part of the large Godey family—including Sandra's former teacher, Emma Godey— that principally settled in Georgetown, he had built a lime-and-plaster kiln a few blocks away in the Georgetown canal's terminus over the past few weeks. He always needed some odd or end, and such an errand had again brought him into the store that day. A friendly man, he responded, "It is going to be a long time before this country goes Democrat again. For generations, we will associate that party with slavery and the Confederacy. With the poverty down there, no one wants to see that happen here."

Old-time Washington resident Christian Hines chimed in with a voice that belied his age, "I lived around here a long time and political parties come and go. We had the Federalist, Whig, and Democratic Republic parties before, and they have all died out. I wouldn't be so sure about the long-term strength of the Republican Party. An 83-year-old man like me may not be around to see the next shift in the political climate, but time always leads to changes. Personally, I think Andrew Johnson served himself proud as the symbol of the slave states and the remaining Democrats in the United States."

Burrough listened intently and reviewed a newspaper before responding, "Mr. Hines, I take your point and defer to your knowledge and experience. I agree that Johnson represented a contingent of moderate Democrats, but a number of their brethren remain as extreme as those that left to form the Confederacy. Today's *Philadelphia Inquirer* has a quote from Democratic Congressman Thomas Hendricks of Indiana, 'While the tendency of the white race is upward, the tendency of the colored race is downward, and I've always supposed it is because in that race the physical predominates over the moral and intellectual qualities."'

Godey joined back in as he shook his head, "Yes, that wing of the Democratic party has no moral interest in abolition. But, you must admit that Johnson worked within the Washington system to prevent too much regulation coming out of the federal government. Without his efforts, I suspect slavery would have been abolished by now. The Slavery Modification Act—or SMA—did grant freedom to all slaves over forty years of age, but it didn't free newly born slave children. It also forbade any slave trading across borders with the Confederacy. In other words, Johnson has helped keep some form of slavery alive here in the United States."

Hines rejoined the group, "I think you may give too much credit to Johnson on that. The timing of the SMA could not have been any more dire for the United States. By early 1863, most of the European powers—including England and France—had placed economic sanctions on any country that had not abolished slavery or was not in the active process of moving in that direction. Seeing the Confederacy's economy spiraling downward with its insistence on unfettered slavery and even the resumption of the slave trade from Africa and the Caribbean, the United States knew it had to pass something relatively significant and quick. This gave Johnson the bargaining chip he needed. Once the bill passed, though, you saw Johnson's power dissipate, as we quickly passed our own trade sanctions against countries refusing to move towards abolition."

Godey smiled and bowed majestically toward Christian Hines, "I stand corrected. Thank you, Mr. Hines. The Confederacy continues to weaken with each new trade sanction passed by the major countries. I don't think there is much fear that citizens of the United States will move to the Confederacy anymore. Rather, the opposite direction of movement will provide a continual headache for Jefferson Davis if Judah Benjamin's impassioned defense of him can help avoid impeachment."

By now, others had joined the conversation, as Christian Hines made his way slowly across the store. A frequent customer and recognizable to the Steuben family, he turned to Nathan and Benton, who were sitting on the counter rolling their eyes. "Boys, you probably think all of this election stuff is kind of boring. Would you like me to tell you about how much more fun it was back in the old days?"

Both Nathan and Benton smiled, and Nathan said, "Yes, please."

"Thank you. It is the habit of old men like me to tell our stories to young children. I hope the two of you will find such a good audience when you reach my age. Anyway, this story happened sixty-four years ago, the election of 1800. Do you remember who ran for president that year?" Christian asked.

While the boys scratched their heads, Sandra walked over and said with a smile, "John Adams lost to Thomas Jefferson. Actually, Aaron Burr tied Jefferson in electoral votes and he became vice president." She also took advantage of the occasion to lightly smack both of her brothers on the head for not answering the question correctly. This led to some good-natured wrestling, where Sandra could still use her strength and coordination to ward of her little brothers' coordinated attacks. After a few minutes of screaming and rolling around in the dirt, the kids focused their attention back on Christian Hines.

"A little wrestling provides a good break during a story. Anyway, that's right, Sandra. Jefferson won that election. Between math and history, you will go far. Your brothers may be another matter," Christian joked. "But, as I was saying, back then everyone in Georgetown voted in Suter's Tavern. It's not here anymore, but it was on High Street between Bridge and Water Streets—basically right near where Mr. George Wilson, the blacksmith, now lives. A large crowd gathered at Suter's as they counted the ballots, and the men drank a lot of whiskey. I remember that the rain had made the sidewalks full of mud. It was a very muddy city back then. In fact, Benton could have gone swimming in some of the larger puddles."

Nathan and Benton laughed, while Sandra joined them to hear the rest of the story. "So, did the men cheer for Mr. Adams and Mr. Jefferson?" Nathan asked.

Christian replied, "It started that way, but when you cheer for one team, it also means you cheer against the other team. So, the Adams men and the Jefferson men started pushing and shoving each other. It even got a bit rougher than your wrestling matches here. I still remember clear as day when a man named Shipley stood in the middle of the crowd and challenged anyone from the other party to a fight."

"Which side was Shipley on?" Sandra asked.

"I actually don't remember. It has been sixty-four years," he laughed. "But, one way or another, the whole crowd got the message. A few minutes later, a man named Lovejoy came out to challenge Shipley."

The boys were mesmerized. "So, was it a fair fight, or was one of them a big bully that was ready to clobber the other one?" Nathan asked.

Christian smiled. "As I remember it, both men were tall, but Lovejoy was stouter. Hopefully, your parents won't mind me telling you this, but back in those days, people fought pretty rough. Usually, it ended up in some type of wrestling, and they would each try to gouge out the others' eyes with their thumbs and fingers."

Benton stood transfixed. "So, who lost an eye? I have never seen someone with a missing eye."

Christian laughed. "The men did fight very hard, and they tumbled into the mud. Lovejoy used his strength, but Shipley used his speed. Soon, Shipley jumped on top of Lovejoy, and he smeared Lovejoy's eyes with mud. Then, the crowd separated the men. When Lovejoy cleaned off his face, he couldn't see anymore."

"That is terrible. Did his sight come back?" Sandra asked.

"No, he was blind for the rest of his life. I would see him walking through Georgetown for many years with a young man guiding him around. Shipley also remained here for a number of years and became a tailor. So, be thankful that today's election quarrels don't reach those levels." Christian stood up and got ready to leave.

"Mr. Hines, who was president when you were my age?" Benton asked.

Christian smiled as he walked out the door. "Why I am so old that they hadn't even invented presidents when I was your age, Benton."

All of the children were speechless as their favorite storyteller left the store.

Abraham Lincoln instituted more of his policies in the second term with a strong Republican majority in congress. Nathan was able to report perhaps the crowning achievement of Lincoln's first term late that year after learning the current events at school, "Guess what? We can now take a railroad all of the way across the United States straight through to California. Maybe when I am older I will get to take that train."

"Train? I want to go too," said the soon-to-be four-year-old Benton.

"No one in this family will ride the cross-country train today. Besides, Nathan, what would you be doing out in California? Playing baseball like you do with all of your free time here?" Katia asked.

"That's a great idea, mom. Baseball in California. Maybe, I should start practicing now," Nathan replied.

Katia only rolled her eyes.

Jonas smiled, "I guess everyone should sit down for a second for a little announcement. I just sold my shares in the Washington and Georgetown Railroad. We made a little bit of money from it. Your mother and I plan to save most of the money, but we also plan to take the whole family on the train out to California next summer!"

About the only thing that could stop Nathan from playing baseball the next few years was the family train trip across the country. Nathan had recently picked up the game of baseball with Harry Burrough and other friends in Georgetown. They first saw it while attending a fair at Georgetown University. Approximately eight blocks from Steuben's Ordinary, the highly respected university had been founded in 1789. But, Nathan and Harry only cared about the food at the fair until they saw a group of young men on a diamond-shaped grass field with a stick and a ball.

What they saw showed some alterations to a recently devised British sport known as rounders. It also bore a resemblance to some earlier folk games from England that had been played for centuries. The American version did not yet have a unified set of rules, but it typically included a batter, a pitcher, fielders, and four bases. The batter would attempt to hit the ball thrown by the pitcher with a stick knows as a bat. Watching this, Nathan and Harry could not believe how fast the ball was thrown and how hard it would be hit.

From that point forward, Nathan devoted every spare minute to baseball. The boys watched games and soon began playing as well. They would talk about baseball all the way to school and search for any mention of games or scores in the newspapers at Steuben's Ordinary.

Over the next few years, Nathan worked hard and became a strong ballplayer. The City of Washington elected him as the captain of one of the teams that would play a demonstration game in front of the Washington Monument completion ceremonies in 1866. The first pitch was scheduled right after the parade and the speeches by Virginia's Congressional delegation. Following the game, President Lincoln would make the final address:

This is a proud day in my life. It is also a proud day for the great state of Virginia, Vice President Seward, and the entire United States.

President Washington stood for something much larger than himself and I could think of no finer tributes to him than the success of his United States and this dedication of the world's tallest building in his memory.

This is a day of celebration, and it is altogether fitting and proper that we recognize all of those who helped build this great country that President Washington was instrumental in founding. Our former citizens that now constitute the nine Confederate states were instrumental in helping forge this country. Our prayers go out to their citizens that face economic deprivation, suffering from trade sanctions and limited industry. We hope with Congressman Lucius Lamar's fiery and courageous speech that saved Jefferson Davis from impeachment; political stability will reign in the Confederacy.

Now, please join me in standing to applaud the many fine men and women seated to my right that helped build this monument over these years. You have created a gift for generations of Americans to take pride in for centuries to come. Hip, hip, hooray!

Decades later, Washingtonians would mark the unveiling of the Washington monument with the parades, speeches, and activities as a seminal event in their memories. Remembering where they were that day, who they saw, and what they remembered would animate conversations well into the 20th century. But, before the Steuben children would engage in such conversations, they would first have to finish their schooling.

Benton had followed in Nathan's shoes as a diligent student in primary school, although he proved to be more of a magnet for fights than his older brother. Less inclined to join the other boys in games of baseball, Benton preferred exploring the buildings or parks and investigating people around the school. Occasionally joined by a friend or two, Benton felt it to be his calling to learn everything he could about the neighborhood. A few of the baseball players mistook Benton's interests for weakness and prodded him into fights. They quickly found Benton did not need much prodding. Years of wrestling with his older brother and having an active lifestyle made Benton a difficult foe on the playgrounds. After delivering more than a few bloody noses and receiving a similar number of rebukes from his teachers, Benton was fully accepted by his classmates.

Sandra's issues at school as she was completing her secondary (high school) education did not involve fights, but rather mathematics. Nearing seventeen and having exhausted the math courses available in the school system, Sandra wished to continue her studies at a college. She had even been honored as the top student by Mayor Sayles Brown at the citywide mathematics competition last year beating her top competitor, her sickly and studious friend, John Thomas Williams.

Sandra visited libraries and asked adults about the different colleges where she might be able to further study mathematics. She became extremely discouraged, as nearly all colleges in the United States at that time exclusively catered to male students. In fact, neither Georgetown itself nor any other college in the area would educate women.

"Dad, it is just not fair. I'm the best math student in the area, but I can only attend a few colleges in the entire country. I haven't even had a chance to look for colleges that focus on math because there are just so few options. The University of Michigan plans to admit women for the first time next year. I would love to attend that school, but it's so far away and we don't know anyone in the area. I know you and Mom didn't grow up here, so you probably never read about or visited many colleges besides Georgetown. But, I sure need some help finding a college to study math." Sandra walked toward her room as she mumbled discontentedly to herself about men making college decisions who could not even pass a simple algebra course.

The next morning, Jonas had an idea. He woke up Sandra and told her he remembered that Lincoln gave a speech at a fine engineering college with some female students in attendance. He encouraged Sandra to find out about Cooper Union in New York. Sandra agreed to learn about the school, so Jonas and Katia breathed a temporary sigh of relief.

Later that day, Sandra ran into the store and hugged Jonas. "Dad, you did it. Cooper Union is perfect. It is one of the strongest math departments in the world. They accept women too. They say the founder, Mr. Peter Cooper, is a great man and a friend of President Lincoln. So, that sounds like a perfect fit. I should be able to begin studies there in the fall. Perhaps I can find boarding nearby?" Sandra asked.

Jonas just smiled. He knew just the family. The Jensens from Bernkastel would be happy to host Sandra and take care of her like she was one of their own. The Jensens still lived in the same New York City neighborhood, just a few short blocks from Cooper Union.

Before enrolling at Cooper Union, Sandra had one more important task. She headed to the southwest part of Washington to see her old math competition rival, John Thomas Williams. "John, you are a man and you can attend any college in the country with your brain. But, I think you should join me at Cooper Union. I am really excited about their mathematics, engineering, and architecture. It sounds like a perfect place to really learn and we would have a great time with our classmates exploring New York together."

Gaunt and sickly, John smiled at his friend and rival. "Nothing would please me more than to join you at Cooper Union. That's a tremendous school, and they're lucky to have you as a student. But, as you can probably tell, I do not possess the strength to make the trip or to live on my own. I will stay home with my mother and try to take my studies at Georgetown."

Sandra strained to temporarily avoid tears and present a smile. "Yes, I can see that now. But, I know your health will improve and the two of us will be inventing new math proofs for the next fifty years!" The tears began to pour out immediately on the sidewalk just as Sandra left the Williams house.

That July, before beginning studies at Cooper Union, Sandra joined Katia for a visit with the Jensens. When Sandra toured Cooper Union, she spoke with professors and students. Never had she seen such a group of hardworking people so focused on mathematics. She wanted her schooling to start immediately, but she knew she must first go back home with her mother.

When she joined her mother back at the Jensens, she found out that they were in for a surprise. The Jensens would join them to spend the evening at the Great Hall of Cooper Union to hear Red Cloud, the Chief of the Sioux Nations, speak.

The Steubens had read about Red Cloud for years in their newspapers and journals, but seeing him in person would be a special treat. Sandra would never forget his words that day:

I am representative of the original American race, the first people of this continent. We are good and not bad. The reports that you hear concerning us are all on one side...

Sandra found the speech an inspiration and she looked forward to others such dynamic speakers during her time at Cooper Union. She recounted much of the speech word-for-word to her younger brothers once she got home, "Look at me, I am poor and naked, but I am the Chief of the Nation ..."

"Naked? You mean he wore no clothes in front of all of those people watching him speak?" Benton asked.

Gently slapping her baby brother while laughing, Sandra continued, "No, of course, he wore clothes. He was kind of tall like Dad, but kind of thin. Almost like when you squeeze your cheeks in. Very dark with long black hair, he wore a single feather in his hair. Sorry to disappoint you also, but he didn't carry his bow and arrow for the speech."

Picking up a recent journal, Nathan asked, "Too bad, it would have been fun to see him shoot some arrows. Did he look like this picture?"

Sandra looked closely, "Yes, that's Red Cloud. I don't remember much about his pants, but I remember he wore a long sleeve leather jacket with a necklace of animal teeth."

Nine-year-old Benton looked at the newspaper, "I see something in his eyes that make you want to look at him. I'm not sure how to say it."

Sandra looked intently at Benton, "I noticed that at the speech. I told the Jensens the same thing. But, I am impressed that a nine-year-old like you could see this from a picture without seeing him in person. But, looking around the theater that night, Red Cloud's eyes really kept people focused on him. The whole room remained perfectly quiet. You couldn't even hear a single whisper during his entire speech."

As the boys turned to leave, Nathan said, "We don't care much about the math you will learn in college, but you have to promise to tell us about all of the Indian chiefs you see."

Realizing she would leave her family soon, Sandra choked up a bit before replying "Yes, I promise."

CHAPTER 7

NOVEMBER 15, 1871: PRESIDENT LINCOLN VISITS CHICAGO AFTER FIRE

"What a disaster. I'm not sure I believe the rumors, though, about a single cow knocking over a lantern in a barn," David Trent said to Jonas, as he read the headlines from the *Chicago Tribune*. "I spent some time investigating that fire and another one in Wisconsin. The fire started near the infamous O'Leary barn, but any number of triggers could have started that tinderbox."

Benton joined Jonas at the store on this quiet afternoon, as Jonas tended the shop. They marveled at the photographs of the many buildings and structures that the Chicago Fire had destroyed. But, they also were happy to see the speed of the cleanup in just one month. "I must defer to you on your intimate knowledge of Chicago and the city officials' histrionics involving the O'Leary cow. Many say the kerosene in the O'Leary barn could have been a prank by neighborhood children or just an accident by local boys trying to sneak a cigarette. I really don't know," Jonas replied, as he rearranged some of his dry goods.

"Neither do I at this point. I am not sure we will ever know. A large contingent of Pinkertons have been investigating this matter, but we still don't know a lot about the cause and path of fires. So, we sift through both physical evidence as well as trying to read people. That is exactly the type of work that attracted me to the Pinkerton Agency, but this is a hard case," David said, as he looked towards Benton.

"How do you read people, Mr. Trent?" Benton asked.

"That's a good question. Reading a person means trying to figure out his thoughts based on the expression on his face and by his body movements. Most people smile when they are happy and cry when they are sad, but facial expressions and movements can be much more complicated for different people when they are lying, nervous, or scared. Some people are obvious with their expressions and movements, while others are very hard to detect. We sometimes say those people possess a 'poker face' because an opponent finds it hard to tell such a person's thoughts when they compete in poker. Pinkerton training involves a lot of study on reading people, and an observant person learns that from experience as they get older by just watching people," David replied.

Benton looked at his father, "You mean like when I can tell if my father is mad at me for not cleaning my room, just by the expression on his face?"

"Exactly. And a good detective will remember that knowledge and apply it elsewhere. For example, maybe you can tell on the playground which boys will look to start a fight with you by his expression as he walks up to you," David explained, as he and Benton leaned over a counter holding rock candy and nuts.

Jonas shuffled through the newspaper. "David, is this your Wisconsin fire? They buried this article over here on the back page. I can barely make out the words," Jonas asked, as he strained his eyes with the small print.

Putting on his glasses that he now needed for reading as he had reached his early 40s, David reviewed the article, "Exactly! Northeastern Wisconsin suffered the so-called Peshtigo Fire. I'm told that it killed more people of any fire in American history—over a thousand. Apparently, several railroad workers inadvertently started a brush fire that quickly spread. My reports are that the Peshtigo fire destroyed sixteen towns. They named the fire Peshtigo because that town suffered the most damage."

Jonas began straightening the shelves, preparing for the next day. "I guess it is hard to compete for newspaper columns when the bulk of one of the nation's largest cities burns down," he said to David. "Besides, Chicago holds a special place in President Lincoln's heart. He lived in Illinois before being president. The Republican Party first nominated him for President at the convention in Chicago in 1860. Then, in 1868, they nominated him for a third term in Chicago as well. He will probably retire there with his family at the end of his term."

When David didn't respond, Jonas turned around. David looked intently out the window. He whispered, "These two men out on Congress Street are about to brawl, and the man on the left has a knife."

Ten-year-old Benton also focused his attention on the two young men outside. He knelt down next to David and began investigating himself. Within a minute, the two men outside on Congress Street began to punch each other. "Mr. Trent is right. That man has a knife!" Benton shouted.

Soon, David ran out on the street, breaking up the fight before any blood could be shed. Benton and Jonas followed fast on his heels. They restored peace with only the exchange of a couple of black eyes before the men went their separate ways.

"How could you tell that they were about to fight, Mr. Trent? Did you read them?" Benton asked, when they had returned to the store.

"Benton, I read these men based on both observation and experience. I don't simply look at people and events. I study them. I look for something out of the ordinary, even if it may not initially seem out of the ordinary."

"But how do you know what is ordinary so that you can tell this is out of the ordinary?" Benton asked.

"Well, I rely on a mixture of life experiences, research, and study. When you're a Pinkerton detective, you're trained for many years to think like this, and you always look for things that are out of the ordinary. We read and study psychology, medicine, chemistry, and physics as part of our training. Besides books that have been written by other authors, Allan Pinkerton keeps an updated list of information learned in real cases from his own employees. In this case, I noticed that the men were very close to each other when they were talking—at least compared to what I've typically seen. Part of my Pinkerton training in psychology also taught me that typical conversation takes place at a distance of three to five feet, but these men were approximately eighteen inches from each other. So, this one was pretty easy. Now that you know this, you will probably be able to see a number of fights before they happen," David replied.

"I hope so. The boys love to fight during recess at Primary No. 2. The teachers must not have the Pinkerton training because they only seem to break them up *after* a lot of punches are thrown or after the boys are wrestling on the ground," Benton said.

Jonas jumped in displaying his parental skills, "But, you don't get into fights in school anymore, do you, Benton?"

Benton struggled to answer in a truthful way that would avoid punishment. "Well, I don't start fights, but I finish them pretty well when I have to."

Sensing his young protégé might be getting into a bit of hot water, David cleared his throat. "Getting back to the case of the fight we just broke up on Congress Street ... I also observed the two men facing each other head-on. People usually converse at a slight angle to each other so as not to stare too intently. Once I knew it was out of the ordinary, I began to search for logical explanations for this behavior. The most logical explanation I found was that the men were arguing. About to fight."

Mr. Trent was Benton's favorite adult besides his parents, especially since he had moved the conversation away from the fights Benton had been having at school. Benton had studied the weaknesses of the other boys in school so that he could quickly win most of his fights without having too much "evidence" to hide on his face when he arrived home. Primary No. 2 believed "boys will be boys" so they did not report his fights to Jonas and Katia. Benton knew ultimately that his father would approve of his standing up for himself, but he preferred not to discuss his playground fights with his parents. He was relieved when the conversation topic had moved away from his fighting and followed up with David Trent. "Mr. Trent, that's truly amazing. But doesn't luck play a big party in your work? You guessed right this time, but you cannot be right all of the time. For example, I think some people are just 'close talkers' and sometimes brothers, fathers, and grandfathers may talk by staring directly at each other?" Benton asked.

Jonas turned to his son, with a serious look on his face. "Benton, please. Mr. Trent is a longstanding expert in his field. A ten-year-old boy should not question him about his work. Please be more respectful. Benton, apologize to Mr. Trent."

"I'm sorry, Mr. Trent," Benton said with a frown.

David gently touched Benton's arm. "Jonas thank you, but with all due respect, we Pinkertons value questioning. We treat our learning differently from most schools where students memorize dates, names, and formulas. We want our students to fully understand what they are learning and accept that our students often can provide new knowledge to the teachers. So, any curious mind like yours, Benton, should feel free to ask me questions. In fact, you're correct. We detectives focus on likelihoods, not certainty. We just play the odds. In this case, my experience and training told me that about 95 percent of adult men that are 'close talkers' are preparing for a fight."

Benton brightened considerably. "Wow, I really want to be able to do that when I'm grown up."

"It's an honorable profession, and I'm sure your parents would be proud if you entered our field. But, I must tell you, when you're a Pinkerton detective, you cannot turn off your analytical tools. You find yourself always investigating even when you are eating at a restaurant, taking a walk in the park, or working at your parents' store. Very often, you may annoy or insult other people by this behavior. But, mostly, it is a lot of fun for me. Why, I even found myself investigating a duck and a dog the other day. The duck tried to reach the edge of a pond to fly away, while the dog raced around the pond trying to pounce on the duck. Instead of just enjoying this game that popped up in nature, my mind focused on calculating the speed the dog would require to keep the duck from flying away. But, I never did. The math was too difficult for me. Maybe you can ask your math genius sister, Sandra." He smiled then and invited Benton outside, to the scene of the fight.

Jonas watched his best friend and his youngest son reviewing footprints, sun angles, wind directions, and the colors of the dirt in the neighborhood. Observing how intently Benton listened and how excited he looked, Jonas knew that Benton would happily follow David Trent's example and become a Pinkerton detective.

Jonas and Katia wanted the best for their children, and they encouraged them to find an occupation that interested them. By the time they approached their teenage years, the children had developed passions that would probably be parts of their lives for many years.

Nathan devoted every free minute to baseball. Gloves, overhand pitching, and a standardized number of strikes and balls established a formalized set of rules played consistently around the country. Some teams continued to play slight alterations to the game, but earlier versions like rounders and town ball were becoming obsolete. Cities, towns, and colleges began creating their own teams. Nathan spent so much time hanging around the diamond at Georgetown University that they made him an assistant manager. They played their first game against Columbian

College from Washington City in 1870, but they only played a sporadic schedule against other schools. Still only fourteen, Nathan hoped to attend Georgetown in a few years to lead their baseball team to glory.

"When you attend Georgetown, what do you intend for your major field of study? Perhaps chemistry, mathematics, or history?" Katia had asked Nathan at dinner the other night.

"Mathematics? Who would want to study mathematics—besides Sandra up at Cooper Union, of course? When I finish up at Secondary No. 2, I hope to never see any more mathematics, chemistry, or history. Baseball is all I need, Mom. Professional leagues will pop up all over the country, and then you can read about your famous ballplayer son. You have to promise to follow my progress in your newspapers every single day," Nathan replied.

Katia could only shake her head and laugh.

Sandra continued her studies with limited interruptions for summer vacation. She had successfully passed courses in calculus, trigonometry, and advanced algebra.

In the summer of 1873 while helping at the store, Sandra told her mother about her experiences at Cooper Union, "I thought there would be a lot of rich and fancy people in college like you read about in books, but Cooper Union is not like that. Many of the students come from families with businesses. A lot of their parents worked as clerks, salesmen, and engineers. Many of them speak with stronger accents than even you and dad."

"Really, I didn't realize we had such accents. So far, we seem to be getting along just fine," Katia laughed.

"Of course, and so do my fellow students. They compete really hard on the math competitions there, but I really enjoy it."

Just then, Benton walked in with a long face carrying *The Washington Star* for that day, June 12, 1873. "Speaking of math competition, I have some bad news to report. Your big math competitor back when you were in high school, John Thomas Williams, just passed away. Only twenty-one-years-old. I remember he always looked so sick from consumption, but he was really smart and a great friend to you."

While hugging her crying daughter, Katia looked at the announcement in the newspaper, "We must join poor Mrs. Williams tomorrow for the service at 3 PM after the burial at Congressional Cemetery. I remember that she lives right across from the Orange & Alexandria Railroad Depot."

Sandra just nodded through her sobs.

The Steuben family prevailed upon David Trent to watch their store while they attended the Williams funeral.

Mrs. Williams was nearly inconsolable when the Steubens arrived, but she recognized Sandra immediately. She called her over and offered Sandra a hug, "My John always thought so highly of you. Any time he could beat you, it would make his day. But, even when he lost to you, he would not get upset. He would just say, 'That Sandra Steuben is really smart. She is the toughest competition in Washington.'"

"Mrs. Williams, I am so sorry. I will always have great memories of your son, John. You don't make friends like him very easily. I really wanted him to join me up at Cooper Union. He would have loved it there," Sandra replied.

Mrs. Williams looked upward, "Sandra, I think he is in a place just like that right now. I will sure miss him, though. He doted so much on me, especially after Mr. Williams passed away."

"Mrs. Williams, what can I do to help you or to honor John's memory?" Sandra said.

Mrs. Williams gently held Sandra's hands. "He would want you to make a successful career out of mathematics. If you can use your friendship with him as inspiration, please do that. But, don't you worry about me."

Sandra put her arm around Mrs. Williams, "Will you return to your family in South Carolina now?"

"I'm afraid that is not a real option anymore. Twelve years of Confederate rule with their insistence on the Southern way of life has made it tough to live for most people down there. Many of the western ones have moved to Mexico, while a lot of the other Confederates have moved up here. Robert Toombs is a good man, but it doesn't look like his Presidency is going to be any more successful than Jefferson Davis's. I don't even think he wants to try to run again next year," Mrs. Williams muttered.

"Yes, I guess you're right. With all of the prosperity here from our businesses and the millions of Europeans coming to the United States to work, Washington provides a better location for you," Sandra replied.

"I think some of my cousins may even come up here to live with me. They said it's hard to put a finger on, but there is a movement afoot of dangerous bad men who aim to cause harm if they don't get their way. My family even says the movement has grown so much that their leader may get elected President next year. A man by the name of Nathan Forrest," Mrs. Williams whispered.

"That would really be a shame for the Confederacy. Cooper Union hosted Judah Benjamin for a speech last year. He was articulate and polite even when he disagreed with the person asking him questions. I don't agree with everything he stands for, but I would think he would make a good President," Sandra countered.

"They say he is the Confederacy's top lawyer and I might even move back if Benjamin were elected. But, Forrest's movement is growing ever so fast. And Benjamin is ..." Mrs. Williams hesitated.

"Jewish?" Sandra offered.

Mrs. Williams just nodded her head.

"Well, we will keep our fingers crossed for better fortunes here in the United States. Starting with our new President, James Blaine, and whether he can follow in the large footsteps of Abraham Lincoln," Sandra replied.

"I saw his footsteps and you are right. They are huge," Mrs. Williams laughed for the first time all day.

"I promise to come visit again soon and then again when I finish up at Cooper Union. Goodbye, Mrs. Williams," Sandra whispered as she walked across the room to join her family.

America's tremendous growth throughout the Lincoln administrations and the beginning of the Blaine administration could be tracked through population and business. Larger and larger businesses arose in all of the major cities, as large families and European immigration added millions to the population. In addition, America now extended outside of its contiguous states with the acquisition of Alaska from Russia in 1867. Newspapers had estimated that Alaska held twice the acreage of Texas, but less than 30,000 people inhabited this vast land mass. Many criticized the purchase as wasteful by then-Secretary of State, Andrew Johnson. They called it "Johnson's Blunder."

These developments and good, consistent management had caused business to boom at Steuben's Ordinary. The Steubens decided to open a second, larger store on the main corner in the Georgetown neighborhood. This store would focus more on produce, dry food, and clothing than the original. On the Southwest corner of Wisconsin and M Streets, the new store would cater to both the university and local businesses. Steuben's Extraordinary had opened its doors on July 4, 1874, amidst patriotic displays of flags, music, and fireworks. Jonas dressed up as George

Washington—white wig and all—and passed out candy to neighborhood children while standing on top of a fire truck.

Jonas knew he couldn't be in two places at the same time, so he had asked Katia to hire a manager for Steuben's Ordinary. Katia agreed, but had quickly became frustrated with the process. Too many candidates simply could not speak English well enough. Those that could speak well often showed no mathematical skills to keep the books. In addition, she was most concerned with finding someone trustworthy. Twelve applicants had interviewed, and Katia did not approve of any of them. But a solution came from an unlikely source. Katia had run into David Trent and confided her problem.

"There may be a solution for you," he said. "Next month, my nephew, Sean Trent, will move here from Scotland to live with me. He has clerked at an establishment back home for several years and would be looking for a position here. I never met the lad so I cannot vouch for his competence, but I can vouch for his trustworthiness. Maybe you could speak with him?"

And so she did. Twenty-one-year-old Sean Trent turned out to be the perfect fit. His strong Scottish accent and formal mannerisms made a good impression on Katia and Jonas. They thought he would present a respectable look to the customers, and they could completely trust any nephew of David Trent.

Sean Trent eventually took charge of Steuben's Ordinary in early January 1875. The Steubens quickly found him to be a competent and trustworthy manager. Sean followed the business closely, which included reviewing the news to be able to converse with customers, "Mr. Steuben, this recent election in the Confederacy seems crooked even by the standards we saw back in Scotland. How is it possible that one candidate can simply place guards with guns at polling places to ensure that only his loyal voters get through? The American papers all suggest Benjamin would have easily won a fair election. But, the Confederate papers show much more restraint in what they write. Perhaps, they fear repercussions from the new President Forrest?"

Jonas looked at Sean. "Sean, I just don't know. It is hard to believe that the Confederate states were part of our country just 14 years ago. Now, they have elected a totalitarian extremist who will punish all of the moderates that don't think his way. I suspect more and more Confederate political and business leaders will move up here to the United States. My friend, Mr. Jensen, told me that he even ran into Judah Benjamin himself at the market near his home in New York."

"I didn't realize that. A proud man with such service to the Confederacy doesn't even feel comfortable in his own country just because of his moderate views?" Sean asked.

"In the case of Benjamin, it was not just his policies. He served as Forrest's competition in the election, and he's Jewish. Forrest continues to make life difficult for Jews and immigrants. Military and police roam throughout the Confederacy to enforce his doctrines," Jonas replied.

"That Nathan Bedford Forrest is extreme. I sure hope he doesn't try anything up here in Washington," Sean replied, as he went back to work.

Nathan had matriculated to Georgetown by the time Steuben's Extraordinary opened in 1875. He informed his parents that he intended to focus on his studies, but they knew studying only meant one word—baseball—to their older son. Nathan quickly earned accolades as a star of the school team. He set his sights on a professional career in the newly formed National League of baseball. But he first promised his parents that he would complete his college degree.

Fourteen-year-old Benton spent less time with Nathan once his older brother entered college, and Benton missed the time they used to spend together. Benton had not developed a long athletic body like Nathan, but he had developed wide shoulders and strong muscles. While Benton couldn't compete with Nathan on the baseball diamond, he could now equal his brother at wrestling matches.

Benton had now reached an age where he would watch the stores whenever Katia, Jonas, or Sean Trent needed a break. Less focused than the others on marketing and customer service, he took his role as security for the stores very seriously. When watching the stores, Benton made sure to "read" all of the customers.

One afternoon in the summer of 1875, Jonas took Katia out for lunch while young Benton watched Steuben's Extraordinary. A family that Benton did not recognize entered the store. Benton overhead the father telling the mother, "Why this is a beautiful store with everything that we could ever need. What a convenience for us around the corner from our new home."

Always suspicious to a fault, Benton thought to himself, "This couple just created this animated conversation to distract me while their kids rob the store. A classic criminal trick. But, they chose the wrong store today."

Just then, the family's seven-year-old boy picked up a large piece of rock candy and was about to put it in his mouth when Benton jumped up from behind the counter and snatched the candy from the boy. "I caught you! I knew you were up to something."

At this, the fourteen-year-old daughter glared intently at Benton and protectively pushed him away from her little brother onto the ground. Seeing the look of shock and horror on the face of the girl and her parents, Benton realized he had made a big mistake. Fortunately, the parents walked over to calm things down, "We apologize. In our old hometown store in Amherst, Massachusetts, our little Scott would just take food and the clerks would add it to the bill. We hadn't established that practice here now that we have moved to Georgetown."

Beet red with embarrassment, Benton stepped back behind the counter, "It's I who need to apologize to you and your son—and your daughter. I spend a lot of time investigating and observing people. I still require much more study and work before I can become a detective. Please take a bag of that candy on my account for your son. My parents and I would also like to welcome you to our store anytime you wish. My name is Benton Steuben," as he reached out his hand.

"We understand and you had good intentions at least to protect your family's store. I am Ariel Goldman, and this is my wife, Tamara. Our candy-eating son is named Scott. His older sister who is still glaring at you after pushing you to the floor is Kristina," as Mr. Goldman shook Benton's hand while trying to calm the situation.

"I am pleased to meet you. My parents, Jonas and Katia, run this store and our original down the street, Steuben's Ordinary," Benton replied, as his face started to regain its natural color.

Tamara Goldman smiled at Benton. "I liked the way your parents named the stores, Benton. By any chance, do you or your siblings attend Secondary #3 in Washington City?"

"Well, my sister graduated from there several years ago, and then she went to college at Cooper Union to study math. Sandra will begin teaching at Georgetown in a few weeks. This worries my brother, Nathan, who is a current student at Georgetown," Benton laughed. "But, I still attend Secondary #3. We now just call the main part of the city 'Washington,' but some of the old-timers still use the old Washington City name. They began changing the street signs in Georgetown so that we look like one larger city, but it takes time for people to adjust..."

Now, Benton's observational skills started to operate much more accurately. He noticed the fear, trepidation, and anger in the face of Kristina Goldman, as she listened to her mother. "Perhaps you wouldn't mind walking Kristina to school until she learns the route for herself?"

As Kristina's look turned to full exasperation, Benton replied, "I would be happy to, but it might be nice to have Kristina meet some of the girls in the neighborhood. Sally Barnes lives a few blocks away. I can ask her and her friends to meet Kristina here at 7 AM next Monday morning to walk together for that first day of school. Would that be OK?"

Seeing a calm expression return to Kristina's face (and even during this stressful experience, Benton had to admit she had a very pretty face) where he thought he might have even detected a very faint "thank you" look in her eyes, Benton turned to listen to Mrs. Goldman, "Why, Benton, that would be perfect. Thank you. We look forward to meeting your parents as well."

Benton waved goodbye as the Goldmans left the store. But, the normally unflappable teenager noticed that he was still shaking.

Sandra marched resolutely down M Street. A Cooper Union graduate, she had moved back to Georgetown to begin her position as an instructor in mathematics at Georgetown University in the fall of 1875. Like some other universities, Georgetown would not allow women to enroll as students, but they employed a few educated women on the staff. With very few men or women in the United States boasting her training and record in mathematics, Georgetown felt lucky to bring her on staff.

Sandra missed her colleagues and life in New York. She focused on and enjoyed her research and the other mathematics professors, but found the students disappointing. Polite, respectful, and wealthy; the Georgetown students did not show the hunger, intensity, or quantitative skills of the students she had befriended at Cooper Union.

Her parents' new home on O Street only required a short ten-minute walk to the university, but this day, Sandra had an appointment in a different direction. Though she avoided her old day-to-day role assisting her parents with the accounting at Steuben's Ordinary—or Steuben's Extraordinary—she couldn't resist reviewing the financial books at least once a quarter.

During her years of study at Cooper Union, Steuben's Ordinary had adopted a new accounting process. Sandra had not seen this process applied before and questioned her parents about it. Jonas referred her to Sean Trent, who had taken over the accounting duties for both stores by that time.

"We'll see what this new employee thinks he is doing to our books," she thought. Sandra had limited formal knowledge of accounting, but with her mathematical skills and her earlier experience with the stores, she felt some personal connection to this part of her parents' business.

So focused was Sandra on this accounting change that she barely noticed her brother Benton walking home from school until he had nearly walked right into her. Then, she noticed something quite peculiar. Instead of walking home with the boys in the neighborhood or a large group mixed with boys and girls, Benton walked alone with a single girl. Sandra noticed them talking earnestly without the nervous tension that one would typically see between a fourteen-year-old boy and girl. "Hi, little brother. I almost missed you there. Who is your friend?"

"Sandra, I would like you to meet Kristina Goldman. Her family moved here recently from Massachusetts. Mr. Goldman had taught up at Amherst College, and now he secured a position in the Treasury Department here in Washington."

Sandra, still in shock seeing her fourteen-year-old baby brother walking alone with a girl, could only reply, "Yes, Mom and Dad had mentioned that."

"Mom and Dad probably told you the story of how I met the Goldmans? Well, now I walk home with Kristina in case I run into a bully and need someone to push him down for me," Benton joked, without any embarrassment.

Holding out her hand, Sandra looked at Kristina, "It's my pleasure to meet you, Kristina. Our family laughed about that story when you pushed Benton down for weeks. The boys at school don't even try to push Benton around, so you really must have a lot of spunk. I must apologize, though. Benton's suspicious and investigative nature may be well suited for detective work, but not so much for running a store."

Kristina also seemed quite natural and at ease with the conversation, "No need to apologize, Sandra. Things have changed a lot since that first day. I have found more to your brother than his interests in arresting seven-year-old candy eating boys. I admit our first meeting does not provide the most romantic story that you will ever hear, but at least our families get to laugh about it. I now find myself a bit of an amateur detective as well, spending all of this time with your brother. But, I am glad to meet you, Sandra. I have heard a great many things about you from your parents— and from Benton," as she smiled.

"Thank you and make sure to come find me if you have any trouble with this one, Kristina," Sandra joked, as she shifted her neck toward Benton. "Well, I don't want to disturb the two of you and I must rush over to Steuben's Ordinary."

The teenagers both waved goodbye to Sandra. In the distance, she thought she could see them holding hands. Too focused on the task on hand to consider Benton's new friendship any further, Sandra just shook her head, smiled, and continued walking.

When Sandra arrived at the store, the handsome blonde clerk Sean Trent greeted her cordially and showed her the ledgers. After she inspected the books, she turned and raised her voice to Trent. "What type of accounting process have you instituted here? My parents had gotten along very well with their prior system for more than fifteen years. Why would you change it?"

Sean was taken aback for several reasons. First, he took a lot of pride in his work, so harsh criticism always made him sensitive. Second, he had never met a young woman so knowledgeable or confident in the fields of business or accounting. But, beyond all of that, he simply could not take his eyes off of Sandra. He could only offer a weak response. "Well …" was his only response. He simply could not think of anything else to say.

"As I understand it, you have moved to accrual accounting. This requires us to depreciate certain types of expenditures. Why couldn't we just stick to our old cash accounting basis so that our results can tie to our monthly bank statements?" Sandra demanded.

Still quite mesmerized with Sandra, Sean finally caught his breath. "You're right about that, Miss Steuben, but each approach offers its own benefits with its own costs. The expansion to Steuben's Extraordinary with its startup costs and the slower turnover of some of that inventory made me initially think a switch would be profitable. But, before I implemented the accrual approach, I analyzed each approach with the last two year's financial records and our business plan's projections for the next five years."

"Then, please show me the math," she said. Sandra knew that she would be convinced of this new accounting process from the numbers.

Sean spent several hours over each of the next few weekends walking Sandra through his calculations. She noticed a few minor errors, but generally, she left the sessions quite impressed. Ultimately, she fully agreed with Sean's decision to switch the accounting process.

Sean enjoyed his business discussions with Sandra, but he also quickly formed romantic intentions. Soon, he made all of the proper inquiries with the Steubens and Sandra, so that he and Sandra began courting. It didn't take long for Sean to ask Jonas's permission to marry Sandra. Jonas happily offered his blessing, and he expected Sandra to quickly say yes as well.

Sandra had developed similar feelings for Sean, and she gladly accepted his marriage proposal. First, however, she required some conditions. "You know how much math means to me, so I wanted it to be an important part of my wedding. With that theme, I wanted to get married on pi day when my age is a prime number," Sandra countered with a wink.

"Sandra Steuben, I'm happy to marry you under any condition," Sean gushed.

"Well then, Mr. Sean Trent, when should I expect to see you at church?" Sandra asked, as she would similarly quiz one of her students.

"I suspect this will not be the last of our mathematics conversations nor the last time you try to quiz me or any children we may have. Pi day represents the value of pi, or rounded to 3.14. The third month of the year and the fourteenth day occur on March 14. In the near future, your age will only represent a prime number on March 14 in the year 1876. Next year. Then, you can see me waiting at the church for my twenty-three-year-old bride! Unless you want to wait another six years until you're twenty-nine and prime again!" Sean exclaimed.

CHAPTER 8

MARCH 14, 1876: GEORGETOWN COUPLE TO MARRY

"Our little girl marries today. A mother dreams of this day. And Sean Trent is such a fine man!" Katia was nearly crying as she uttered these words to Jonas.

"Yes, now if we can only manage to see our boys cleaned up and dressed at church, it will truly be a miracle," Jonas joked, as he started playfully swatting the boys with his folded copy of *The Washington Daily Capital* that announced Sandra's wedding.

"Don't worry, Dad. Kristina will make sure that Benton looks presentable," Nathan teased.

"Thank god for that. That girl is the best thing to ever happen to your brother. I can't exactly say the same for you and the girls that follow you and your baseball friends around. Single women getting dressed up to watch a game and then screaming for their team? Not in my day," Katia replied.

"Oh mom, in your day there was no baseball. Don't worry, I'm sure you will love the girl that I end up marrying," Nathan replied.

"We'll see, Nathan Steuben. Now, in the meantime, get dressed and hurry over to the church," Katia replied as she stepped outside.

Unfazed, Benton continued working his hair with a small black comb while looking in the mirror. He knew Kristina would arrive soon.

On their walk to church, Jonas smiled at an early campaign sign in the window of Steuben's Extraordinary, "Re-elect Blaine 1876." Occupying a large space at the busiest street corner in the Georgetown neighborhood, the banner made all of the local citizens aware of the Steubens' political leanings. Steuben's Extraordinary had displayed a similar banner four years earlier, when Blaine became the seventeenth president as Lincoln's successor.

Jonas and Katia saw David Trent on their way to St. John's Episcopal Church. "I believe this will be the most secure wedding this year with more than ten of my Pinkerton colleagues joining us," David laughed.

"I suspect they will only need to enjoy themselves as guests without investigating any troubles. Georgetown in the middle of the day has always been very safe," Katia replied.

"Yes, I suspect you and your colleagues will face more difficult challenges keeping security this summer at the Republican Convention in Cincinnati. I look forward to attending my first convention as well. I don't think President Blaine will face much competition with the nomination, though," Jonas replied.

David smirked, "I agree. Blaine's political career has truly experienced a second life. I thought it ended when his supporter described Democrats as the party of 'rum, Romanism, and rebellion.' His quick reaction to clarify that the Democrats represented the party of the Confederacy turned out to be a brilliant political move."

"Yes, I agree. Republicans face tougher obstacles to win than we did during Lincoln's time, but I think Blaine and Wheeler will secure a second term in November," Jonas replied.

"You know, Jonas, when we get to talking—you especially—we can forget ourselves pretty easily. You may have noticed a throng of people gathered outside of the church. Perhaps, we should make our way over there also." David smiled.

The Steuben children had already arrived at the church and begun preparations for their roles in the ceremony. Sandra was so busy that her memories would always be a blur. Nathan enjoyed himself, but kept checking his watch to see if he would have time to play in a late afternoon baseball.

Benton's experience on his sister's wedding day, however, brought a more serious and lasting memory. The fifteen-year-old had been walking Kristina Goldman to and from school for the past five months. He had initially organized for Kristina to walk with a large group of girls, but soon Benton and Kristina started spending a lot of time together at school. While the other girls tried to get the older boys' attention with giggles and blushes, Kristina found Benton's seriousness and focus interesting. Kristina's initial hatred of Benton for his treatment of her brother at their first meeting had cooled and eventually turned into friendship. In turn, Kristina's love of life rubbed off on Benton. Soon, Benton joined the walking groups with Kristina. But, eventually, Benton and Kristina split off on their own. Kristina would also arrange for them to explore the city on its streetcars visiting important government buildings and walking through some of the old city parks. By the end of 1875, classmates and family could clearly see the development of their courtship.

Besides his schoolwork and investigative detective research, Benton spent nearly all of his time with Kristina. Their romance remained physically innocent and had not advanced past holding hands, but their long conversations made them much closer than most married couples.

The young couple found a small area between the church and the Linthicum Institute School for buys where they could speak privately during the wedding reception. Kristina smiled with a serious tone, as she gently pulled Benton towards her and pressed her lips upon his for their first kiss, "Benton Steuben, I love you. Once we are old enough, I want to marry you."

Benton could barely believe his luck as he listened to the words being whispered in his ears. This tall girl with curly brown hair and freckles was everything he could ever ask for in life. "I love you too, Kristina. I will happily marry you as soon as we can," Benton said with a face fresh with excitement.

Jonas sorely wanted someone in his family to join him at the Republican Convention that summer. He knew that David Trent would be there, but David's work schedule would make it hard for them to spend time together.

Katia didn't enjoy traveling.

Sandra was a newlywed.

Nathan could not leave in the middle of baseball season.

That left Benton to join his father.

After many hours on their train to the Queen City, Jonas and Benton spent time exploring Cincinnati and dining together. Father and son enjoyed their time together, but Jonas could truly spend all day in the back room meetings and listening to the political speeches. Benton ended up spending much of his time watching and talking with the Pinkerton team working the convention.

"Mr. Trent, when I grow up, I want to be the best Pinkerton man ever. Except for you of course," Benton said.

"Benton, you flatter me. I work hard, and I hope that I can help many people, but I don't think of myself as the best Pinkerton ever," David replied.

"But, you know so much. Who else could be that great of a detective?" Benton asked.

"Well, look around at this Exposition Hall. Many of my finest colleagues fill this hall. One of the greatest detectives is our founder Allan Pinkerton behind me with the receding hairline and the long thick beard. A friend to honesty and a foe to crime, he has organized all of our operations, and his skill at finding good people and training them is unparalleled," David stated.

"Yes, I guess, Mr. Pinkerton is a great detective too. So, I can aspire to get to your levels," Benton countered.

"I'm not sure I belong in Mr. Pinkerton's league. In fact, the best "Pinkerton man" was not even a man. Her name was Kate Warne. You have probably read of some of her big cases, like the Adams Express Company and the foiled Lincoln train assassination attempt in Baltimore. I had the honor to work with this great woman for several years in Chicago before I moved down to Washington. A small woman with dark hair, she could run circles around our colleagues in the field. We all lost a great detective and wonderful woman eight years ago when she passed away. I will never forget her," David said wistfully.

"Wow," Benton said. Benton had already been picking up some of the mannerisms like a seasoned detective, including knowing when to keep talking and when to let a conversation end. He could tell that David Trent held strong feelings for Kate Warne that extended far beyond her professional skills. He made a mental note to himself to ask David Trent about her at a later time. For now, he would focus on the acceptance speech being made by President Blaine:

…Vice President Wheeler and I look forward to continuing the fifth straight term of Republican rule in the United States. We owe a large debt to our many supporters who have worked tirelessly on the campaign. I particularly want to single out one man whose speech excited this crowd yesterday, Mr. Judah Benjamin. This former Democrat who saw his own presidential election stolen in the Confederacy two years ago serves as a fine asset to Republicans across the country in this election season.

I want to celebrate that this will be the last convention where we have to address slavery. Recognizing international pressure and slavery's lowered need in our industrialized economy, in just one year, the Quadruple 7 will be enacted. Slavery will cease forever in the United States on July 7, 1877.

Finally, my last point involves my own career. Unlike President Lincoln, I do not intend to seek a third term. Looking around the hall today, I know the future remains bright for the Republican Party.

Jonas smiled contentedly from a vantage point across the convention floor. Noticing Benton across the hall, Jonas realized he and Katia had provided a very different life to this fifteen-year-old than the provincial lives they faced at that age back in Bernkastel and Kues.

Jonas walked to the large desk at the back of the store and turned the calendar to March 1879, eagerly counting down the days until Katia's forty-seventh birthday on the fifteenth. He and Katia did not celebrate prime number birthdays with quite the gusto that Sandra did, but they would look forward to a night out on the town.

Benton walked into Steuben's Extraordinary and approached Jonas at his calendar. "Dad, did you just turn to the March calendar to mark the time when Nathan will be going away to join his teammates on the Boston Red Caps again?"

"Well, I am still surprised that he can earn a living at sport, but we are sure proud of him. It sounds like he has focused himself on third base, but they play him wherever they need him." Jonas replied.

"Dad, you have become a true baseball fan. Yes, I know Nathan is excited, and I will follow his results every day in the newspapers. Hopefully, they can win a championship just like they did the last two years," Benton replied.

"Dad, I actually wanted to talk to you a little about my own future and profession. You know I have started my training with the Pinkerton Agency since I turned eighteen in January," Benton began.

Jonas didn't know where Benton was leading with the conversation, so he remained cautious as the two of them sat down. "Yes."

Benton jumped right in. "With the strong growth of our country and the size of the government, Washington needs more and more detectives. In fact, the Pinkerton Agency today offered me a position based here in May when I graduate."

Jonas hugged his barrel-chested youngest son. "Congratulations, Benton! You have fulfilled your dream."

"Thank you, dad. I do have a dream to be a Pinkerton detective. But, another dream far exceeds that in my mind. I want to marry Kristina and raise a family with her. She has made my life so much better for almost four years now. I know most men wait until they are older to marry, but I don't need any more time to know my feelings for Kristina. We will, of course, ask her parents, but we are hoping to get married this summer after I start work. I think she also plans to work—but here with you at Steuben's Extraordinary," Benton replied.

Jonas just smiled. "Of course, we could not be happier."

Benton and Kristina went through many changes that summer. They finished secondary school, secured jobs, wed, and found a place to live all within a few short weeks. Then, they left for their honeymoon.

Benton had suggested renting a small cabin by a nearby lake, but Kristina wanted more adventure. "Within a short time, travel will be more difficult with children. We can spend time just the two of us during our honeymoon. Your sister Sandra tells so many exciting stories of her time at Cooper Union, so I always wanted to see New York City!"

The travel sounded a lot more glamorous when Kristina described it, and Benton knew he would enjoy every moment of it.

"The first place I want to visit is Central Park. They say it feels like a forest or a country estate, but right in the middle of the city," Kristina whispered, as the couple walked down 5th Avenue from 60th to 66th Street.

Entering the park with his right hand clasped in Kristina's left, Benton could not believe its size. "It is truly amazing. You can barely look through the trees to see any buildings once you get in the middle of the park."

"Yes, eventually the trees will get more grown in and even taller once they mature. Then, the park will offer no views of city buildings—unless they decide to build a few Washington Monuments here in New York," Kristina laughed, as she felt Benton adjusting her new wedding ring.

"Well, I don't know about that, but if you look south, I can already see the tops of a couple of very tall buildings. I guess the New York views will depend on whether the buildings grow faster than the trees," Benton replied as they exited the park on 59th Street at Broadway.

"Well, it just so happens that we are heading in the direction of those buildings downtown. I hope Mr. Pinkerton keeps you in shape. We will be walking several miles, Benton. Let's stay on Broadway for a while. It reminds me of our Pennsylvania Avenue with its wide lanes, but there are so many more people and stores. There is barely enough room on the sidewalks for us to walk next to each other," Kristina panted as she kept up a quick walking pace.

"Wow, I just can't get used to the sheer number of people here. Let's take a seat for a couple of minutes on this park bench," Benton said as he enjoyed transforming the weight of his body from his legs to the green wooden bench. "Hey, do you see that structure over there on top of the white brick building? It looks like an arm holding a torch."

"You sit here and rest. I will find out for you," Kristina whispered, as she gently kissed the top of Benton's head.

Benton watched Kristina moving through the crowd. Efficiently, she located the person in charge and made a direct line to speak with him. Then, she hurried back with the information while sitting with Benton on the green bench, "That's the torch-bearing arm of the Statue of Liberty gift from France. Apparently, funds to complete the rest of the statue did not materialize, and it has been on display here in New York since the Centennial celebration in Philadelphia a few years ago. It will remain on display in this park here at Madison Square until New York secures enough donations from its citizens and tourists to complete the project."

Benton laughed. "Why don't we drop a couple of quarters in the box over there? I doubt our small donation will have much impact, but a man on his honeymoon can be generous. We will always remember our honeymoon contribution if it ever gets completed."

Kristina pushed her husband along to the arm where they dropped their quarters into the box for donations. "We still have a few more stops on this walking tour, Mr. Steuben. Then, you may rest for the remainder of the day," Kristina laughed.

"That sounds like a perfect day. I see we have continued farther and farther downtown. I thought it was crowded uptown, but down in this area, you can barely walk at all," Benton observed as they continued down past 8th Street.

A few minutes later, Kristina asked her husband, "Does that large rectangular building on the left look familiar?"

"No, but the sign over to the right gave me a big hint. The Foundation Building and Great Hall at Cooper Union. So, Sandra spent four years studying and attending lectures at this building? It is quite an impressive structure. Are we going in here?" Benton asked.

"No, this just happened to be on the path of our walk. So, I wanted to make sure we saw it. We must walk another fifteen blocks or so down Bowery for the next stop," Kristina smiled.

But, Benton already knew as he looked east towards Brooklyn, "It's the bridge! Wow, those towers just rise up to the sky. It reminds me when they built the Washington Monument and we school kids kept track of its height. But, this bridge will actually hold vehicles. That will be something to see."

"It looks like they've set up pathways to let you walk to the towers and across to Brooklyn. I would love to do that, but I would rather walk across the completed bridge itself with our children when we come back," Kristina noted.

"I can see the completed bridge now with us walking across hand-in-hand. As soon as we can, we will bring our whole family back here for that walk," Benton replied.

"Well, we made it almost back to our hotel, but I wanted to take a short walk down Pearl Street. My parents told me about Castle Garden and I wanted to see it for myself," Benton requested as they approached Battery Park.

"I always imagined the building to be bigger. It extends out in a circle towards the water with its flags waving above. That must be quite a sight for immigrants after a long journey at sea. I can just imagine your parents and Sandra walking through the building 24 years ago and changing your last name to Steuben. I am glad they did—it is a lot easier to pronounce," Kristina observed.

"Yes, you're right. It's a bit underwhelming. I can't imagine how this building functions as the main depot for U.S. immigration," Benton continued.

"Well, that walk tired me out. Now that we're back near our hotel, perhaps you will allow your new bride the courtesy of a short nap. Perfect timing, I see a pub right here for you to sit and have a beer—The Dry Dollar," Kristina noted, as she walked into the hotel.

Benton thought to himself that it seemed like each corner in New York City had at least one pub. Being tired and thirsty, he took a seat at the dimly lit bar and ordered a beer. Benton noticed several customers and the bartender giving him unfriendly looks.

"Thank you," Benton said as he received his beer and darted his eyes around the room.

Three men came up behind and grabbed him. He could feel a revolver placed at his head.

The man seated to his right at the bar walked up to him with a menacing copper attachment to his right thumb ring. "Mister, who are you with? You know whose place this is?"

Remembering his Pinkerton research, he tried to think of the names of the brutal and vicious gangs in New York that worked the Wharfs, the Five Points, and the other notorious neighborhoods. But he couldn't remember their names or recognize anything specific to identify these particular gang members. "Steuben. Benton Steuben is my name. I just came in for a drink on my honeymoon with my wife. If you look in my left jacket pocket, you will see that I work for the Pinkerton Agency based in Washington," he continued with his arms raised slowly.

"What are you investigating here, spy?" one of the thugs behind him growled.

"I'm not working. You can probably tell that my wedding ring is brand new. I didn't mean to interrupt a private meeting. I just wanted to sit and get a beer while my wife took a nap at our hotel down the street," Benton responded without changing expression, knowing that a forceful truth typically offered the best option in difficult situations.

"Boss, he ain't packing. I seen his business card, so his story checks out," the thug informed the man at the bar with the thumb ring.

"All right, let him go. Let the man drink his beer in peace. Mr. Steuben, my name is McGloin, Mike McGloin. We face a lot of competition for this territory, so my friends and I don't show good manners to the customers in our bar. But, we ain't here to harass tourists," McGloin began while passing Benton's dime back to him. "Your money is no good here. The drinks are on me."

"Thank you, Mr. McGloin. In my profession, you don't survive long without being very suspicious either. In fact, my suspicious nature got me into a lot of trouble once, but it all worked out. In fact, that is how I met my wife," Benton replied, as he recounted the story to McGloin and his friends of his first meeting with the Goldman family four years earlier.

Laughing after hearing the story, McGloin put his arm around the broad-shouldered Benton, "It is a shame you didn't grow up in our neighborhood, Benton. We sure could have used you on the Whyos with that poker face and those wide shoulders."

Benton smiled, as he finished his second beer. Feeling more comfortable, he followed his Pinkerton training—provide a personal story so that others feel comfortable with you, but make sure to show interest in them by asking them something specific. "You may be right. Our work is not all that different from yours. I know we have worked with a number of gangs to help on our cases, and I know we will again. But, Mike, I wanted to ask you about your thumb ring. I've never seen anything like it."

McGloin took off the ring to show it to Benton with obvious pride. "It is not just a ring. Our old boss, Dandy Johnny Dolan used to wear it before he was hanged a few years back at the Tombs. His ring works as an eye gouger that just plops in there and takes out someone's eye. He wore one on each thumb."

That gruesome image reminded Benton of the story Christian Hines had told him as a little boy. "My condolences about your old boss. But, that reminds me of a story an old man once told me about the 1800 election for president ..."

McGloin could not stop laughing. "Times don't change much. People still fight and kill each other over politics and money."

Benton stood up to offer the bartender two dollars as a tip, as he got up to leave. "Gentlemen, thank you again. Here's my card. Please call on me if I can ever provide you a favor. And I'll be sure to look you up when I come up here next."

Looking around the bar, McGloin said, "And you know where to find us. But, I wanted to give you something before you go. I only need one of these thumb rings. You keep the other. As you said, your business may not be all that different from mine. You may need it someday. Please enjoy the rest of your honeymoon in our fair city."

Benton received the ring graciously and bowed to his new friends, "I will pass on your kind words to my wife. If I arrive back at the hotel any later, she may soon be my ex-wife."

The men laughed cheerfully as Benton left the bar.

Back in the hotel room, Benton lightly kissed Kristina's forehead and held her hand while he lied down on the bed next to her. "Now, maybe, I could use a short nap also."

Upon the return from the honeymoon, the young Steuben couple moved into their rented unit in the same building where Kristina's dressmaker, Annie Ward, lived. Kristina also quickly befriended others in their Georgetown neighborhood. The neighbors felt a sense of comfort being around Kristina despite her only being eighteen years old.

One of her favorites was upstairs neighbor, Mary Hanckel. "You have the look of a newlywed, Mrs. Steuben. How long have you been married?"

"Yes, we only got married in May. We recently finished secondary school and started working," Kristina replied.

"I am glad that you both completed your studies. After all, I am a teacher and I am a stickler for education. I particularly like math," Mary replied.

"I must introduce you to my sister-in-law. She gained some fame as a math star here in secondary school and then went to Cooper Union to study mathematics. For the past four years, she has been teaching at Georgetown." Kristina smiled.

"I think I know of her. Sandra Trent? She is a local legend here. Between her friendship and competition with the late John Williams and her advancement in mathematics since then, I would love to meet her to ask for some tips." Mary smiled as they both spotted Benton walking home from work.

Kristina offered a proper and formal introduction. "Miss Hanckel, this is my husband, Benton Steuben."

Mary replied in turn. "Mr. Steuben, it is my pleasure. But, please call me Mary."

Benton smiled at the two women. "Thank you, Mary. Please also call me by my first name as well. Benton. My parents thought it was a strong name in honor of a courageous politician—and I have grown to like the sound of it these nineteen years."

As they entered their apartment and sat down, Benton smiled at Kristina. "It's like the neighbors have already crowned you the belle of the ball on 3045 Dumbarton Street. I also met two gentlemen from our building, however. I will be sure to introduce you to Daniel Coombs and Joseph Lewis. You will like them too."

Kristina giggled. "Actually … I already met too. You are right. I do like them. They know so much about all of the new homes being built here in Georgetown. They say they stay busy building six days a week. But, your timing is perfect. Dinner is all ready."

Benton sat down to his plate of grilled chicken, mashed potatoes, and green peas. "Yes, Coombs recently moved up from South Carolina. He said he had never ridden on a train before then. Now, he takes a train almost every week. He still marvels at all of the modern conveniences here compared to his little hometown in the country. He couldn't believe it when he saw a telephone in use at the Treasury Building calling President Blaine's office."

"Yes, he's very thankful to be here. Coombs told me he never saw factories in South Carolina except for guns. People can feed themselves on the land, but can't find many other ways to make a living down in the Confederacy. President Forrest has drawn such a clear line in the sand against Negroes, Jews, Mexicans, and other foreigners that few people want to move there. And, many good people like Coombs move away," Kristina said with a frown.

"In fact, the instability down in the Confederacy has caused concern up here. The upcoming Republican Convention will need as much security as space will allow. I just found out that I have been selected to join the Pinkerton contingent being represented in Chicago this summer," Benton said.

"I am so proud of you. Only nineteen years old and protecting some of our most important politicians. You must tell me how well Chicago has recovered from the fire. The newspaper reports in the store make it seem like nothing less than a miraculous transformation. I will miss you during the trip, but I knew what I was getting into when I married a Pinkerton man." Kristina smiled.

"I do love the work, and I learn something new every day," Benton replied.

Kristina smiled and looked Benton in the eye. "Maybe once you return, we can start thinking about expanding on the family?"

During early June 1880 while Benton was away at the convention, Kristina was reviewing the papers on her morning shift at Steuben's Ordinary when a well-dressed professional woman with curly brown hair, in her late twenties walked in. "Welcome. May I offer my assistance, Ma'm?"

Using a strong country/mountain accent more commonly heard in the vacation parkland areas of western Virginia or western Maryland than by a well-dressed lady in the city, the woman replied, "Why, yes, thank you. I would like to purchase three dozen large pads of papers and the same number of sketch pencils."

"That will be my pleasure, but we don't have those immediately in stock. If you would leave a card here, I will contact you when your order arrives. My name is Kristina Steuben. My husband's parents own the two Steuben stores," Kristina replied with an outreached arm to shake the woman's hand.

With her right arm out to shake Kristina's, the woman reached into her bag with her left arm. "Thank you, Mrs. Steuben. Laura White. You will have all of my contact information on my business card."

Laura White, Architect

Corcoran Building

Washington, DC

Noting the lack of a wedding ring, Kristina responded, "Pleased to meet you, Miss White. A female architect with an accent from the hill country. You don't see that every day."

Smiling at Kristina, Laura continued, "You're right, and please call me Laura. We have two female architects in Washington—Alice Bogert and me. She operates out of an office on Rhode Island Avenue near Iowa Circle right off of the streetcar line. But, I sincerely doubt my home state of Kentucky employs any female architects."

Stunned and amazed, Kristina continued asking questions. "Kentucky! You must be from Louisville where they just started holding that big horse race every year or perhaps Lexington where Mary Todd Lincoln grew up."

This caused Laura to laugh, "Oh, no. Only the fancy Kentuckians live in those fancy cities. I come from the southern part of the state just a little ways up from the Tennessee state line. A little place known as Manchester in Clay County. Probably not more than a couple of thousand people in our whole county. My family has run a salt works there for many years," Laura added sarcastically, "You may have noticed that I have a bit of a country accent?"

Trying to understand how a woman from such humble beginnings could become an architect, Kristina pressed on with more questions, "I didn't think there were many schools in that area with all of the mountains and not too many people. How did you get the training there to become an architect? You must have excelled as a student."

Flattered by the interest from this warm young lady, Laura replied. "Many architects come to our field through their artistic ability and creativity. For example, that is Alice Bogert's specialty. She makes the most beautiful and innovative drawings I have even seen. Other architects like me find the work to be a useful application of our math skills …"

Kristina added, "But surely, Clay County did not have schooling for the type of advanced mathematics that you speak of?"

Laura laughed. "No, you are right about that. Fortuitously, just as I finished secondary school, the University of Michigan began to admit women. My older brother, John, was studying there at the time, so I moved up to Ann Arbor, Michigan. Eight women made up that first contingent back in 1870. After that, I continued my studies at the Massachusetts Institute of Technology in Boston and then on to Paris …"

Kristina politely interrupted. "That sounds like a lot of schooling and a lot of math. Remind me to tell you about my sister-in-law when you come back to receive your order. I apologize for taking so much of your time. Please call me Kristina."

Walking out the store with a wave, Laura smiled. "It was my pleasure to meet you, Kristina Steuben."

Benton had always been proud of his sister, but he dreaded sitting through her math competitions. Kristina had made the experience more pleasant in recent years, as they could hold hands and he could daydream while the competitors tried to solve impossible problems. Today, however, he truly looked forward to the competition. For his wife, Kristina, had concocted a plan. He held Kristina's hand as they escorted their new friend Laura White to the entrance booth.

September 10, 1879, was the annual Washington math competition. Secondary students would compete for the title that Sandra had earned years before, and an "open" division had been added in recent years where college students could compete with adult residents. For the fifth straight year, the organizers billed the competition as, "The John Thomas Williams Memorial Math Competition of Washington."

Georgetown University would be co-sponsoring the tournament along with the Linthicum Institute, the free school for boys which also served as the setting for Benton's first kiss with Kristina. Sandra and her colleagues would ask the questions for the secondary school students before the city officials would conduct the college/adult competition.

"Remember, just stay in the shadows as much as you can. We don't want to let Sandra know anything about you until the competition," Kristina reminded her new friend Laura White.

"OK. That sounds like a good plan. I am not much for shadows and detective work, so I will follow Benton's lead," Laura responded.

As they entered Healy Hall, Benton guided Laura to the right where she signed up and then watched the secondary school competition hunched down in a back row.

After a fifteen-year-old boy took home the first prize, sixteen contestants competed for the open division prize. Sandra was surprised to see another woman in the group for the first time. Not recognizing this woman, she saw Laura correctly answer the first question against her initial competitor. "That woman is quick on the draw, but what an accent!"

Accent or not, Laura continued to advance towards the finals. Sandra couldn't believe when Laura easily beat Henry Tarr, the 1878 runner-up and her Georgetown mathematics faculty colleague, by a score of 9 to 4 in the semifinals. After she won her own semifinal match, Sandra said to herself, "This woman looks like my toughest competition here since my school days with John Thomas Williams."

Soon, the finals began with Sandra Trent facing Laura White. Neither woman would give an inch, and the competitors each had scored nine points leading into the last question.

Benton realized he had now been smiling for nearly the entire math competition, as he turned to Kristina. "I knew you would transform my life, but even in my wildest dreams, I never thought you could get me to enjoy a math competition."

Kristina lightly touched Benton's knee and whispered in his ear, "Quiet, this is it. The last question."

Typically, no one could answer the last question in the allotted time, so the spectators expected that the competition would end in a nine to nine tie. But, Sandra smiled when she heard the last question. A long and difficult question involving lockers and students, Sandra had seen a similar problem before. So, she knew the trick to solving it quickly. Without that trick, it would be nearly impossible to solve. Looking on Laura's face, Sandra knew this problem was totally new to her competitor. Sandra turned in her answer of "31" and watched Laura scribble something on her paper before turning it in.

Josiah Dent, President of Washington's Board of Commissioners, took the final answers and advanced to the podium:

On behalf of Georgetown, the city of Washington, and the Linthicum Institute, I am happy to announce the grand prize winner. I am sorry that my father-in-law, Edward Linthicum, missed this event. He loved

Georgetown, and especially the two stores run by Jonas and Katia Steuben. Their daughter, Sandra Trent, has won her fifth straight title … But … this year she will share this title with Laura White. Congratulations to both women on their perfect scores. Please come up to accept your prize.

The two women walked up on the left and right sides of John Thomas Williams' mother who would place ceremonial ribbons on each of them. After shaking Laura's hand, Mrs. Williams hugged Sandra and whispered in her ear, "That reminded me of the competition between you and John. Miss White provided a worthy competition for you. John sure got some entertainment looking down on the two of you."

Sandra kissed Mrs. Williams on the forehead as they finished hugging. Then, she moved over to meet Laura White.

Benton and Kristina smiled and laughed when they relayed their story of meeting Laura White to Sandra. Then, they properly introduced the winners right after the competition, and a mutual respect and friendship was born. The girl from the backwoods of Kentucky and the girl from a small town in Prussia had become some of the first female university graduates in the United States. Their professional focus in mathematical fields isolated them even more from other women in Washington.

Kristina could rarely understand the math that these two women would discuss with each other, but she felt good about introducing them and spending time with each of them. The three spent time at each other's homes and out together in the Georgetown neighborhood, as they developed a fast friendship. Quickly, Laura White became part of the larger "Steuben" family of which Kristina was becoming the centerpiece. As 1880 moved into 1881, the three women would soon welcome Laura's brother John and his wife Alice to Washington with John's election to Congress. But, even more than the new friends, Kristina would look forward to the final piece of her adult life as a mother.

CHAPTER 9

SEPTEMBER 11, 1881: TWO WOMEN KIDNAPPED IN GEORGETOWN

"We'll find them or die trying. You have my word, Jonas," David Trent assured Jonas, whose tears had stained *The Washington Daily Critic*.

Four days. It seemed like an eternity to Jonas. He had never been away from Katia for this long before. But, this was much worse than being away for a two-day business trip or a three-day convention trip. He always knew when he would be home on those trips and that Katia would be there for him. Now, he didn't even know if Katia was alive, anywhere. As much as he tried to remain strong for his family—especially Benton—Jonas was simply unable to do anything but cry and to stare off into the distance.

The comfortable life that Jonas had created for his family in Georgetown had been shattered four days ago when a group of kidnappers took Katia and Kristina. Just like thousands of women were doing on that same otherwise peaceful day, Katia and Kristina were walking home after lunch with Sandra, but they never returned home.

The authorities had learned very little since that time. David Trent led the investigation for the Pinkerton Agency, assisted by the young detective, Benton Steuben.

Trying his best to move forward with his logical, analytical process for solving crimes, David began. "Kidnappings can be economical, personal, or political."

"I hope that we can rule out personal here. No one in our family would have been involved with this, and I'm fairly sure Mom had no real enemies that would do this. Let's focus on my mother first and then see if Kristina provides an additional angle," a thoroughly distracted Benton responded.

"Perhaps you're right," David said carefully. "But I don't want to rule anything out just yet. I think we can rule out your sister's family, your father, your brother, and you. But, we should at least think about people your mother or your father may have upset over the past twenty-five years while running their business."

Benton shifted in his chair and did his best to continue to concentrate his full efforts at rescue. "Well, certainly Mom and Dad argued with suppliers over prices, quality, and returns over the years. But I think in all cases, those suppliers continued to work with my parents. Similarly, some customers returned a product or tried to negotiate lower prices. But, I can't think of any instance where one of them might have held a long-term resentment. Those all seemed to be normal business operations that ended with a discount, credit, or exchange."

David thought about Benton's conclusions and agreed that the kidnapping did not arise from a personal grudge. He continued to move down his logical list. "We should explore both political and economic reasons," he said. "First, your family owns a well-known successful business right in the heart of Georgetown. Some may even remember your father as being an early investor in the highly successful streetcar venture, the Washington and Georgetown Railroad. So, your family could potentially be a target of someone trying to find a wealthy business owner. Also, your parents have consistently supported the Republican Party for decades. Their stores display large banners supporting Republican candidates. Like this one that you haven't taken down even though Judah Benjamin has been inaugurated as the 18th President."

JOIN JUDAH IN 1880

"Yes, I see your point. The Steuben stores have not flown a Democratic banner since … Thomas Hart Benton in 1858," Benton recalled the banner from the late Missouri lawmaker whose name he had been given.

Jonas listened to the two detectives, but did not participate in the conversation. Not a religious man, Jonas still found himself praying in silence for the safety of his wife and daughter-in-law. "Come, my friend," David said to Jonas with an outstretched arm. "I'll walk you home."

Jonas simply nodded. He turned to Benton. "Are you coming, son?"

Benton knew he couldn't face a whole night back at home without his wife. "I'll take care of locking up," Benton said. "I just want to think for a little."

Jonas waved absently, and David nodded. When they left, Benton let his head rest in his hands and then began sketching out the significant political factors that may have impacted the kidnapping.

As Benton began his analysis, a knock on the door interrupted him. Benton's neighbor, the policeman—coincidentally named William Benton—had arrived along with Laura White and Sandra Trent. "I saw these two loitering outside of the store, Benton. I thought four brains might be better than one—especially with these women."

Benton offered a weak smile revealing the heavy bags under his eyes while he opened the door to his three visitors.

"Your sister and I analyzed newspaper stories, speeches and travel surrounding Confederate President Forrest. He garners huge crowds wherever he goes and that helped him win re-election easily last year. He gets so worked up in his speeches that he would drip with sweat while his eyes focused around the crowd. But, the key point is that the crowds also get worked up by his speeches that focus on hatred and revenge. Forrest gets the best responses when he blames Negroes, Jews, Mexicans, foreign trade sanctions, or the United States for all of the Confederacy's problems," Laura White began.

"So, you think he targeted Mom and Kristina based on this hatred?" Benton asked.

Sandra joined in. "Not directly. I think they represent the person he hates most in this world. Judah Benjamin. After Forrest stole the election of 1874 from Benjamin, he thought Benjamin would slither away to nothing with the laws imposed against Jews and other groups in the Confederacy. He hadn't counted on Benjamin moving up here and becoming the President of a much stronger country. The newspapers from the last few years continue to quote Forrest and his hate for Benjamin as a "dandy", a "Jew", and a "lying lawyer." Forrest can't accept his defeated competitor holding a superior position than him. But, Forrest is too cowardly, and his country is too weak to take on Benjamin and the United States directly. So, he infuses terror in Benjamin's country. First, by loss of property. Second, by the kidnapping of prominent women known for supporting his nemesis, Judah Benjamin."

"But, why so much hatred to Benjamin? Forrest beat Benjamin and Benjamin has not targeted Forrest or the Confederacy specifically since his inauguration," Benton asked.

Officer William Benton stepped forward and placed a large hand on Benton's shoulder, "My friend, I think I can answer that. Forrest knows deep down that Benjamin is a better man than he is. Forrest mocks Benjamin's abilities in the courtroom, but he ultimately knows that he can't compete with Benjamin's analytical mind. Benjamin's success means Forrest's own failure in Forrest's mind. He takes joy in these small victories and counts on Benjamin not responding in kind."

Laura White continued. "A reasoned analyst would understand that Benjamin quickly divorced himself from the Confederacy after he left. First, he switched out of the Democrat Party. Then, he represented Blaine's Cabinet in July 1877 by making a public speech at the Washington Monument formally announcing the end of all forms of slavery in the United States. Symbolic to have a former Confederate make such a speech, Forrest may have considered this action to be disloyal for a Confederate as well."

Sandra concluded. "Not many people predicted Benjamin would become the President, but newspapers clearly recognized his seniority in the Republican Party with Rutherford Hayes and John Sherman."

Benton picked his head back up to join in. "Even in the United States, many people expressed surprise with Benjamin's election. Roscoe Conkling endorsed and campaigned for Benjamin while saying, 'a Jewish Confederate representing the Republican Party? Now I've seen everything.'"

"Forrest reacted a lot more strongly to the election, though. He said: The United States elected a nigger-loving dirty Jew as their president. He and his Republican sympathizers offend all good white men of the Confederacy," William Benton added.

"Forrest made his intentions clear, and he appears to be following up on that now. We know that Forrest likely organized the violence to buildings, bridges, and monuments around the country. But, have you found any relationship between this kidnapping and that violence?" Benton asked the two women.

Sandra responded. "The destruction focuses on people who represent in Forrest's mind an enemy of the Confederate way of life. So, the Charles Sumner School here in Washington. The late President Lincoln's home in Springfield, Illinois. The ship known as USRC Salmon P Chase. Forrest could take pride in damaging the reputations of men who stood for abolition and other causes at the heart of Forrest's Confederacy—even though, none of these men are still alive."

"Forrest has simply moved on to his next step with live people. Kidnapping defenseless women provides no military risk to Forrest. It also offers the added benefit of amplifying the level of terror being felt here," Laura continued.

By now, David Trent had returned to join the other four in a heated discussion. "We must now focus on the specific geography of the streets where the women were taken. In terms of an escape route for the kidnappers, they would have trouble with bridges over to Virginia. The military and Pinkerton personnel monitor the Chain Bridge, the Aqueduct Bridge, and the Long Bridge; and that monitoring has ramped up since the kidnapping. With so many eyes on the bridges and the waters of the Potomac, we can safely rule out them crossing the river anywhere near Washington," David said, pushing aside the maps on his desk.

"Yes, especially holding two women in broad daylight, I think they must be on foot or in a carriage," Benton ran his hands through his uncombed hair. "Which means they probably boarded somewhere here locally or nearby in Maryland. If they head further north, their escape route back to the Confederacy will become much more difficult. With so many dark alleys, small streets, and old tucked-away houses, Washington provides a number of safe hiding places for the kidnappers. They can also use homes with basements and attics that are hidden from the street view."

"Officer Benton, would you mind walking us through the physical evidence again?" David asked.

Pulling out his black notebook, William Benton responded. "Katia and Kristina Steuben had just met Sandra Trent for lunch at a café abutting the Georgetown campus and the Georgetown Market. It had taken police several hours to locate Sandra Trent after Jonas Trent had reported his wife and daughter-in-law missing. Professor Trent was not in her office, as she had apparently decided to call on her mentor, the Rev. James Clark. Professor Clark had helped Sandra through her early years of teaching, but had recently suffered a stroke.

Sandra Trent informed the police and the Pinkertons that her mother and sister-in-law had started walking back to Georgetown's commercial district at 1:15 PM. The three women had just completed a standard Wednesday weekly lunch, so the routine would have potentially been known to kidnappers that had studied their behavior. Katia and Kristina Steuben would always walk back through the neighborhoods on N Street until they reached the commercial district on Wisconsin Avenue. The six-block walk would usually take fifteen minutes at a leisurely pace."

"Why would a kidnapper grab someone in broad daylight in the middle of the day? I realize fewer potential witnesses would be walking along N Street than M Street with its commercial traffic or O Street with its streetcar route. But, there must also have been something special about this day to make it attractive to a kidnapper," David considered.

"I think I know. I have been analyzing the weather reports. September 7, 1881, was the hottest day in recent memory in Washington. The kidnappers knew the streets would be deserted with that heat in the middle of the day," Laura responded, while reviewing a large stack of weather reports.

While looking at the weather reports in Laura's hands, Benton replied, "Yes, you found it, Laura. So, that tells us that our kidnappers showed some planning and sophistication. Let's see what we can find next."

The conversation had lasted until sunrise, and the group soon moved out onto the street to inspect the physical evidence.

At 3414 N Street, Benton and David stopped cold. The plants had been disturbed and a small tree had been knocked down.

"I bet the kidnappers first came upon Katia and Kristina here," David said.

"We need to investigate every home on or near N street between Georgetown University and Wisconsin Avenue," Benton said, displaying the energy that made the "We Never Sleep" Pinkertons famous.

"My colleagues and I also investigated all of the businesses on Wisconsin and M Streets on or near Katia's and Kristina's route," Officer Benton reminded him in between yawns.

"Yes, let's get started with the home canvassing," Benton said, knocking on a door.

Mr. and Mrs. Alexander Tenant, the residents of 3414 N, had been out of the house at the time of the kidnapping. Mr. Tenant, a plumber, had been busy on calls all afternoon. His wife was visiting with friends a few blocks away. Neither appeared to have a role in the kidnapping, and they cooperated with authorities over the physical changes to their garden and property.

The authorities similarly questioned all of the neighbors. Addie Johnson, who lived across the street at 3413 N Street, was also at work—as a washer. Laborer, washer, and cigar maker, respectively, Eugene Brown, Kate Brown, and Alexander Paul could also provide no additional information from the vantage points of their home at 3415 N Street. At work at the time, they could only remember the blistering temperatures during that afternoon.

This process continued down the block, with carpenters, nurses, painters, grocers, servants, sailors, bricklayers, shoemakers, milkmen, and engineers. Full of working people, the block canvassing offered no sight witnesses to the kidnapping—the kidnappers had chosen the location wisely.

The investigation revealed that the kidnappers seemed to be dragging the two women based upon the paths of dirt in the alley. Whether the women were resisting or were forced at gunpoint or with chloroform was not clear. Ultimately, the trail went cold after the initial abduction because the kidnappers had taken the women through an alley behind N Street, then proceeded north up 34th Street towards O and P Streets. From there, the authorities lost their tracks. David and Benton believed the kidnappers proceeded east, as the west offered little housing and commerce except for the university.

David decided to apply and leverage his connections in Washington's criminal underworld. Confidence men George Gardiner and Isaac Vail cooperated by asking information of their friends in the underworld, but neither provided any direct information. David then secured the services of the infamous and petite Negro pickpocket, Ida Prather. In particular, Prather agreed to provide her "services" as a favor to David Trent when the time arose.

Urgent knocking at the door startled Jonas out of a light sleep.

"Just a minute," he muttered, slowly getting up out of the chair and shuffling across the room to the door.

"Telegram!" the young man announced. He wore a red tie over a white shirt and black pants. A black Swift Safety bicycle rested against the porch pillar. He held out the telegram, with both arm's outstretched.

Jonas reached out to sign. He thanked the boy with a nickel and quickly shut the door.

Jonas immediately read the telegram where the kidnappers asked for $20,000 with the promise of a second telegram the next day to announce the location of the exchange. Forgetting his hat, he ran out the front door and down the street. He had to find Benton.

A nervous Steuben family woke up on September 12, hoping for some progress.

Like all of the young adults in the neighborhood, William Benton had experienced the kindness of Kristina Steuben. She had baked him pies and invited him over to their home for dinner on a number of occasions. But mostly, he remembered just sitting on his front porch in the cool spring evenings talking with her and Benton. He remained almost as distraught at Benton himself. "The kidnappers must realize that we would monitor the telegraph office where they made their initial contact. In our canvassing of that neighborhood, we only located a single eyewitness. Fred Daly, a bacon cutter from the L Street market. He had just arrived home at 723 9th Street NE and was sitting with his daughter, Brooke, on the front porch when he saw two men approach a little boy with money. Daly could not identify the men, who hid their faces, but he identified and located the small boy who received the money. The boy named Jack Toliver never got a good look at the kidnappers except to confirm they gave him money to bring the telegram to the office."

The Pinkertons faced a tough problem in trying to predict the next telegraph office the kidnappers would use. They knew the kidnappers could send telegrams from many places. By 1880, Washington had 1,266 telegraph poles, over thirty separate lines, and 436 wires. In addition, of course, the kidnappers could send a telegram from Maryland or another state.

In the backroom, David and Benton discussed the telegrams.

Benton reasoned that the September 12 telegram would come from Maryland or farther north. A kidnapper could easily take a horse or train north out of Washington—especially if one of his partners stayed with the victims, presumably still somewhere in Washington.

David Trent knew they had to play the odds. Once on a train, a kidnapper could send a telegram from any big city like Baltimore, Philadelphia, or New York. In addition, he could ride multiple trains to smaller towns. Monitoring all of those possibilities would require thousands of men.

David reasoned, "Regardless of where the kidnapper sends the telegram from, there's a good chance that he will be coming back to Washington for the exchange. So, we can likely restrict our circle to be within hours of Washington. We can review the train schedules and search for a single man traveling east and south towards the Baltimore and Potomac Railroad Station."

The telegram came from Newark, Delaware at 12:21 PM. The kidnappers would exchange the prisoners at 7 PM that night for the ransom money at the southwest corner of 1st and C Streets NE.

David sent men to consult the train schedule, and the Pinkertons determined that a person in or near Newark around 12:21 would need to be on the train arriving in Washington at 5:44 that evening to participate in the 7 PM exchange. Gas streetlamps densely populated the area around the Baltimore and Potomac Railroad Station and they extended east on B Street consistently for approximately nine blocks. However, after sunset, the eastern part of the city would turn dark very quickly.

The Pinkertons and police staked out the train station that afternoon. David and William Benton first walked to Vienna Bakery, which advertised "An Excellent Cup Coffee with Cream for 5 Cents" on 6th and D Streets NW and filled up on coffee and pastries.

The train arrived on time at 5:44 PM. Throngs of passengers exited with most on foot or heading to the electric streetcars. However, no streetcar line would take a passenger directly from the railroad station to the 15th Street NE area where the first telegram was sent. One of the Pinkertons followed a passenger taking the 7th Street line north. However, the passenger did not change streetcars to proceed east. Instead, he stayed on the northbound car toward LeDroit Park. The Pinkerton man followed him, but it turned out to be a dead end. William Jones had been returning from a business trip to acquire supplies in Baltimore for his cigar shop at 1004 7th Street NW.

William Benton, David Trent, and Benton Steuben hurried into the eastbound streetcar at 6th street to follow four passengers. David's pickpocket contact, Ida Prather, had fleeced all four of them and passed the wallets to the Pinkerton detectives. Their wallets contained some information (and some cash, which Ida accepted as payment for her services) but nothing immediately definitive on any of their names.

From this group of four eastbound streetcar passengers, two exited on stops at the northern edge of the Capitol, where the policemen followed them.

Both entered offices in the Capitol building where they were employed in the U.S. Senate. Edwin Dickenson worked as the private secretary of the senate president, U.S. Vice President William Wheeler. Francis Shober worked as chief clerk to the secretary of the senate, John Burch. Neither of these train passengers appeared to have any ties to the kidnapping.

Both of the remaining passengers exited the streetcar at its final stop at the corner of 9th and East Capitol Streets. One gentleman walked east two blocks and veered left at the six-square-block grassy area known as Lincoln Park. Benton followed him on a slow walk East and South of the train station. Finally, he stopped at Joseph Crandall's florist shop at 636 8th Street NE. There, Benton inquired of the proprietor as the suspect walked out.

"My name is Steuben. Benton Steuben. I'm investigating a crime with the police and the Pinkerton Agency. Can you tell me about your latest customer?"

The middle-aged florist with graying hair focused intently on the young detective. Seeing a sense of seriousness and purpose that belied Benton's age gave Crandall the comfort to answer directly. "That there was Edward Flaherty. He comes by the shop to buy flowers for his wife every couple of weeks or so."

Benton found nothing particularly indicting about that information that later corresponded with Ida Prather's pickpocketing research, so he probed further. "Do you know anything else about his family, friends, or employment?"

Surprised with all of the questions about Mr. Flaherty, Crandall considered everything he could remember. "I remember him filling out cards attached to flower arrangements made out to his wife and daughters. I have a record back here somewhere." He rummaged a few minutes. "Yes, Riley is his wife, and his daughters are Haven and Samantha. He lists 107 11th Street NE as his address."

Though it looked more and more like a dead end with the suspect being a local citizen devoted to his wife and children, Benton followed Pinkerton protocol to leave no stone unturned, "Any knowledge of his employment or travel?"

Crandall was running out of information, but offered what he could, "He works as a salesman of some sort. I remember him discussing trips to Philadelphia and New York. Beyond that, I'm not sure."

Benton thanked Crandall for his time and made his way to 107 11th Street NE. A short discussion with Mr. Flaherty confirmed Crandall's information. Benton could find no association with the kidnapping. He then followed David's path behind the final passenger on the streetcar. David had proceeded along the northern edge of Lincoln Park before veering northeast on Harrison (formerly North Carolina) Avenue. At 13th Street, the potential kidnapper turned left (north) and proceeded for a block until stopping at an abandoned row house at 900 13th Street NE. The suspect sat on the porch, carefully looking up and down the street to make sure he wasn't being followed.

David had been watching the suspect from a distance inside a newsstand on Harrison Avenue. Even with David's experience and training, he struggled to avoid being seen.

Eventually, however, the suspect satisfied himself that he had not been followed, and he entered the house. David waited at his hiding spot until Benton reached him.

When Benton arrived, David filled him in on their situation. David had gotten the newsstand proprietor to walk down to a nearby police station where they would inform their colleagues and the Pinkertons around the city. Soon, fifteen police and Pinkertons would join them at the back door to the newsstand to stake out the suspect's house.

David and Benton devised their plan. They would first need to cut off all routes of escape by placing men at strategically located nearby homes. One of them, 904 13th Street, home to watchman Gotlieb Eisenbram and laborer William Gingells, offered a porch with a clear line of sight to the back of the suspect's home. Across the street at 831 13th Street, the home of barber James Gordon, servant Maria Smith, and laborer Charles Wilson, provided the perfect line of sight to the front of the suspected kidnapper's home.

The Pinkertons knew that capturing the kidnappers would be far easier than keeping Katia and Kristina safe. They wanted to "have eyes on" the women throughout the process. The police took a position from the back of paver William Morrison's house at 911 12th Street NE. Working with Morrison's wife, Robin, and his son, Nicholas, the Pinkertons set up operations from the kitchen of the Morrison's home. There, they thought they could see movement in the basement of the suspect's house. From that vantage point, they couldn't verify Katia's or Kristina's identities. But, they could do no better at that stage.

Benton paced back and forth showing his impatience, and David had to tell him to calm down.

"I think we should go in the front and just take them by surprise," Benton said.

"No." David shook his head emphatically. "We need to go in the back to ensure the women's safety."

"With all of the men we have, we should be able to do both," William Benton said. "Then there's no escape."

Benton and David decided to enter the suspect's home from the front and back, fully armed and supported by three policemen on either side. Coordinating their entrances, they both rushed and broke down the front and back doors at 6:37 PM.

Crashing through the back door, Benton frantically looked around the room. Nothing.

Benton's team quietly moved down the stairs into another room, a basement. A dim light pierced the damp air. He saw the faint outline of a woman. His mother! Heavy chains held an extremely fatigued Katia to a heavy metal beam.

"Mother! Mother! Are you all right?" He took her hand in his, quickly trying to ascertain how to set her free.

"Oh, Benton! I'm fine, I'm fine," she said, while she started crying.

Katia hugged Benton tightly and whispered in his ear, "Your dear wife. It was very hard on us being dragged around on that hot day without any water after being chloroformed. Poor Kristina did not have the strength to continue. She told me she was pregnant. The last thing she said was 'Tell Benton that we will always love him whether we are here or not.' Oh, Benton, it's my fault that I couldn't save her!"

Katia in her weakened state kept Benton upright, as his entire body went limp. One he recovered his voice, Benton reached out to Katia. "Mother, I don't know how I'll be from this day forward, but rest assured I'll always love you. And, I know you did everything in your power to save my wife," Benton cried, as he noticed a door ajar leading to another room.

In the adjacent room, Benton came upon Kristina's lifeless body stretched out as if begging for water. The body was Kristina, but the life inside of it that Benton loved had expired days earlier. He held her for ten minutes until the medical team came to take her away and to look after Katia.

David Trent had missed the horrors downstairs, as he helped capture the kidnappers upstairs. The Pinkertons apprehended the first suspect, Jubal Larson, with several punches. The other suspect, Myron Breakstone, aimed his pistol when a shot rang out.

Breakstone grabbed his abdomen, blood seeping through his hand. William Benton went over to him, and, without pity, began to interrogate him.

"Who sent you to kidnap these women?" he demanded.

"I need a doctor," Breakstone gasped.

"No doctors until you answer all of our questions."

"Please, a doctor! My…my wife, m-m-my daughters…"

Myron slumped, his eyes taking on the glassy look of someone no longer fully in this world, and he expired before taking another breath.

The heat had built up in the windowless room at the abandoned home, and David and Benton had periodically walked into the hallway to drink coffee or water. Adrenaline kept them going, as they shot question after question at Jubal Larson.

Jubal Larson may have prayed for peace, but for the next seventy-two hours, his prayers would not be answered. Most of the police had left the home with the body of Myron Breakstone and had taken Katia to a local doctor. She would not sustain any life-altering injuries, but the terror of this incident would haunt her for the rest of her life.

Benton and David would leave the abandoned home for twelve hours to bury Kristina. During this time, Officer William Benton stood guard to ensure that Larson received no water or food either.

Benton and David rotated in and out with questions and various means of persuasion. "You have not told us anything about your family, Mr. Larson. You may think you're clever withholding that information, but it is not us you need fear. Your bosses know where your family is. Surely, they will seek them out after the newspapers reveal that Jubal Larson has leaked the names of all of the Confederates involved in the kidnapping," Benton said.

"But, that's a lie," Larson protested.

"Perhaps, but the press will never know that," Benton replied.

With a look of terror, Larson replied, "But, they might harm my wife and my family."

"Oh, they most certainly will kill your wife and children—immediately and violently," Benton responded without any expression.

"You have two minutes," David said.

Larson grew silent, his bravado gone. His shoulders slumped, and he rubbed his face. "I will tell you everything I know. Breakstone and I lived in a small town just south of Montgomery, known as Prattville. We had both been working at farms up in the area the past ten or twelve years. Anyway, a man named Rafer Allison lived in the area also. He worked somewhere in the government in Montgomery. We met him at a tavern in town a couple of years back, and he had gotten us to do some mechanical and carpentry work for him. A couple of months back, he offered us each five thousand dollars to kidnap Katia Steuben in Washington, DC. Well, we ain't never thought of kidnapping anyone, but times are tough. Five thousand dollars goes a long way toward setting up a man for life."

David jumped in. "Did you meet with anyone besides Allison on this plan?"

Larson continued, "We never met no one else, but he always referred to his boss. Frankly, he sounded scared of that man. He wasn't real clear, but it sounded like there was something wrong with his boss's face that Allison couldn't even look at him. Allison made it clear that his boss reported directly to President Forrest, but I don't think he had any official job in the Confederacy.

Anyway, we could never find Katia Steuben alone, so we took the other lady as well. She was never part of the plan, but it was the best we could come up with. We didn't want to kill no one, but that heat just kept coming that day, and we had a hard time dragging them where we needed to go. Even with the chloroform, we could barely carry their weight in the heat. I don't know if the heat or the chloroform caused it, but the other lady never came to after we got back to the house."

With a knowing eye, William Benton whispered to Benton and David. "I'll alert my superiors that the prisoner never regained consciousness."

Benton nodded to William, and then pulled out a paper bag from a drawer. Before placing the bag over Larson's head, Benton whispered, "That other lady was my wife, Kristina Steuben, pregnant with our first child. You have ended their lives and essentially mine as well."

The authorities would not notify the press about the deaths of Breakstone and Larson for several weeks. The press eventually reported that both Breakstone and Larson died from gunshot wounds before either had a chance to speak with the authorities. The less Rafer Allison and his bosses knew, the better.

CHAPTER 10

SEPTEMBER 26, 1881: TWO CONFEDERATE KIDNAPPERS KILLED BY POLICE

An out of town business traveler in Steuben's Extraordinary searched the racks for his hometown paper. Finding the *Philadelphia Inquirer*, he moved over toward the window and read the first story.

"We avoided war in '61 due to the strength of Abraham Lincoln—may he rest in peace. Benjamin will find it difficult to resist war with the Confederates kidnapping and killing American women."

Four men quickly moved toward the stranger.

"Hey, what are you doing?" the man said. "Don't push."

They jostled him out the door quickly but gently. A man said, "We know you meant no harm, but this here is Jonas Steuben's store. They kidnapped his wife and daughter-in-law. Only his wife made it back alive. We will offer your apologies to Jonas, but you would show respect by remaining out of his stores for now. Thank you."

The stranger did as he was told, and he would soon learn the whole harrowing tale when he read through the newspaper still in his hand.

eved for Kristina and assisted with Katia's recovery.
ome quickly after hearing of the kidnapping. In his
e Boston Red Caps in the National League, he had
ra Sutton in the middle of 1881 as the starting third
baseman. After ... ft the team, they immediately lost four straight games
on their way to a poor 6–11 record in September. Twenty-four and single,
Nathan would provide great comfort to his family in the days ahead.

Sandra had brought her two children and Jonas to meet Katia at the
doctor's offices. Her one- and three-year-olds—Geraldine and Augustus,
respectively—made Katia smile during this harrowing time.

The family reunion was bittersweet under the circumstances, but
they knew that having Katia back and healthy was the first important task
immediately at hand. Jonas never left her side, bringing her food and reading her their prized Brothers Grimm books to pass the time. She showed a
healthy appetite, and soon the color was restored to her cheeks. After two
weeks, her strength had improved enough that she felt she could go back
to work. But she would never walk more than a block without an escort for
the rest of her life.

Now fifty-one years old, Jonas was starting to slow down just a bit,
but this would be a time that would define him. First, he finished nurs-
ing his wife back to health. He worked around the clock to cater to her
every need despite the fatigue he felt, but his hard work paid off with Katia
regaining her health.

However, Jonas feared his next task would prove to be far more difficult, as he thought about his youngest son.

Never had Jonas seen a wife so important to a husband as Kristina
had been to Benton. She opened him up to the outside world and created

happiness for his introverted personality. Losing Kristina would potentially have tragic consequences for Benton for the rest of his life. Jonas knew he had a responsibility and desire to find a way to convince Benton to continue to find meaning in his life. As he approached his son's home, he saw Benton sitting on a chair on the front porch looking out into the sky.

Benton saw his father walk up. "Dad, so many people have come to wish their condolences. They've told me that I'll feel better with the passage of time. They also tell me that I can do many things to honor Kristina's life. They even said I'll start to find other parts of life to give me peace and happiness. But, I don't think so. Kristina and I would talk about everything. She had the perfect mix of being able to listen intently, but also to respond with an important point to consider."

Jonas scratched his head and thought deeply before responding. "It is altogether fitting and proper that your friends and neighbors have come to see you and wish you their best regards. They mean well and I know you don't fault them for trying to help. It is difficult to find the right words to say, so people fall back on common sayings. But, I came here to tell you the truth. As difficult as you find it, please listen to me all of the way through."

Benton just nodded.

"You have experienced a horrible event such as very few people will in their lifetimes. When you lose a loved one of natural causes after they have lived a full and worthy life, you can recover even if you will still miss them dearly. You may not recover as well, but you may still recover when a younger relative passes away from disease or natural causes. People find it difficult to recover from accidental deaths of loved ones, but deaths due to evils acts of men are particularly hard on the family. Compounding that with a young wife as dear to you as Kristina taken in such horrible and public circumstances will just not make it feasible to forget or comfortably accept your situation. For the rest of your days, you will mark your life as the happiness before September 7, 1881, and how the world differed afterward." Jonas then took a long breath and continued. "But, Kristina's love will sustain you whether you can see her or not. You must understand, though, that you can't magically fix yourself and your feelings by searching for new happiness. You can, however, find relevance and purpose in what you do day by day. I can't tell you how to do that, but I will try my best to help. First, our family needs you. Your mother and I, your sister's family, your brother. Second, you may find fulfillment in your career in helping other people avoid what your mother and Kristina experienced. You may get enough fulfillment from these things to live what we call a normal life, but you cannot deceive yourself. You can never be the same."

"I will never lose my love for Kristina, but I want to be able to talk about her and her passing. I know I can talk to you, Dad, but very few people feel comfortable enough to talk about her. And those that do, will not truly understand her loss to me," Benton replied, as he lifted his head out of his hands.

"There is a saying that 'misery loves company' that may apply here. It may very well be that with your investigative skills, you will identify people who have experienced a similar loss in their lives. Or, perhaps you may simply hear of such losses when you meet these people. If the saying is true, you may form a closer relationship with these people because of your common loss. But, remember, you can always come to me. A father's love is forever," Jonas replied.

Benton just hugged his father tightly, as he had one other thought. Whatever his life prospects might be, he knew he could have no true peace while Rafer Allison and his boss still lived.

CHAPTER 11

JUNE 10, 1882: NO LEADS ON STRING OF KIDNAPPINGS

"I just can't believe the number of kidnappings we keep reading about all over the country. Hopefully, the authorities can find the source of the kidnappings quickly." Officer William Benton said as he read *The Daily Dispatch* from Richmond.

Daniel Coombs, Benton Steuben's housemate, walked into Steuben's Extraordinary and waved to Officer Benton, "Good morning Officer. I came in to pick up a couple of papers for our friend, Benton. Joseph Lewis and I are taking Benton to hike the falls out in Potomac and stay overnight. We hope the fresh air, water, and horses will help clear his mind for at least a few hours."

Sean Trent walked over to the group from behind the counter. "Good morning, gentlemen. Yes, my uncle David tells me that Benton shows more focus than any Pinkerton he has ever known. The kidnappings just obsess him. But, outside of that, we have difficulty carrying on conversations with him. When he babysits our children, he lights up, but he darkens again as soon as the children leave."

"Benton will adjust on his own schedule. Don't expect his old personality to come back. Deep down, he appreciates our loyalty, but too much pity or support will not make him feel any better. Sadly, I have seen it before when criminals have killed my fellow officers. We rightly honor them as fallen heroes, but the lives of their young wives and children are never the same," William Benton replied.

Benton and David had just walked over the M Street Bridge on their way home from the Pinkerton office a few weeks later.

"We need to go after Allison. That bastard must pay for what he has done," David said, puffing on his pipe.

"Yes, but I need a couple of drinks before we discuss this," Benton replied, as they veered onto M Street into John Albert's Saloon at 2907.

Benton soon had a shot of whiskey and a mug of beer in front of him at the bar lit by a dozen gas lamps. By this time, John Albert knew Benton's order by just a nod.

Benton continued. "At the right time, we will take Allison down. I can't wait too long because the delay is killing me inside. But, our training instructs us to avoid emotional actions in favor of reasoned and analytical actions. I need some more time to lessen the emotional impact and research the analytical approach to this."

"Benton, I feel like a brother to your mother and father. Similarly, I treated Kristina as I would my own daughter. I know that I can't fully comprehend what you are going through, but please also understand that I do share your pain as well. Any time you need me, I will drop everything and join you immediately," David replied while finishing his own shot of whiskey.

Benton considered all of the possibilities that awaited him and David on the other side of the entrance to the room where they stood this Friday morning, October 6, 1882. They waited without showing emotion, just outside President Benjamin's private offices on the second floor of the Executive Mansion.

A door opened further down the corridor, piercing the silence, and a man dressed in black came to them. He politely opened the door where President Benjamin rose from his rectangular desk to meet Benton and David near his large mirrored bookcase. Benjamin sat at the only desk in a room that included two other smaller bookshelves, a large mirror to the left of President Benjamin's desk, and a fireplace directly under the mirror.

Six wooden chairs with black leather cushions faced President Benjamin's desk in a semi-circle beneath the six-light chandelier overhead. The two end chairs on either side were taken by men who introduced themselves. Then, David and Benton sat down in the unoccupied middle seats.

President Benjamin walked back behind his desk and placed himself in his wooden swivel chair. He began to speak as he would to a jury by moving his eye contact from one participant to the other. "Gentlemen, we face a time of crisis today. But, our enemy does not have the courage to face us directly. Rather, they terrorize undefended citizens and structures. I don't propose to let this continue, but I don't believe a military invasion is our best course. In fact, I think our enemy, President Forrest, wishes us to do just that. It would make him, and his struggling country feel more relevant. We would win such a war, but being able to fight a defensive war would strengthen their odds. And it would force us to sacrifice many good men."

General William T. Sherman, the most senior general in the armed services and the brother of the Ohio Senator who had been a presidential contender, shifted in his chair, his hair slightly unkempt and his expression just a shade away from a scowl. "If we don't engage the army or navy in an invasion, what other option do you suggest, Mr. President?"

Benjamin had little physical presence when he stood at barely five feet tall, but his voice and presence at his desk were commanding. He quickly responded to the cigar-chewing General Sherman. "You can only fight terrorists by inflicting terror and chaos upon that terrorist. Remember the story of Moses. He and the Jewish people didn't defeat the tyranny of Egypt's persecution by fighting the Pharaoh's army with a traditional army. They received miracles from the Lord in the form of ten plagues to defeat Egypt. These plagues created chaos in Egypt's businesses, food supply, and eventually their families as well."

No sound could be heard from any of the six chairs facing President Benjamin, as thoughts of Kristina and the kidnapping filled Benton's head.

The President continued. "We don't have the option of the ten plagues today, but we have other means to create chaos and terror in the Confederacy. First, I will ask our Congress to sign a law that grants immediate citizenship to all Confederate slaves that reach American soil. We can call it the Freedmen Citizen Act. Confederate citizens will surely think of this as a precursor to mass slave revolts. Second, as any snake hunter will tell you, we must literally 'cut off their head.' Forrest must be assassinated."

General Sherman raised his eyebrows in disbelief. "Mr. President, do you really suggest we murder Forrest? The president of a sovereign nation? Wouldn't the Confederacy rise up and fight us?"

Attorney General Benjamin Harrison, looking larger and stronger seated in a chair than his 5'6" frame would suggest, spoke next. Grandson of the late President William Henry Harrison, Benjamin Harrison was one of the country's top lawyers. "I don't think so. Without a leader, they would struggle for direction. There might be some sentiment for war, but these very independent-minded states would not likely be cohesive. The potential for millions of escaping slaves would only exacerbate the confusion."

President Benjamin added, "And, if after all of that, a very weak Confederacy wanted to engage in war, they would need to invade us. We could fight a strong defensive war utilizing our forts along the Virginia, Tennessee, and Missouri borders with fewer casualties. Besides, we will take no formal credit for the assassination and will do everything we can to make his assassins a mystery who simply vanish into thin air."

John Mosby of Virginia, a forty-eight-year-old highly educated lawyer from Virginia, served as the Secretary of War. He had angular features, with wiry brown hair. Like many Virginians of his generation, he had hardened against the Confederacy in the past twenty years. Poverty and extremism taking hold in the Confederacy had ripped apart the old ideals of Southern society from which Mosby and his fellow Virginians grew up. Mosby responded, "I like the idea, but first I want to formally offer my condolences to Benton Steuben. None of us can understand your pain, but a few years ago, I lost my wife and two of my children. I would not wish that pain on anyone—not even Nathan Bedford Forrest."

"Thank you, Secretary Mosby. My father recently told me that misery loves company, and I can tell you that I also appreciate your support," Benton replied.

David cleared his throat. "Mr. President, Mr. Steuben and I loyally support your administration and our country. But what purpose do you have for us in this meeting?"

"I think I can answer that." A broad-shouldered man with a dark, bushy gray beard replied from the far right of the semi-circle of chairs. General Jeb Stuart immediately stood up and motioned for Benton and David to join him in an adjoining room.

Benton knew of Stuart as one of the top-ranking generals in the army. Newspapers reported Stuart to have keen powers of observation, a trait most prized by Pinkerton detectives.

After the Pinkertons had said their goodbyes to the President and joined General Stuart in the adjoining room, Stuart turned to Benton. "I'm very sorry for your loss, Mr. Steuben," he said in a very soft yet very articulate voice. "I swear to you both that Forrest will regret it but once, and that will be continually. Gentlemen, you're looking at the team that will provide this world a service by removing President Forrest."

"It will be my honor," David replied.

"Thank you for this opportunity," Benton added.

"Don't thank me yet. We must work around the clock until we can finalize and execute this plan. And, there is no time like the present. So, let's get to work," Stuart replied, as a whirl of emotions moved through Benton's head.

David and Benton had been hard at work with General Stuart on their "De-Forrest" assignment for several weeks through October of 1882. Meeting at Stuart's office in the State, War, and Navy Building just a few blocks east down Pennsylvania Avenue from Benton's old primary and secondary schools, the trio poured over maps, itineraries, personnel, and dates. Finally, the day arrived when the location of the assassination needed to be decided.

General Stuart thanked the young private who brought him more maps for the Confederacy. "Gentleman," he said, unfolding the map in front of Benton and David. "We must make our initial focus the Confederate capital of Montgomery, Alabama. Forrest spends most of his time there, so it offers us many more opportunities than other venues where he might travel."

"The transportation looks challenging. There's no easy access point," David said.

"We would travel about two hundred miles from Montgomery to even reach the U.S. border in Tennessee afterward," Benton added.

Stuart then concurred. "Accessing Montgomery from the west and east would prove no easier, as Georgia, the Gulf of Mexico, Mississippi, Louisiana, Arkansas, and Texas surround Alabama. Destin, Florida provides a potential point of southern access about 150 miles from Montgomery. However, reaching Destin through the Gulf of Mexico and around the tip of Florida would be a very risky venture."

Benton poured over newspapers and joined the conversation. "If we can't reach him in Montgomery, we must follow his travel schedule. The Confederacy had advertised Forrest's 'Southern Pride' tour of speeches early next year. That should be our best opportunity."

General Stuart brought in two of his best intelligence officers to assist their group.

Alexander Clements, a smart and serious-looking older man with glasses, was a Captain and neighbor of Benton's in Georgetown, "Forrest plans to concentrate this tour on the states where he needs the most political support. He knows the Deep South—the first six seceding states that formed the Confederacy of Alabama, Florida, Georgia, Louisiana, Mississippi, and South Carolina—are clearly behind him politically."

"That leaves Arkansas, Texas, and North Carolina," Major William Huxford added. Continuing, while scratching his forehead where his hair parted in the middle, "Texas is so big that it is hard to generalize. Its eastern sections aligned more strongly with the Confederacy than the southern and western sections, where people could live more than five hundred miles away from another Confederate state. Citizens in Amarillo, Odessa, and El Paso live much closer to Mexico, New Mexico Territory, Indian Territory, Kansas, and Colorado than to other Confederate states. Forrest knows that he needs to strengthen his support in these areas of Texas, but the logistics of such a trip would require too much time. There just aren't enough railroads."

Captain Clements replied. "Arkansas had joined the Confederacy late, but it has seemed to ingrain itself more into the Confederate culture than Texas. Having no coastline, New Orleans provides its main access for commerce. As such, Arkansas became essentially a northern branch of Louisiana. The western Arkansas citizens may have had less access to the Mississippi River, but they have faced negative exposure to the United States. They share a long border with the Indian Territory and constantly fight off hunting parties of Cherokee, Choctaw, and Chickasaw Indians that had crossed the borders. Arkansans despise the American government for allowing their state to be overrun with Indians who delight in looting the Arkansas border towns for food, clothing, and especially cigars."

Benton jotted down some notes and responded. "North Carolina is a lot closer for us, but will Forrest travel there in a convenient spot?"

Major Huxford, tugged at his thick moustache and pointed at the map in front of Benton. "North Carolina definitely has divided loyalties. It remained in the United States for more than a year after the Confederacy was formed, and it shared long borders with the United States across the states of Tennessee and Virginia. Forrest needs more support there, and he can move around the state fairly easily by railroad. Our intelligence has him traveling there in February next year, but we will have to confirm the dates and details."

As October moved into November, the plan became more structured and finalized. The team evaluated the likelihood of mission success based on where Forrest would be speaking, the terrain of the land, and the political leanings of the local population.

The spies learned the details of the North Carolina trip from an informant in Greensboro who was presumably arranging a dinner for Forrest. Dr. L. J. Montague considered himself to be a patriotic Confederate, but he had no love for the extreme tactics of President Forrest that now included terrorizing innocent women as a revenge tactic against his fierce enemy, Judah Benjamin. Montague had been a supporter of Davis and Toombs but could not abide by his country turning into a terrorist regime. He let the Pinkertons know that Forrest would speak at a banquet and then spend the evening in Greensboro on February 2.

General Stuart appreciated this intelligence. "Greensboro is a perfect location for us. Only forty miles from the border, it is also close to our Southern Virginia army bases in Danville and Appomattox. The Confederate citizens near the border already carefully avoid our army base in Danville. Also, a sizeable Quaker population lives in Greensboro. They have never warmed to the Confederacy."

"We still must learn more about Greensboro and potential escape routes back to Virginia. Forty miles on horse and foot at night will test a man's stamina. If we get diverted off course or we miss an important bridge, that could doom the mission," David said.

"I think I can help with that. I was born and raised just over the border in a little town known as Ararat in Patrick County, Virginia. I am sure if I mentioned that to President Benjamin, he would have been sure to tell us the story of Noah from the Bible," Stuart laughed, as he continued. "I know a lot of friends and kin out there that can help you with anything you need. They will arrange to show us the roads, rivers, bridges, and other key spots well before February 2. I will start with my brother, William Alexander—he owns more land than anyone in those parts."

The team spent the next several weeks with General Stuart's family, Dr. Montague, and several other Forrest opponents in Greensboro. Addison Coffin, an older member of the Quaker church, had worked the Underground Railroad with his father Vestal, brother Alfred, and cousin Levi for more than half of a century. The young Moravian Reverend Edward Rondtheler with the wire-rimmed glasses allowed the Pinkerton team to use his Salem Congregation Church for meetings and a safe haven. With this assistance, the team prepared for their mission.

The men huddled around the large, hand-drawn map, studying the details. "We need to make sure that telegrams do not arrive north announcing the assassination while we remain on the escape route. If the citizens in the northern towns of North Carolina don't know about the assassination, we have very little danger. But, that means we have to control the telegraph lines," David said.

"Let's start with this telegraph map. You must first avoid any major settlements right around Greensboro. These include the western settlements of Stokesdale and Summerfield. Next, on your potential route will be Reidsville, which is serviced by telegraph. You can miss that by staying due north," General Stuart's heavyset brother, William Alexander Stuart, said.

Benton joined him at the map. "So, it looks like we can proceed due north until the border near Ridgeway, Virginia." He pointed to the town, lost in thought.

"Perhaps, but the lines of the path may need to be adjusted. For example, we must also consider water. Are there any big rivers to cross, Henry?" General Stuart asked in the direction of his nephew, the fancily-dressed Henry Carter Stuart.

Twenty-seven years old and the most eligible bachelor in Virginia, Henry Carter Stuart was heir to the fortunes of both his Stuart family as well as the larger fortune of his mother's Carter fortune. His uncle hoped to extract information from his well-known encyclopedic mind. "Only one, but it is a big one that will be hard to pass. The Dan River blocks your progress on nearly every path you go. The Leaksville Covered Bridge crosses the river near Spray and Draper. I can think of no other reasonable way to cross over the water in the height of winter." He lightly marked these points on the map that would veer a bit west.

David thought for a moment. "It looks like we will stay west of Wentworth and then veer east over the bridge. That bridge becomes the key point in our escape. Leaksville may have received a telegram of the assassination by then, and they may place guards on the bridge," David said.

"Yes, we will need some military presence nearby on the road from Leaksville to Stoneville and on up to Matrimony. We don't want to cause an incident with local citizens if we can avoid it, but it might be necessary," General Stuart replied.

"To be safe, I would recommend cutting the telegraph wires in and out of Leaksville that evening. It will take at least a day to fix. We may still see a contingent from Stoneville, but it is much less likely," David said.

Southern Virginia farm country had suffered a fierce winter during the early weeks of January 1883. Adjusting to the environment and climate, David and Benton had become accustomed to the swift gusts of cold air that would sweep across unobstructed terrain.

General Stuart, David, and Benton would spend six weeks living on the Flanagan family farm in Ridgeway, Virginia—just over the border from North Carolina. Their time on the farm provided an opportunity to familiarize themselves with the geography. The Flanagans—Beverly and Nancy—served as the perfect hosts. Nancy made the team feel welcome in her home with warm blankets on the beds and hearty meals at the dining table. Beverly, a self-taught veterinarian, knew the local paths as well as anyone, as he spent much of his time searching the area for medicinal herbs. Benton would often join Beverly on these trips into the local woods, where he learned the roads and waterways.

The rest of the plan focused on the route out of Greensboro. Working with Dr. Montague and Addison Coffin, he learned the routes out of the city and the best trails for horses north. Mostly, they would follow the routes established by the heavily trafficked so-called Underground Railroad. Walking the path one day, Coffin stopped. "Come feel this tree. There is a nail halfway around back towards the left. It tells you the direction to go in places like this—where there is a fork in the road."

Benton smiled, remembering the family photograph and his father's story of Lincoln facing a fork in the road at his first inauguration. "Thank you, Mr. Coffin. How do I know I'm looking at the right tree, and how will I know the height where the nail is placed?"

Adjusting his traditional skull cap and lower beard, Coffin continued. "The nail will always be three and a half feet off of the ground. If there is no tree when you get to a fork, then look for a fence or a stake in the ground that blend in easily to the surroundings. We have always done this since the railroad began before I was born. My father, Vestal, started the system here in Greensboro. He passed away as a young man, but his cousin and my brothers have followed in his footsteps."

By late January 1883, the team made final preparations to execute their plan. After Forrest's contingent had passed their spot, Benton would create a large distraction by detonating two hand grenades on the street about three miles north of the railroad tracks. The main road north of town, Summit Street, would eventually lead to Danville and Lynchburg, Virginia. But, in the dead of winter, the road would be deserted. The farther one ventured north of the railroad tracks and the city of Greensboro, the sparser the traffic became. With this isolated locale, Benton's hand grenades would not cause a disturbance to anyone but Forrest's party. During the disturbance of the smoke and sounds, David and General Stuart would emerge from the woods and fire their rifles.

The three of them would carefully walk through the small forest of trees on the eastern side of the street, where they would have fresh horses waiting. From there, they would wind through various old horse trails between Lakes Brandt and Townsend, proceeding north and avoiding the main access road of Summit Street. They expected to reach the Leaksville Covered Bridge within approximately five hours.

Expecting to confront Forrest's party at 3:15, they would be in the darkness well before they made it to the Dan River. Nearing the height of the full moon in that cycle, they would benefit from a heavy dose of natural light to assist with their movements. Another five-hour walk from the river would land them back in the safety of U.S. territory before sunrise—if all went according to plan.

When February 2 arrived, David, Benton, and General Stuart couldn't believe what they saw on Summit Street. Four riders crested a small hill. An American president would travel with a large entourage of military and political personnel on occasions like this. Forrest only traveled with three other riders. Either Forrest was highly confident of his own shooting ability (and his popularity in the area), or the Confederacy was even poorer than the newspapers reported.

Benton began to run along one side of the street. Then, he pulled the pin out of the grenade and rolled it toward the four horses. Quickly, he repeated this exercise with his second grenade. Then, he sprinted into the trees as fast as he could.

Ten seconds later, the first grenade detonated. The horses reared up as the men tried frantically to control them. Forrest picked himself off the ground and tried to move around the grenade. The other men fell from their horses. The crowd looked around, trying to find who threw the grenade. But, they only had two seconds of clarity before the second grenade went off.

At this point, Forrest and his party prepared themselves for a third grenade or whatever else came at them. Once the smoke finally cleared, though, the Forrest party had nowhere to hide from the two assassins. Benton heard the shots coming from the still popular Winchester 1873 model rifles. In all, each man fired 15 shots in the one minute they remained at the scene. Many shots missed, but a good many hit their targets from a distance of 80 yards.

The bullets hit Forrest once in the upper abdomen and at least once in the lower abdomen. Benton knew those shots would prove fatal. The remaining shots found the legs and bodies of the others in Forrest's party. They might survive, but no one could chase after David, Benton, and General Stuart. Nor could Forrest's party move quickly to alert authorities.

As the men made their way through the patch of trees back to their horses, adrenaline helped carry them north. The horse path was flat and clear, and Stuart's years of cavalry experience proved invaluable at this stage. Benton and David struggled to keep up with Stuart, but the team covered its distance quickly, moving between the lakes. They passed a few riders traveling south, but they all passed without incident. The riding slowed down to a slow walk north of the lakes, so the men left their horses outside a pre-designated farmhouse. They then took the rest of their journey on foot, mostly sticking to the Underground Railroad path.

On the south side of the Leaksville Covered Bridge, the group met two lieutenants from the U.S. army base at Danville. Before proceeding back to their base, the lieutenants reported that the coast was clear to proceed across the bridge and then north-northwest to the Virginia line.

The trio breathed a sigh of relief and felt some relaxation as they neared the bridge. Suddenly, out of the bush darted a group of people. Benton and his group had no time to draw their pistols or otherwise defend themselves.

Benton braced for a bullet, when he heard a familiar voice, as the stern, honest face of Addison Coffin appeared in the middle of the group. "Well, Mr. Steuben, I have come bearing some good news and some bad news for you. The good news is that my group is not looking to hurt you. The bad news is that I need to ask you a large favor."

Benton exhaled and turned to Coffin. "Your guidance through these roads has been invaluable. I will happily help however I can."

Coffin gestured to his party of three Negro children. "These children are escaping to your country for freedom. I think they have dogs following them, though. I can safely spend the night at a church nearby, but with the dogs in hot pursuit, the children must keep moving all night. They need the assistance of younger men like you with more strength—and more firepower—than this pacifist can provide." He continued while pointing to himself. "Their parents were killed by a group known as the Red Shirts in South Carolina while they walked through town on an errand for their master. They don't know the man's name who led that Red Shirts group, but they say he has only one eye."

Benton, David, and General Stuart introduced themselves to the children known as Jeffrey, Terri, and Matthew. "Do you have a last name?" David asked.

Matthew, the oldest, stepped forward. "We use the name of our master, but we want to start fresh."

Benton looked around the group. "I could think of no better last name than Coffin," as he pointed to Addison.

"Yes, that would be an honor. Thank you, Mr. Coffin," Terri responded.

After a quick goodbye to Coffin, the group of six proceeded north. They heard the faint bark of dogs, just as they reached the tube-like bridge. Because of the bright moon, the group could see a faint light at the end of the tunnel as they stepped onto the bridge.

The well-built wooden bridge was moist and damp, but it held steady, as the group walked slowly across the river. Benton waited for the other five to cross. Then, he pulled the pin from his last grenade and set it at the foot of the bridge. Sprinting across the bridge, he had to jump to make it across before the bridge collapsed. By the time he crossed, the dogs and search party had arrived at the remains of the bridge. All that remained was a stone piling in the middle of the river with large pieces of wood floating on the water. With the river half frozen, Benton knew they were safe for the time being. None of his party turned around to give the search party a look at their faces, but they needed to hurry across the border.

Hurry they did. The adults thought the children would slow them down. But eight-year-old Jeffrey was the fastest of the bunch.

Fatigued and cold, the group finally made their way across the border at 4:45 AM. A group of eight undercover Pinkertons and uniformed military personnel quickly transported them back to the Flanagan farm, where a large fire blazed. Stuart marveled at how Benton and David had so much energy after a dangerous night without any sleep.

David responded, "It is part of our training. The first week we all learn the Pinkerton motto. We never sleep."

"Well, I hate to dishonor your fine agency's motto, but I think sleep is probably a good idea about now. Things will be in chaos in the morning," General Stuart said, as the group dispersed to lie down for a few hours of rest.

CHAPTER 12

FEBRUARY 3, 1883: CONFEDERATE PRESIDENT FORREST MURDERED

Jonas gently placed his arm around his wife's shoulders and pointed to *The Raleigh News and Observer*. "Katia, you must see this paper from North Carolina."

Katia looked up from behind the counter of Steuben's Extraordinary with her mouth open. "Jonas, I don't feel sorry for Nathan Forrest. His name, of course, reminds me of those horrible days. I still have nightmares being stuck in that room with poor Kristina's body just over in the next room. Maybe with Forrest gone now, I'll be able to sleep a bit better at night."

Fifty-year-old Katia had returned to normal physically working in the stores, helping around the house, and visiting with her grandchildren. Thankful for that, she would take long walks around the city and on the river—always with an escort (Jonas usually volunteered for this duty.) But, in quiet times and at night, she would remember her abduction and being chained in the dark basement. The faces of the kidnappers and her late daughter-in-law burned deeply in her memory. Doctors could provide little assistance or guidance for her mental state. They hoped she would improve over time, but they really didn't know.

While newspapers and telegraphs around the world were beginning to report on the assassination of the Confederate President, Benton and his group were just waking up in Southern Virginia. Leaving the Coffin children in the care of the Flanagans, the three men prepared for a long debriefing beginning at 10:00 AM.

First, General Stuart provided details of the assassination, the initial miles on horseback, the route north along the Underground Railroad, the Coffin children, the tracking by dogs, and the grenade exploding the bridge. He gave a thorough briefing that left out few details, but finished the story efficiently within 15 minutes.

Pinkerton's Frank Geyer then stood up, neatly dressed and looking refreshed. "First, I want to confirm to you that Forrest did not survive. The first shot hit him in the back while he was looking at the grenade. He turned around to look for the shooter, and the second bullet went into his heart. A third shot hit him in the stomach from the front as well. Two of his colleagues died at the scene before anyone arrived. The last one in the party has not yet regained consciousness and is not expected to survive. I commend you for very accurate shooting and escaping without detection, gentlemen."

"The Confederacy announced a national hunt for the assassins. We have engaged the Danville army base to thwart any searches over the border, and they will arrest anyone suspicious persons crossing the line. We will adopt similar measures with our other military bases near borders in Tennessee and Missouri," Geyer replied.

"Do they report on any physical account of our group?" Stuart asked.

"No, we do not believe so. The group with dogs chasing the slave children may have seen you, but we have picked up nothing over the wires," Geyer offered.

"I don't think they could see anything clearly across the water at that hour of the night, especially with the smoke from the grenade," General Stuart replied.

"One person definitely saw me, though. Before I fired the second shot, Forrest looked me right in the eyes. That must have been his final vision on earth," David replied.

Over the next few weeks, the Confederacy's search continued. To be safe, the group of assassins and escaping slave children stayed inside the Flanagan compound during the daytime. In the evenings, they would venture outside a bit more.

Ultimately, without the resources or a good lead as to the looks or locations of the assassins, the Confederate interest waned. The official investigation continued, but the active investigation stage had passed. No one ever identified or described Benton, David, or Stuart in connection with the assassination. With such a small group of Pinkertons, military personnel, and senior government administrators knowing their identities; Benton, David, and General Stuart did not expect their identities to be compromised at any time in the future.

By this time, the group had also dismissed concern that the slave catchers might try to cross the border and look for the Coffin children. The six that had walked those many miles the night of February 2 - 3, 1883 could now resume their lives.

Benton approached the children, as the group prepared to leave. "I made a promise to Mr. Coffin and I intend to keep it. I will remain with you until you are safely living in a good home. Do you have any plans for where you want to go and live?"

Terri stepped up, "Mr. Benton, thank you. We have been talking about that these past few weeks. We had to leave quickly, so we never had a plan beyond getting out of the Confederacy. I guess we need to look for a place to work."

The eleven-year-old's clear thinking impressed Benton, and he approached the three children cautiously. "You make a good point, Terri. But, I think it will be difficult for an eight-, eleven-, and fourteen-year-old to find good work. I have an idea for you to consider. My family has some money, and we can use it to purchase a home where you could live with me. I would hire an older woman to help around the house as well. Then, you could spend the next few years attending the colored school in Washington until you are old enough to provide for yourselves."

Terri stood in shock. "But, Mr. Benton, that's a big sacrifice for you. Are you sure you want to have the responsibility of three children?"

Benton had clearly thought about this the past few weeks and answered slowly but forcefully. "Yes. Since my wife passed away, I find myself with a lot of time and energy but with no clear purpose. I always spend too much time feeling sorry for myself. I will never forget my dear Kristina, but when Mr. Coffin brought you three to me, I realized many others face this type of extreme suffering as well. I realize that I can help, and I want to try."

The three children spoke among themselves, and Matthew arose. "This is a very hard decision for us to make. We have always lived together, but I think we each face different paths now, Mr. Benton. I think the city would not agree with me and I am too old to begin school. Being here with the Flanagans reminds me how much I love the animals and being on the farm. Mr. Beverly has taken me all around the grounds showing me the herbs and teaching me about being a veterinarian. He told me I could stay here and learn from him. He and Miss Nancy said they have no kids, and would pass the farm on to me. I really thank you for your offer, but I think I will make my life down here on the Flanagan farm."

Benton saw tears in each of the children's faces and felt some of his own fall on his cheek. "That's a brave decision, Matthew, but the Flanagans are good people. I know General Stuart's family in the area will provide you any help you need as well. You have my promise that I will take care of your little sister and little brother. We will visit you as often as we can and if you change your mind, my house always has room for you."

The children bid each other a tearful farewell, as the Flanagans and Matthew waved goodbye to their friends and family. The trip home would cover many more miles than the trip from Greensboro that night, but it would prove much easier resting inside a railroad car without Confederate pursuit.

―――――――⋘⋙―――――――

Just after the New Year, 1886, family and friends took Benton Steuben out to celebrate his 25th birthday at his favorite restaurant, John W. Ohl's, at 20th and Pennsylvania. Katia and Jonas brought along Sandra Trent, Sean Trent, and David Trent. Nathan's new bride, Claire, would also join the family.

Before the meal, Laura White joined Benton and Sandra. "Happy birthday, Benton. Nights like this make me sad to leave Washington, but I must move back to Manchester, Kentucky to run the family salt works. My mother Sarah finds the operations difficult with Dad gone now and her children scattered around the country. As the only unmarried one of the brood, I got drafted for this duty. I love Kentucky and I will stay active with the suffrage movement there, but I will certainly miss my life and friends here."

Sandra wiped her eyes. "I have never had a friend like you, Laura. We will make sure to stay in touch and I hope to get to Kentucky one day to visit you. Maybe, you will move back here someday as well."

"Perhaps. But, in the meantime, I will think of you as I follow this new company you just joined. I don't know how many people or businesses can afford $475, but that big black Burroughs Adding Machine with the crank is really impressive. Perhaps, if I had that with me for our math competitions, I could have beaten you," Laura joked.

Benton responded, "Laura, thank you for the birthday wishes and all that you have done. The time you have spent working with the Coffin children at my house has been invaluable. Terri is now the star pupil at the secondary school, and Jeffrey will soon be joining her there. Their faces light up when you come into the room."

"Kind of like the way, your face lights up when you see those children?" Sandra asked with a knowing smile.

"Yes. I hope I have been good for them, but they have certainly been good for me. I really enjoyed seeing their older brother, Matthew, up for Christmas this year. He is almost a full-grown man," Benton replied.

As Laura left the group, Nathan brought Claire over to his brother and sister. "Happy birthday, little brother. You sure have your hands full with work and taking care of the Coffin kids."

"Yes, but it looks like you do too." Benton looked toward Claire's expanded abdomen.

"Two more months. Just in time for the beginning of spring training for the Beaneaters' season!" Claire exclaimed, showing support for her hometown baseball team.

"I miss Washington, so I hope to be traded down here to the Nationals, but Claire still enjoys living in Boston near her family," Nathan remarked.

As the group broke up, Benton passed by David Trent who gave him a knowing nod and passed him a folded sheet of paper.

Benton just nodded back as he read the note:

TEXARKANA

More than four years had come and gone without any solid information on Rafer Allison. Intelligence gathering in the sparsely populated Confederacy was difficult, and Allison was not an easy man to track down.

Finally, in late 1885, Pinkerton detectives had come across Allison by chance, living near the Arkansas border with Texas. The Pinkertons had been engaged in that area to monitor disputes between the Indians and Confederates. Border skirmishes were common. For years, slaves had gained freedom by moving into Indian Territory. With the economic depression in the Confederacy, many farmers could not afford to feed and house slaves in recent years. So, escaping slaves were less of an issue for Confederates than Indians roaming through their lands on hunting parties.

The monthly report of the Pinkerton activities in that area sent to senior staff throughout the agency simply included a reference to a former Confederate Treasury official living in the area as a private citizen. Skimming this report as he did with other monthly reports around the country, David immediately recognized Allison's name.

A week after Benton's 25th birthday, David and Benton joined the Pinkerton team in the Indian Territory area and soon began to investigate Allison during their off hours. An older, semi-retired man, Allison spent a lot of his free time fishing. A man of routines, he spent every Wednesday at Pleasant Lake.

One Wednesday fishing expedition did not turn out so pleasant for Allison. With David carefully hunched behind trees carrying his trusty Winchester 1873 model rifle, Benton walked around the lake towards Allison. Slowly but not hesitantly, he asked, "Are you Rafer Allison?"

Allison had been honored as a hero from the Mexican War and did not scare easily. But, he saw something in the sturdy man approaching him that was unnerving. Never one to fear a loud and boastful man, Allison knew a confident man needed no additional histrionics to steel his resolve. This man approaching Allison had a stillness that underscored his competence.

Allison tried his best to be cordial. "Yes, sir. Rafer Allison at your service. I've been fishing in these parts for several years. But, nothing is biting this morning. Pleased to meet you, Mr. ..." He offered his hand for Benton to shake.

Benton did not smile or move. "Steuben. Benton Steuben."

Rafer Allison drew back, his nervous smile fading. He immediately knew the name—Steuben, as in Katia and Kristina Steuben. The greatest mistake of his life haunted him every day. He often pondered whether he would receive his justice in this world or the next. Benton's eyes told him the answer would be in the former. Allison had learned that Benton worked in the Pinkerton Agency, but he had never seen a picture of Benton before.

Allison briefly considered his options. He knew he couldn't lie his way out of this. Escape was unlikely because of his age and the terrain behind him. But, soon that consideration would be moot. Another man with a rifle pointed directly at Allison started to approach from Allison's rear. Allison knew his best option was to be honest and direct.

"I won't deny anything. You know who I am and what I've done, and I can offer no excuse that will satisfy you. All I can offer you are direct answers to any questions and my collection of gold coins," he said, digging in his pocket. "This key works the safe where I keep them at my home. You must know my address at 312 Hazel, at the corner near Clinton. I recently had the coins appraised at fifty thousand dollars."

Benton appreciated the lack of pretense that Allison displayed. He thought for a while before responding. "I cannot spare your life." After letting that sink in, he offered. "I have no need to soil your reputation or harm your family if you continue to cooperate, though."

Knowing these would be the last acts and decisions of a long life, Allison teared up while accepting his fate. He knew he couldn't save himself, so he decided to do his best for his family. "How can I cooperate with you?"

Not the type of man to beat someone when they are down, Benton simply nodded solemnly. "I have been trying to find all of the kidnapping conspirators for years. We know it went all of the way up to President Forrest. Larson fingered you as the direct supervisor, but he also said that you took your orders from someone else. It sounded like perhaps someone with a physical deformity that you found difficult to view? What can you tell me about this man? I need to find this man next," Benton replied.

Allison could not immediately reply. He looked calm, but he also knew the man they were talking about. And the memories of this man made Allison anything but calm.

Finally joining the other two, David said, "Tell us as much as you can remember about that time."

Allison had tried to forget those terrible months. His country living and fishing helped with his state of mind, but he still had vivid memories and nightmares of that time. "Forrest was a demonic man, but he employed some competent people in the Confederate government. You probably hear otherwise in your newspapers, but a lot of good people still live down here in the Confederacy. Anyway, living in the area, I knew some of these government executives, and they asked me to take on a position with their treasury in 1878. For a couple of years, I had a great situation with an interesting job. But, everything changed in November 1880. Forrest just became crazed once y'all elected that Jew, Benjamin, as president."

"President Judah Benjamin. A great man. May he rest in peace. We each had the great honor of receiving one of the casings from the twenty-one-gun salute at his funeral. Your country's loss was our gain when Benjamin moved from New Orleans to New York. Please go on," David replied.

Allison had forgotten himself. In a conversation among Confederates, Allison knew he could always criticize Jews in general and Judah Benjamin in particular. Between the rhetoric of President Forrest and the Confederates' jealousy toward the United States, Judah Benjamin had replaced Abraham Lincoln as the most hated American in the Confederacy.

But, Allison could tell that Benton Steuben and his partner were clearly not Confederates. He knew he would not have many more chances to make mistakes like that. "Yes, the late President Benjamin. Forrest's administration became focused exclusively on terror and military buildup. The economy kept declining—people even freed their slaves because they didn't have the money to feed and clothe them. Well, since we had no money—I was in the treasury after all—terrorism seemed like the cheaper solution to Forrest than establishing trade relations or developing our own economy. It also fit his style—guerilla warfare, he called it. He brought in a handful of loyal henchmen to carry out the bombings, fires, and kidnappings. Some of us government employees were forced to join as well. We didn't join the terrorists to keep our jobs. We did it to keep our lives."

"I see. Which henchman did you report to?" Benton asked.

"A young man from South Carolina who had suffered some accident a few years ago. He didn't have a left eye. The bastard didn't even bother to wear a patch. We just had to look directly at the red scars whenever he came to meet with us. They called him 'Pitchfork' Ben Tillman. He was just a wild young man—the type that would shoot his mother if she looked at him the wrong way. Forrest loved him, though. They both shared a fierce hatred for all slaves, Jews, and Americans. There was no limit to what they were capable of when they felt they were wronged. Tillman felt it our patriotic duty to carry out these kidnappings as quickly as possible. Boy, could he stir up a crowd when he spoke!" Allison replied.

"The same Tillman that led the Red Shirts that killed all of those Negroes in South Carolina around that time?" Benton asked.

Impressed with Benton's level of research and knowledge of activities in the Confederacy, Allison continued, "Exactly. He loved those Red Shirts—they were his people. Eventually, President Forrest instructed me to follow Tillman's direction for his special projects. First, they involved looting. Then, they graduated to burning and bombing buildings, bridges, and railroads. Eventually, they got to kidnapping."

Benton took out a small notebook from his pocket and wrote notes. "Do you know where Tillman lives or what he does now?"

Allison nodded. "He must have been in his early thirties in 1880 when I first met him. So, he must be forty or so these days. Once Forrest was assassinated, of course, Tillman's role would only continue if a Forrest loyalist took over. Once Rufus Cobb took over the Presidency from Forrest-loyalist John Morgan, Tillman left Montgomery quickly."

David nodded knowingly, "Yes, the days surrounding the Forrest assassination were hectic for us as well."

Something about David's nod let Allison know these two Pinkertons played some role in the Forrest assassination. He wanted to inquire further, but knew he was on a short leash, "Since those days, I have not kept up with Tillman and would like to avoid him forever. But, I understand he runs some illegal slave ships between Cuba, Brazil and the Confederacy. They say the market for slaves has bottomed out, but it still seems that some slavers continue to profit handsomely like Tillman. I don't know if he keeps a home in the Confederacy or just lives on one of the slave ships."

Benton responded, "Anything else?"

Allison thought a while before he answered, "Don't look at that left eye, though. As trained as I know you are, it still takes some time to get accustomed to."

Benton nodded. "I think we have enough."

"May I use a piece of paper from your notepad? We all want to avoid Tillman knowing that you found me. So, a suicide note can clear that up. It will keep my family safe from Tillman and provide you with the element of surprise in your pursuit of him," Allison replied.

David and Benton conferred and agreed with the suicide idea. David had a plan. "You can fill up your knapsack with rocks and then tie it around your neck. We'll leave you on your own to paddle the boat out to the middle of the lake. But, I think we will avoid the note. The suicide will be obvious with the bag of rocks if anyone finds your body."

"Very well," Allison replied as he walked over to his boat while he filled up his knapsack with heavy rocks around the shoreline.

"I don't expect forgiveness. You men have been fair with me. My life started with such promise, but in the end, it concludes with shame," Allison shouted his last words while rowing.

A few minutes later, David and Benton saw Allison tie the knapsack around his neck and fall into the water. For what seemed like a minute, they could spot air bubbles, but the bubbles soon stopped. Finally, the lake was still again. David didn't talk while Benton stared off into the distance for ten minutes.

David convinced Benton to take Allison's gold coins. "You never know when you'll need them. A good detective always carries a big belt with a lot of tools. Fifty thousand dollars of gold coins may be just the tool you need some day."

As they left Allison's home at 312 Hazel that evening with the sack of gold coins, Benton thought. "Only one left, but he will be the most difficult."

CHAPTER 13

NOVEMBER 9, 1888: VOTE IS CONFIRMED, AS GARFIELD BEATS CLEVELAND IN CLOSEST ELECTION IN 40 YEARS

"Eight consecutive wins for the Republican Party!" Katia held up *The Cleveland Plain Dealer.* "By the end of his term, the Republicans will have held the office for 32 years. We always knew it would be hard for Democrats to win a national election once they were associated with the Confederacy, but finally, they are getting close."

"I have a feeling our good-luck streak might end soon," Jonas said, as he curled one of the few locks of hair remaining on his head.

Katia, still tentative outside of her family and immediate friends, just smiled at her husband and squeezed his hand. She knew that Jonas had planned a special dinner that Wednesday night. Their children and their spouses would join Jonas and Katia.

Sean and Sandra Trent rushed home from work to get prepared for the family dinner. Sean did a little bit of everything from accounting to buying to managing at the Steuben stores. He lived a busy life either working, helping out with his family, or sleeping. He and Sandra were raising four children. Still active with her teaching at Georgetown, Sandra showed off the new calculator she was promoting to her husband. "Look, we call it the Comptometer. It has green and white push buttons."

Sean placed his eyeglasses on and examined the bulky machine for a few minutes by typing in numbers and cranking out results. "It definitely improves upon the P100 Burroughs machine, but it still doesn't match humans. Or at least mathematical humans like you and your old friend, Laura White."

Nathan and Claire also prepared themselves to meet the family. Claire was dressing the two girls for a night with their Trent cousins. "Nathan, I sure miss Boston with my family, the Commons, and of course the Beaneaters. But, having your family around has proven to be a great help in raising the girls. The kids love visiting Uncle Benton's house to see him or to be babysat by Terri and Jeffrey Coffin."

"Except for that one time," Nathan laughed.

"Yes, being placed on top of the icebox as punishment for screaming at her cousins will be an experience little Kira will not soon forget," Claire chuckled, as she finished up the last button of Kira's dress.

Nathan struggled with his bow tie, a much more delicate operation than putting on a baseball uniform. "I love being home in Washington with my family. But, the Nationals just don't field competitive teams like the Beaneaters. With the hitting advice from my young catcher, Connie Mack, I hope to finally wrest that batting crown from Cap Anson, Dan Brouthers, and King Kelly next year. But, I suspect we will still end up near the cellar. I feel worse for our pitchers—poor Hank O'Day had to pitch more than 400 innings last year and still lost 29 games."

Claire kept moving around the house trying to push everyone out the front door, while she smiled at Nathan. "You know I am usually a sucker for all of your baseball talk, but tonight we celebrate and focus on your family, Nathan. Remember, we are still in the offseason."

Benton had spent the past seventy-two hours investigating the rumors of potential ballot stuffing that always seemed to surround New

York's Democratic political machine, Tammany Hall. One of the few places in the United States to consistently vote Democratic, New York City had suffered through decades of political corruption. Benton had never spent so much time listening in on newly installed telephone lines. The corruption the Pinkertons found had not provided enough "votes" by deceased and imaginary citizens for New York's Democratic Governor, Grover Cleveland, to win the election. A competent governor with a new young wife and baby, Cleveland's personal scandals—he had been accused of fathering a child from an unwed mother—turned off many voters in rural districts.

Back at home, Benton sat with Terri and Jeffrey. "Are you sure you two can handle all six of my nieces and nephews? Some of them are a handful."

Terri laughed. "Don't worry Mr. Benton. You go have fun. Jeffrey and I will be fine. Remember, we're not the same little kids that came to live with you six years ago. I will finish secondary school soon, and we have both been working in your parents' stores for years. If we can handle the political arguments going on there, we cannot imagine any problems with your nieces and nephews. Besides, Geraldine and Augustus are old enough now to help. So, we really have four babysitters for four kids."

Benton smiled. "Yes, I should not worry. I have a lot of faith in you both. Feel free to put the kids to bed anywhere you want if we run late. Even in my bed. We will be eating up the river in Potomac, Maryland at The Old Angler's Inn. I know we have many good restaurants much closer to us, but my father loves that place."

Terri replied, "Don't worry. Besides, with all of their cousins around, those kids won't be sleeping anytime soon. The hardest part of my evening will be to pull Jeffrey away from your Pinkerton detective books to help."

Just then, the three of them heard a knock on the front door. "I think our first guests have arrived," Jeffrey said.

"Not quite. I just swung by to pick up Mr. Steuben," said David Trent, as he entered the foyer with a smile.

"Mr. Trent! You take care of Mr. Benton. We will handle everything here," the children yelled in unison, as they ran over to give him a hug.

"Thank you two. And remember, I host us for Thanksgiving in a few weeks. I just heard that your brother, Matthew, will come up from Ridgeway. Maybe, he can bring some of those herbs he grows on the farm to give me a little energy. I am not as young as I used to be," David replied, as he and Benton walked out the front door.

The Steubens and friends walked around the deck of the boat, as the group enjoyed the fresh air and the sunset view of the falls. David Trent passed around glasses of wine. He also turned around carefully to only be in Benton's vantage point where he pulled out a flask filled with Irish whiskey. He took a long slug and whispered to Benton, "I love your father like a brother, but the long toasts he has prepared for the evening will go down a lot easier after a little whiskey."

Benton knew that he could use more than a little whiskey himself that evening. He nodded to David and quickly took a long slug from the flask. "I just sit back and enjoy it. I could listen to my Dad talk all night. Some families tend to cut off long toasts by the old grandfathers, but you can always learn something about them or about history if you listen patiently."

David nodded. "Yes, your father teaches me something new almost every day."

By 7:00 PM, the entire party had made its way over from the falls to the cozy fireplaces of The Old Angler's Inn. After slowly walking up the spiral staircase to their private room with a window facing the river, Jonas walked to the head of the table to begin his toasts. "We are so honored to have our family and close friends with us tonight and we have a lot to celebrate. First, let's offer a toast to President Garfield's good health in his second term. He has proven to be a worthy successor to Lincoln, Blaine, and Benjamin."

Cries of "Here, here" echoed around the table, as David and Benton exchanged knowing glances with the mention of the late President Benjamin.

"Now, you may be sad to hear that I only prepared three more announcements for this evening." Pausing a few moments for everyone to laugh, Jonas continued, "First and foremost, I want to congratulate our dear friend, David Trent. He will be retiring from the Pinkerton Agency next year after more than thirty-five years. This man has made the United States a safer and better country. Katia and I could not ask for a better friend. Of course, Benton could not have had a better mentor in the agency as well. We are forever indebted to you, our dear friend. As a small token of our appreciation, I promise that we will always keep a well-padded rocking chair out for your use in our home during your retirement."

David felt so moved by Jonas's kind words that he felt he must offer a response. Nearing sixty with a full head of gray hair, David slowly stood up. "I never had time to get married or have children. But, I've never felt wanting for a family because you have always accepted me as part of your family. I can also assure you that the Pinkerton Agency remains in good hands with young men like Benton. He needed very little mentoring from me, but it has been my honor to work with him. I'm not quite ready for the rocking chair yet, Jonas, but I vow to spend more time at the ballpark next summer cheering for the Nationals to stay out of the cellar," David laughed.

The rest of the table—with the exception of Nathan—laughed as well.

Benton had mastered the ability to hide his emotions, but he teared up during the speeches and gave a hug to both of his parents as well as David.

Jonas stood up again. "Thank you, David. We know Nathan will lead the Nationals to the pennant in 1889 and take home his first batting title. My second announcement also concerns the Trent family. Sean, you have provided a great service to our stores these many years. From now on, we'll change the names of all of the new stores to Steuben & Trent, as we will be partners. We have plans to open up three new stores in the next five years."

Sean Trent did not feel comfortable speaking in front of a large group of people, and this occasion provided no exception to that rule. His jaw dropped at this announcement, as he stared at his wife in surprise. He impulsively stood up and offered a short toast, "Thank you, Jonas. As we begin this new venture here in 1888, I would like to offer a toast that Steuben & Trent will still be serving Washington in 1988."

After the toast, Benton noticed something awkward with Sean Trent. He had a suspicion, and when things had settled down, he moved over toward Sean after gesturing for Nathan to join him.

"Sean, Nathan and I want to thank you for all of the hard work you have done that have created the successes in the business. My parents could not have asked for a better partner. Congratulations," Benton whispered quietly while Jonas reviewed his scribbled notes for his next toast.

"Your family has been very good to me, Benton. But I feel uncomfortable being named partner and successor for this successful business. Your parents have two sons that would stand to inherit such wealth. I'm always used to sons inheriting businesses, land, and wealth from their parents," Sean replied.

Nathan smiled warmly. "Sean, you're our brother. This is as much your family as it is ours, and we know you will take care of the business our parents started. Besides, what would a baseball player and a detective do with a bunch of stores? I would talk about baseball all day with the customers, and we have all heard stories of Benton working at the stores."

The last story reminded Benton of the first time he met Kristina. He found that he missed her most during celebratory evenings like this night.

Benton didn't show his emotions about Kristina and Sean Trent felt better. So, the three "brothers" clinked whiskey glasses and turned their attention back to Jonas.

Jonas was far from done, and he saved his longest toast for last. "Katia and I arrived here with Sandra thirty-three years ago. We love the United States, but we have never traveled back to Bernkastel and Kues in all that time. Our parents are no longer with us, but we keep in contact with family and friends who have remained in the area, which is now part of the unified Germany. We only knew Prussia in our time. Katia has planned our travel and we will spend the months of July and August in Europe next year. On the way back home from Germany, we plan to spend three days in Paris for the Exposition Universelle. We look forward to Paris, but we have one reservation. We have been so proud to live in a city with the world's tallest man-made structure these past twenty-two years and the Eiffel Tower in Paris will eclipse it. But, I must confess that I really want to see this Eiffel Tower that will be nearly twice as tall. A final stop in England, and we should make it home in time for the end of the baseball season."

After the last toast and a long dinner, the guests made their way back to the boat. The temperature had dropped a bit, but with light jackets, the guests enjoyed the fresh air and views from the deck.

David joined Benton looking out into the distance towards Langley, Virginia. "I just checked again, and we don't have any leads on Tillman. I know it will be difficult, but you must remain patient and carry out a reasoned analytical plan to take him down."

"David, thank you, but I think it's time for you to enjoy your retirement. I plan to handle this one alone. But rest assured, I will come to you for advice. You've trained me well," Benton replied.

"I may not be your Pinkerton partner anymore, but I always remain your loyal friend. That will never change. Besides, in a few years, you will train a new young partner, I suspect," David replied.

"Jeffrey?" Benton asked.

David just nodded.

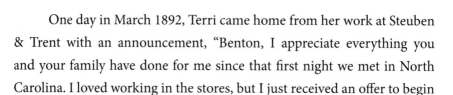

One day in March 1892, Terri came home from her work at Steuben & Trent with an announcement, "Benton, I appreciate everything you and your family have done for me since that first night we met in North Carolina. I loved working in the stores, but I just received an offer to begin work at the *Washington Star*."

Benton smiled and gave Terri a hug. "I'm so proud of you, Terri. But, I will miss you when you move out next month. New job and getting married at the same time? I remember those days. Exciting times for a twenty-year-old."

"Thank you. The election coming in the fall makes the timing with the newspaper perfect," Terri responded.

"Not just here, but in the Confederacy as well. It looks like they will finally set the slaves free there, but you can bet that will be heavily debated down there," Benton said.

"Congratulations, sis. Our house here will certainly get a lot messier here with you gone and we will be eating out a lot more if I can finish all of my schoolwork. But, I think you have trained us well. You and Ulysses have a great start in your marriage," Jeffrey said.

Two years later, Jeffrey Coffin walked into the house. "I now officially represent the Pinkerton Agency. I completed my final training today!"

Benton shook Jeffrey's hand, as David Trent walked in the front door. "I guess they don't need me back at Pinkerton's after all. Three generations of Pinkertons around this table."

Benton asked, "So, what's your first assignment?"

"I guess like most of us these days, I handle labor strife. I head to Pullman, Chicago on June 1. Will you be with us, Benton?" Jeffrey answered.

"Not quite. I have a twelve-month assignment trying to quell that family feud on the Kentucky-Virginia border. You know, the Hatfields and the McCoys?" Benton replied.

Pikesville, Kentucky would serve as Benton's base of operations for the next year of his life. Nestled in the Appalachian Mountains just over the Virginia state line, Pikesville was one of the two larger towns in the area. He and the Pinkertons would also learn the smaller hamlets, as well as the other relatively larger town known as Williamson, on the Virginia side of the Tug Fork River.

Tensions ran high in the area, but the mountainous terrain made transportation and communication difficult. The Pinkertons did not expect to forestall any violence in the hill communities, but they hoped to at least keep the town centers of Pikesville and Williamson safe. Nonetheless, they spent much of their time investigating the hills.

During one of these investigations, Benton found himself ambushed by two young men as he walked near a moonshine still. Despite Benton's training and experience, the two men knew the terrain much better. By the time he reached the still, one of the men pointed a rifle at Benton's head, "Pretty dangerous having cops up here looking around for shiners?" Twenty-two-year-old B.G. Ratliff snarled.

Benton didn't move as he assessed his options. Ratliff and his partner, Ray Bowling, could easily shoot him and no one could find him for days. So, he tried his best to lessen the tension by first raising his hands slowly, "Benton Steuben, gentlemen. I am no cop, but I am a Pinkerton detective." Seeing their eye-rolling pass back and forth to each other, he continued. "We have no interest in moonshine and we don't have the authority to arrest shiners anyway. Our engagement here only involves the violence between the Hatfields and McCoys."

Twenty-three-year-old Bowling replied, "We get awful cautious of people we don't know up here. Federal agents and even some confederate agents snoop around in these hills sometimes. They usually don't bother us much, but we don't want to take no chances."

Benton nodded slowly and tried his best to continue to diffuse the situation. "Look, gentlemen, I have no interest in disturbing your business. Please look me up when you come into town in Pikeville, and I will buy you a couple of drinks."

Ratliff looked toward the still. "We ain't gonna get a better drink in town than we can offer you right here. Benton, I bet you never tried moonshine?"

As Bowling passed Benton a small cup with a clear liquid, Benton said, "Can't say that I have. How does it compare to whiskey?"

Bowling chuckled, as he laid down his rifle. "Not quite the same thing. When we get moonshine right, you get a drink that is smooth going down, but very strong."

"Wow, you just found yourselves another customer, gentlemen. It tastes kind of sweet like lemonade, but you can feel the burn," Benton observed, as he finished his first sip.

"Even the Hatfields and McCoys don't argue about moonshine. You know, there ain't much to the feud anymore. The families mostly keep to themselves. The Hatfields over the border in Virginia and the McCoys here in Kentucky. Besides us, have you met any of the locals?" Bowling.

"Not exactly. Most people here seem to keep to themselves. I head out a few miles west to Manchester this weekend. Have you ever been out there?" Benton asked.

"Can't say that I have. But, I hear that is a pretty clannish area too. They say some feuds started over there in Clay County over a cow. You city folk may not think much of killing a man over a stolen cow, but when that cow feeds your family, perspectives change. Will you be investigating the Clay County feuds?" Ratliff asked, as a second cup was poured for everyone.

"No, just visiting an old friend. You know, I usually don't talk much with new people, but I feel comfortable up here with you two. Maybe it's the moonshine. Anyway, my sister and my wife made a good friend in Washington, DC years ago. This lady moved back home to Manchester about eight years ago. She sends letters, but none of us have seen her since then," Benton offered, as he twisted his ring.

"Married? I had you pegged for being single. That ring you're twisting don't seem like any wedding ring I have ever seen," Ratliff inquired.

"Well, I'll tell you I got this ring as a gift during my honeymoon. It was the last time I found myself in the wrong place at the wrong time—before the two of you had leveled your rifles at me earlier today," Benton joked "But actually, an old New York gangster gave it to me. The ring actually gouges out eyes. Or so he said—I have never tried it."

"Well, what do you know? I wouldn't let the Hatfields or McCoys see that. It might be just the thing to reignite that feud. And since you are away from home on assignment for a year, why don't you tell us about your wife?" Ratliff asked while eyeing the ring from a safe distance.

Benton teared up as he unfastened the top buttons of his shirt to reveal a necklace holding two wedding rings. "I always wear this necklace and I never plan to take it off. Twelve years ago, kidnappers took my wife, and she didn't survive the ordeal. Kristina was pregnant with our first child."

Ratliff now regretted his question. "I apologize, Benton. We offered you a drink and we want to be good hosts. I doubt you want to keep talking about that tragedy."

Benton had recovered by now and closed his shirt back up. "B.G., I think about Kristina every day. I found that remembering the special things about Kristina makes me feel better than trying to forget her."

The moonshiners could tell Benton needed to get back to town, so Bowling offered, "Benton, any time you want to get away, you just come join us up here for a spell. But, remember to shout our password as you approach next time, so we don't have to get our rifle out again. Just walk up shouting the number eighteen."

Benton stumbled a bit, as he passed his cup back, and slowly made his way back to Pikeville. "Much obliged gentlemen. I will be back soon and often."

After Benton completed his Kentucky assignment and Jeffrey completed his first assignment with the Pullman strike, the two sat at their kitchen table drinking coffee. Sixty-five-year-old David Trent walked in the front door and joined them. He nodded at Benton.

Benton began. "Jeffrey, now that you have reached twenty years of age, David and I want to tell you something. We never wanted to hide it from you, but we wanted you to be older for your own safety. Do you understand?"

A bit confused, but not making any noticeable reaction, Jeffrey just nodded.

David continued. "We met you, your sister, and your brother just after your parents had been murdered by the Red Shirts led by a one-eyed man. As you know, around the same time, a Confederate kidnapping spree also included the kidnapping of Mrs. Steuben and the murder of Benton's wife, Kristina. At the scene of the kidnapping, we learned some of the conspirators in the plot, but it took us many years to find the final piece to the puzzle."

After putting down his cup, Benton continued. "We discovered that a one-eyed man masterminded the kidnapping. It turns out that he is the same one-eyed man from the Red Shirts. Goes by the name of Ben Tillman.

David has helped me track him down over the years, but we haven't gotten anything clear. Tillman had traded slaves for many years, but we lost track of him the past two years with the Confederacy finally outlawing slavery."

"At my age, I cannot provide much help to Benton anymore. Jeffrey, we need you to take my place from this day forward. Remember, none of our conversation leaves this room," David added.

"Of course, you have my full loyalty. That is one terrible man. We must avenge our loved ones and track down Tillman," Jeffrey said with his eyes focused directly on Benton.

Jeffrey walked over to Benton's office at the Pinkerton building carrying a telegram one day in the spring of 1897. "I bring some bad news about our dear friend, Addison Coffin." Benton quickly examined the note and replied, "Yes, it was his time. A great man, and he lived more than the biblical 'three score and ten'. The world will little note, nor long remember the great deeds of Addison, but we must honor this great man. Quite a life."

Jeffrey wished to continue the conversation. "The note comes from his daughter, Ida Coffin Doane. He lived with her out in Indiana these past few years. I believe we should travel out to Indiana to pay our respects to his family."

"Yes, that is the right thing to do. Let's send a telegram out to his daughter and see if your brother and sister can break away for a little trip with us. But, they may find it difficult to travel with their families and their work," Benton replied.

Jeffrey and Benton coordinated their schedules and planned to leave after work on April 23rd on the overnight train to Indianapolis. Benton would alert the office chief of staff, Greg Farquar, as he and Jeffrey were walking out of the office, "Jeffrey Coffin and I will be away during the week of April 26th through 30th. If an emergency arises, we can be reached by telegraph at this station here in Indiana care of Ida Coffin Doane."

"Mr. Steuben, you have not provided the appropriate paperwork to request a leave of absence. The official procedures state that you need to provide three weeks' notice, approval from your supervisor, confirmation from the office manager, and …" Farquar replied sternly.

Benton interrupted, "Perhaps I did not make myself clear, Mr. Farquar. We do not *request* leave. We are simply *telling* you. Good day."

As they left the building, Jeffrey could not help but laugh as he watched Greg Farquar slump back into his chair. "I have seen that Benton Steuben look before when people take themselves too seriously and get corrupted by power. You do not stand for it. I half thought you might try out your ring on his eyes."

"There is a time and place for rules like in the army, but when an office boy who has never been in the field tries to exert influence over operatives that risk their lives, we can't have that. Being power hungry like that is bad, but not bad enough for that ring. I hope I will never have to use it," Benton replied.

Jeffrey and Benton arrived at Union Station in Indianapolis on April 24, where they met Ida Coffin Doane and her husband, John. From there, the four would take a local train for 25 miles west of the city where they would finish the journey by carriage to the small town of Amo.

After a short nap at the Doane house, Ida walked the two Pinkertons out to her father's gravesite. Following several minutes of silent reflection, Benton said, "Your father was a great man. He changed my life and the lives of the three children that took his name. We are always indebted to your family, Mrs. Doane. Please do not hesitate if we may ever be of assistance."

Ida Doane smiled and teared up at the same time, "My father led his life to help others. He would never ask for compensation for such acts, but his heart would warm when people like you, Mr. Steuben, made similar sacrifices."

Jeffrey then asked, "I knew your father only briefly, and I was just a young boy then. I learned some more from his letters over the years, but can you tell us a little more about him?"

Ida continued, "He led a very fulfilling life. As you know, he and his family tried their best to help slaves escape using the Underground Railroad, and he loved to lecture and talk about his experiences. Even in the past few years, he traveled to Europe on a speaking tour. The audiences excited him, but he had a more practical reason for his speaking. So many former slaves have moved into the United States, but they have little preparation for any vocation besides farming. With many of them settling in the large cities, my father felt strongly about educating them. He tried his best, but he always found himself short of money."

"I understand that. We were fortunate Benton and his family supported our education and upbringing, but few former slaves have such a luxury," Jeffrey replied.

Ida smiled. "Yes, my father always spoke so highly of Mr. Steuben. I have now taken over my father's role in the Friends Society coordinating these funds, but we always have a lot more demand for money than supply, I am afraid."

Benton reached into his jacket pocket and took out a leather sack. "My friend once told me that these coins might come in handy one day." Benton paused as he gave a large pile of coins to Ida. "I hope these will help your cause. I have been told they are worth about twenty thousand dollars."

"Bless you. I see my father chose wisely entrusting Jeffrey and his siblings to you," Ida replied, as she hugged Benton and Jeffrey.

CHAPTER 14

AUGUST 6, 1898: CLAY COUNTY'S FEUDS BRING EXPERIENCED PINKERTONS TO MANCHESTER AND THE NEARBY HOLLOWS

"Violence fills this county. With all of the murders, I find myself forgetting that less than 2,000 people live in the whole county," Benton noted to another Pinkerton detective, Charles Myer, also assigned to investigate and quell the fighting in Clay County, Kentucky.

"We had heard about these Hatfield and McCoy feuds for years and years, but this Baker-Howard feud here in Clay County has also been going on for decades. The violence has really escalated recently with six murders. The newspapers love these stories, though, of hillbilly cousins killing each other," Myer replied, as he and Benton faced each other sitting on two tree stumps. He adjusted his glasses and continued reading *The Lexington Morning Herald*.

The local authorities and the governor brought in the Pinkertons along with the Kentucky National Guard following the recent string of murders. Their first order of business was to establish order once the Howard clan took over the town of Manchester, Clay County's county seat, by force. An equally large and armed group from the Baker clan lied in wait three miles out of town. With the many hollows of Clay County, the authorities and the Howard clan would find it difficult to locate and confront the Bakers.

Benton spent much of his time with Laura White at her family's business, Upper Goose Creek Salt Works. A long-running family business, the Whites now had trouble finding workers, with the threat of violence spreading throughout Clay County. Forty-six-year-old Laura could not contain her agitation and fear. "The killing just never ends. The Bakers killed my poor cousin Beverly White, and then we murdered Tom Baker. The law really can't operate here with that type of vigilantism."

"I hope we can help the police put enough of both sides in jail just to provide some calm. But, in these parts, feuds continue for generations. We may only achieve a respite in the feud as opposed to a true ceasefire," Benton replied as the two sat in rocking chairs on Laura White's front porch.

"Yes, I know this feud will continue for a long time. One cannot easily turn off emotions, especially those involving family. For instance, I still miss your dear wife, Kristina. I know I shouldn't keep bringing it up, but she was really special to me. I will never forget her," Laura murmured between sips of iced tea.

"Thank you and you should always feel comfortable discussing Kristina with me. It hurts to think of her with the kidnappers, but I know she touched many lives. My father was right. I have realized my life since September 7, 1881, would never be the same as it was before. I have stayed busy, and I have even enjoyed myself a bit, but I know I can never achieve that same level of happiness. Being able to talk freely with good friends like you provides a good tonic, though," Benton replied.

"I understand and you can always talk to me if it helps provide some tonic. But, you had mentioned to me that two friends from over near Pikeville were coming by later today. Do they know your family?" Laura asked.

"Not exactly. Speaking of tonic … When I worked the Hatfield/McCoy feud back in '94 and '95, I got to be pretty close to these guys. Believe it or not, they operate a moonshine distillery out deep in the mountains," Benton replied.

Laura rolled her eyes, "That doesn't sound like a good start. But, you can read people better than anyone, so I'll trust you."

As they looked down the dirt road and saw two scruffy men approaching the house, Benton whispered to Laura, "Don't worry. They are pretty rough around the edges, but you'll like them."

Bowling walked in first, as he and Ratliff removed their hats. "Ray Bowling and B.G. Ratliff at your disposal, ma'm."

Benton sat down at the table. "Gentlemen, I want to introduce you to Laura White. We have been friends for almost twenty years now. Please trust her as you would me."

Laura noted the men in their mid-twenties dressed like hill country moonshiners, but she also noticed their trustworthy eyes. "Make yourselves at home. I will pour some iced teas for you."

"Thank you. It is our honor. But, first, Miss White, we both want to offer our condolences for your cousin Beverly. We saw how the Hatfield and McCoy feuds tore up the communities where we live, and we hate to see it happen here as well," Bowling began.

Laura replied, "Thank you. I appreciate your kind words. Hopefully, things will calm down before too long."

"Let's hope so," Ratliff replied.

"Gentlemen, how is business?" Benton changed the subject.

"Well, a lot tougher than the last time we saw you. We now have some serious criminal gang types getting in on the moonshine business," Ratliff replied.

"They hire young guys and arm them to keep the authorities away and also to scare us into closing up shop. I dare say quite a few shiners have either closed up shop or joined these large criminal gangs. I guess, if you can't beat 'em, join 'em," Bowling said.

"These operations have really grown. Some of them operate out of our towns around here—mostly Pikeville and Hazard. But, the big guys set up shop across the Virginia lines and into Tennessee. Mostly Johnson City. They can duck into the mountains there and work the Confederacy as well. It don't take much to avoid the law down there," Ratliff continued, while adding a touch of his moonshine to his glass of iced tea.

Benton was intrigued. "When did all this start?"

"Like everything else, it all changed kind of gradually. But I heard a man say the other night the thing that got this whole big business started was when the Confederates finally outlawed slavery a few years back. This man said that the big slave-trading operations needed another business to go into. Some went legit and others set up gambling shops, but most got into moonshine. I guess a man might only pay for a gambling shop every month or so, but he will pay for moonshine ten days out of ten," Ratliff replied, as he put his jar of moonshine back into his pocket.

Benton had a very small, subtle change in expression when Ratliff had brought up slave traders. Barely perceptible. His eyes darted just a bit.

Bowling looked quizzically at Benton. "Something about slave traders sure caused a reaction in you, Benton."

Ratliff added, "It was as if you were trying to hide it, but you couldn't keep the emotion in."

Looking around at all three in the room, Benton hesitated before talking. "This stays a secret among us. Only two other people know this. One of the big slave traders was a one-eyed man named Ben Tillman. He organized my wife's kidnapping and murder. I have been searching for Tillman ever since. Once the slave trade ended, his trail went cold."

Laura jumped in. "No one in your family knows?"

"Well, I do consider David Trent part of my family. But, Jeffrey Coffin also knows. He now works as a Pinkerton also. We found out that this same Ben 'Pitchfork' Tillman led a group of Red Shirts that killed Jeffrey's parents," Benton replied.

Bowling exchanged looks with Ratliff before responding. "Well, Benton, you know you have our full trust. Nothing will leave this group unless you want it to. Maybe this will help. We heard a one-eyed man runs one of the big moonshine operations. I can't remember for sure, but that name Tillman sounds familiar. Besides, how many one-eyed men are there?"

Benton smiled at the good news and immediately began to devise a plan to capture Tillman. Despite Benton's protestations, Laura, Bowling, and Ratliff insisted on being part of the team all of the way through.

The town of Pikeville hosted its big annual party that in later years would be named "Hillbilly Days". Kids walked down the dirt roads eating candy and ice cream. Some of the older crowd sat on benches in front of the simple wooden buildings. Beer, whiskey, and moonshine flowed freely from various tables on Main Street.

Benton and Laura stood near the pig roast, while Bowling and Ratliff watched the awards ceremony from a tent down the street. City Chairman, James Sowards, conferred awards to a dozen local children for perfect attendance and grades.

The large moonshine companies would not meet until later in the evening. Word of mouth quickly spread that the meeting would take place at the western edge of town on the banks of the Levisa Fork Creek after nightfall. Benton, Laura, Bowling, and Ratliff arrived a bit early to see as many moonshiners as possible, and even hoped for a glimpse of their target, Tillman.

Around 5:00 PM, Bowling spotted a group of men that he knew to be part of Tillman's gang. "Over there. Let's take a stroll and see if we can't get a gander on that one-eyed freak. We don't want to freeze in the moment."

The group looked all over and could find no one resembling Tillman's description. Finally isolating one of the gang members who had taken in more than his share of moonshine, they asked about Tillman.

"The boss man. Yeah, I never saw him, but I heard he is a mean son of a bitch," the man said. "They say he just changed his plans and won't be coming to Pikesville today."

Ratliff asked, "Did you hear why?"

"I never got the whole story. But, something about a Senator dying and him being appointed to take over," the man replied.

Laura nudged Benton, as the moonshiner went back to join his friends. "I read about that in the paper. Senator Joseph Earle from South Carolina just died. But, I saw no mention of Tillman replacing him yet."

Exasperation and frustrated boiled over in Benton, "Sixteen years I've been searching. We lost a great chance today. Finding him unprotected in Montgomery will be difficult. I feel like we are back to square one."

Benton had lost his concentration in his frustration, and soon six of the moonshiner's colleagues had circled Benton and his friends. With revolvers pointed at each of them, one of the thugs directed the group to walk through an alley behind a barn.

The moonshiner who appeared to be the boss walked up to Benton with a large knife and said, "We don't need no one poking around in our business."

Before Benton could respond, the moonshiner buried the knife into Benton's gut and ran away with his colleagues.

Bowling picked the stricken Benton up from the ground. "He is bleeding pretty fierce. We better hustle over to Doc Campbell's place.

B.G., you go on ahead and let Doc know. Laura and I will get Benton over there quickly."

By the time Bowling and Laura had brought Benton to Dr. Campbell's place, Ratliff and Kate York Campbell—the doctor's wife—were waiting on the large wooden front porch. They had moved the wicker chairs out of the path to the front door and over near the stained-glass window.

"Much obliged, Mrs. Campbell. If you and B.G. can give a bit of a lift, we can take the patient in to see Dr. Campbell," Bowling replied.

Inside the house, Dr. Campbell fidgeted with his handle-bar moustache while motioning for Benton to be placed on a bed. "Please place him on his side with his wound facing up."

"Now, I need the rest of you to leave my husband with the patient for now. I will assist him here in the examination room, but please just make yourself at home in the parlor or out on the front porch," Kate York Campbell said, as she closed the door to the examination room and propped Benton into examination position, showing uncommon strength for her slight frame.

"Mr. Steuben, we must cut your shirt so that I can stop the bleeding. This may hurt," W.A. Campbell said quickly, as he grabbed his medical scissors.

"W.A., they must have stabbed him with a dirty knife. I will first clean that cut out," Kate York Campbell alerted her husband.

"Then, we have to apply enough pressure to slow down the bleeding. Mr. Steuben must have moved while being stabbed. The incision is isolated to the side of his abdomen. So, that will help us. But the knife went clear through from front to back," Dr. Campbell replied as he examined the knife marks.

Kate York Campbell kept pressing down on the wounds. "I think I've slowed the bleeding down. Should I get your stitching materials?"

"Yes, but we need to make sure he's still breathing. He responded to the smelling salts. The breathing remains faint but consistent," Dr. Campbell continued to speak as he started stitching the back wound first.

Once Dr. Campbell completed the stitching, the Campbells left Benton propped up on his side and let him sleep.

"Thank you, Dr. Campbell. How is Mr. Steuben?" Laura asked nervously.

"He is fortunate to have been in town. He would have bled out if you had to move him from out in the hills. We will leave him to rest here for a couple of weeks before we let him travel anywhere," Dr. Campbell replied.

The group agreed that Bowling and Ratliff would look in on Benton during his recovery while Laura would alert his Pinkerton colleagues back in Clay County.

As Benton prepared to gingerly walk down the steps of the Campbell's front porch after his seventeen-day recovery period, he looked closely at the couple. "You have saved my life. I will never forget this. What can I do to repay you?"

The Campbells looks at each other from the comfort of their wicker chairs and smiled before Dr. Campbell replied, "We would ask nothing of ourselves, but the county recently appointed me to provide public health services to the community. I continually find myself running short of supplies to treat such a sizeable community. So, if you ever come into any money, our community always appreciates a small donation."

Benton shook Dr. Campbell's hand and then reached into a pouch in his bag. He then placed a pile of gold coins into Kate York Campbell's hand. "Please keep up your great work. I hope this can help. I understand them to be worth ten thousand dollars."

"Bless you and keep yourself out of trouble, Mr. Steuben," Kate York Campbell said as Benton left the Campbell house in the company of Bowling and Ratliff.

On the carriage ride over to the train station, Ratliff asked Benton, "Now that you feel better, do you want to go after that moonshiner who worked for Tillman? We got a good look at him."

"Not just yet. I have a better idea," Benton began. "Seeing how your business dried up and you both possess natural investigating skills and work well under pressure, why don't you come back with me to Washington and join the Pinkertons."

Benton happily brought back his two new Pinkerton recruits to Washington when he returned in April 1899. True to his word, he (with the help of David Trent also) managed to secure them both positions.

The Washington to which Benton returned had changed a bit. William McKinley of Ohio remained the President. The Republicans regained that position after four years with the first Democratic President in decades, Grover Cleveland. Nebraskan Williams Jennings Bryan—the Democratic candidate facing McKinley in 1896—was known as the greatest orator in the land, but he offered little rebuttal to McKinley's standard comment, "If you want to see what this country would look like when run by Democrats, look no farther than our friends of the Confederacy at our southern border."

Although the President hadn't changed, the city of Washington and the nation had appeared to grow up and move more into the international spotlight. Engaging in and winning a small war with Spain in 1898—the Spanish-American War—the United States now took on a more central role in world affairs—across the Atlantic and Pacific.

After showing his recruits around the city, Benton introduced them to his family. The new Pinkertons were excited to meet the famous manager of the Senators, even if Nathan had struggled to make them a strong team. Bowling and Ratliff met the rest of the family at the home of Jonas and Katia.

First, young Jeffrey Coffin approached them. "Welcome to the Pinkerton Agency, gentlemen. I look forward to working with you."

Next, they met Sandra. Worried about her reputation as a tough professor of math, the men tried to prepare for math quizzes. Walking over to the men with her latest "Addometer" calculator, Sandra just thanked them for being such loyal friends to her baby brother. Then, they spent fifteen minutes discussing Laura White.

The men had never seen anyone that talked as much as Terri Coffin Jones. However, they enjoyed hearing about her baby girl and her newspaper work.

Jonas and Katia showed off all six of their grandchildren. Then Jonas walked the men down to Steuben & Trent's original store. In the front, Jonas pointed to a yellowed photograph. "That baby is your friend Benton. We all went to see Lincoln's first inaugural address as a family. He sure heard a lot of boos that day. But with our successes coupled with the Confederacy's many failures, not many people question old Abraham anymore."

Bowling was impressed. "Mr. Steuben, how did you manage to make such a business empire with six stores?"

"Mostly through impatience and realizing there is no such thing as a good boss. Mrs. Steuben and I worked very hard in those early years. But, the Trent family, our own children, and the Coffins have helped us plenty over the years. The best employee we ever had, though, was Benton's wife Kristina. She would just light up the store," Jonas replied with tears in his eyes.

CHAPTER 15

JANUARY 5, 1902: CONFEDERATE SENATOR TILLMAN CRITICIZES PRESIDENT ROOSEVELT FOR DINING WITH BOOKER T. WASHINGTON IN THE WHITE HOUSE

"That man can't seem to keep himself out of the newspapers. With people like him leading the Confederacy, I understand why they have such suffering," B.G. Ratliff said while sipping a shot of whiskey at the Ebbitt bar at its new location on F Street. Not quite the potency of his moonshine back home. Ratliff had tried several of the watering holes in town before settling on the Ebbitt. The large "Old English" style bar was convenient to his home and office. It also boasted the best bartenders who knew their whiskey and beer. Ratliff had become fond of the local German brewery's Senate Beer.

Grabbing the *Washington Colored American* from his friend, Ray Bowling said, "I wonder if he truly believes all of the bunk that comes out of his mouth," he laughed in between sips of his fifth bottle of Senate Beer.

"Well, it's about time!" Bowling shouted as Benton Steuben walked into the bar with Jeffrey Coffin. Ratliff hid the newspaper away from Benton's vantage point.

"Yeah, you got a lot of catching up to do," Bowling added while passing Benton and Jeffrey each a new bottle of beer.

"B.G., I appreciate the attempt, but you know you can't hide that newspaper from me. Even if you were sober, I read your 'tells' too well for you to put something past me. But, don't worry, I've seen the papers today. More pronouncements from our favorite Confederate. I'm going to have my hands full getting at him," Benton bemoaned.

"*We* are going to have our hands full," Jeffrey Coffin said, while joining his colleagues.

"Thank you, and I appreciate that more than you know. But, isn't that you, Jeffrey, in the newspaper picture providing security for Booker T. Washington?" Benton offered, as he squinted at the newspaper article.

Ratliff grabbed the newspaper "You're right, I'll be damned. Our Pinkerton brother right there in the picture!"

The four Pinkertons clinked their glasses before the bartender interrupted them. "Mr. Steuben, your colleagues brought these Connecticut Pie Company pies for you earlier. I hope they got it right. Blueberry I think. Happy birthday."

"Thanks, Sam for reminding me I just hit 41. Blueberry is right. That Copperthite fellow who started the company can sure bake a mean pie. Let's dig in," Benton smiled as he replied.

"Not without us," Nathan screamed, as he and Sandra made their way over to the loud group of Pinkertons at the bar.

"I thought you were going to relegate me to the kids' table just like Dad did to me on my fortieth birthday party," Sandra laughed, as she took a choice seat at the bar.

"Yes, and Dad blamed me again for spilling grape juice that same night. This time when the waiter spilled grape juice on the kids," Nathan laughed.

"Let's make sure to save a slice for him and Mom. Dad loves those pies, but at seventy-one, I definitely see him slowing down," Benton countered.

On a cold day in early December 1905, the Steuben family and friends gathered for Jonas' funeral. He had declined in health for several years, but never appeared to suffer. Although the family had time to prepare, when the time came, it was a devastating blow. Katia, in particular, found returning to normal a difficult process, as she had lost her spouse of more than 50 years.

Benton felt a calming sadness in the coming months. He would miss talking with his father. He knew that no one could fill the void for the many conversations Benton could also have with his father. He knew this feeling felt different and more natural than the anger and sadness with Kristina twenty-three years ago. As he told David Trent, "I sorely miss Dad every day and I think about him all of the time. But, most of those thoughts are positive about how proud I am of him, how he had lived a full and worthy life, and how his passing was a natural event. I feel very fortunate to have had him as a father for these forty-four years. No one could ask for more."

David had known Jonas for even longer and this would hit him very hard. "I share some of your thoughts, but I think there is something altogether unique about losing your contemporary and best friend. It really makes you feel old. But, Jonas enhanced my life more than any man. Not by blood, but he was my family."

"Yes, even though it has only been three months, I think I've largely made peace about my father. Twenty-three years has not been long enough to make my peace with Kristina's murder, though," Benton sighed.

"It kills me to hear about Tillman in the Confederate Senate. They make him out as a big man down there, founding a university. Clemson, I think, is the name," David replied.

"Yes, and they just hired a president of the school, a Woodrow Wilson. We will keep tracking Tillman for another chance. There is just too much security down in the Confederacy to catch him like we did to Forrest. We hope he will join some other lawmakers coming to visit the United States or Mexico, but nothing has availed itself yet," Benton said.

"You must keep a deadline in your mind. At some point, you just have to travel down to the Confederacy regardless of the dangers or consequences. Am I right?" David asked.

"Yes. Jeffrey wants to be part of it. Bowling and Ratliff too. But, if it moves forward down in the Confederacy, I will do it alone. But not while Mom is alive, though. She had to bury a daughter-in-law and a husband. I can't add a child to that list," Benton explained.

David nodded sadly.

CHAPTER 16

OCTOBER 29, 1908: CONFEDERATE PRESIDENTIAL CANDIDATE MISSING

"I got scooped on that story, I see," Terri Coffin Grant shouted while glaring at the headlines of the *Miami Herald* at the original Steuben & Trent.

"You don't get scooped too often, Terri. Whenever I think about how hard it has been for me as a female math professor, I think of your many accomplishments, Terri. Yours too, Laura," Sandra Trent responded while smiling at Terri and Laura White.

Laura glanced at the iconic 1861 Steuben family photo hanging at the entrance of the store and replied on her way out of the store. "I don't know about that. But, I hope the current mission that has brought me here will prove more permanent. Giving women the right to vote."

Holding the newspaper, Laura made a beeline straight for Benton Steuben's house. He had asked her to join him at 10 am for an unspecified reason, but now she had her suspicions.

When Laura arrived in the foyer of Benton's house, she felt a little disappointed when she heard Benton explaining labor unions to Bowling, Ratliff, and Jeffrey Coffin. "Well, get this. After all those years leaving those Southerners down in the Confederacy to stoke racial troubles, our own unions up in New York now say the same thing. I saw Samuel Gompers of the American Federated of Labor, just gave this press release: Caucasians are not going to let their standards of living be destroyed by Negroes, Chinamen, Japs, or any others."

Bowling replied, "Bah, we've been working labor strikes for the past five years. Those unions pretty much hate everybody. But, no one as much as we Pinkertons, who have spoiled their parties on many occasions. Well, let's at least be thankful for avoiding any serious violence."

"So far. Europe feels like it may burst at any minute, and I don't know how long the problems in Texas and Mexico can continue without some conflict. But, I think for now Teddy can keep the United States out of these disputes between other countries. We'll see what happens next year with a new President," Benton said.

Ratliff listened to Benton and tried to figure out why he had a feeling of déjà vu. Then, it came to him. "You know, you're not half the man your dad was, but you're growing into his role with them speeches. That just reminded me of him. I didn't get too much time to know him, but I will never forget him. I can't believe it has almost been three years."

Benton paused and then said, "Yes, I stop to look at his favorite family photo from the Lincoln inauguration every morning. Looking at his proud face with his young family, it sometimes seems as if time stands still. If I'm becoming more like him, I'm happy about that."

"OK, gentlemen, I don't think you brought us all here to discuss politics. Benton, there must be something else on your mind," Laura interjected.

Benton paused and looked around his dining table. "Yes, you're right, Laura. You're looking at the only people that knew Ben Tillman as the organizer of my wife's kidnapping and the murderer of Jeffrey's parents. I cannot thank you enough for keeping this confidence for many years. I wish to beg your indulgence to keep the secret a little longer. But, first, David and Laura must hear about our recent trip to New York City."

Now the Washington, DC chief for the Pinkerton Agency, Benton had accepted the assignment of investigating the Port Authority in New York City. Long a place of corruption and criminal activity, the astronomical growth in the city over the past several decades had only worsened the problems. A Democratic stronghold, New York City and its Port Authority remained under the control of Tammany Hall and its boss, Charles Murphy.

"Benton, this seems like pretty standard investigative work. Why is someone so senior like you getting involved in the day-to-day operations?" Bowling asked.

"I have a couple of reasons. Officially, the work exceeds the current capabilities of our depleted New York office. Crime has increased so much in New York that the local authorities truly cannot follow it. Big Tim Sullivan from the Bowery organizes much of the graft, and he has proven to be a very tough nut to crack. But, the other reason is … Tillman. He has scheduled several meetings there without his wife during late October."

Bowling's eyes widened as he said, "Damn, it's about time. That one-eyed crazy man fills the newspapers talking about the honor of the Confederacy and its Southern culture. I remember him actually saying, 'Republicanism means Negro equality, while the Democratic Party means that the white man is supreme. That is why we Southerners are all Democrats.'"

Benton said, "Yes, he makes himself an easy man to hate. I read a similar quote of his the other day, 'If all blacks were shot like wild beasts, the Confederacy would be better off, but that would be unlawful.'"

Ratliff joined in. "I ain't no Democrat. Never have been. Never will be. But, I don't think too many Democrats up here want to associate with that man—even those in Tammany Hall. He keeps barking up that same tree with his speeches to spark support for his run for president, 'We organized the Democratic party with one plan and only one plank, namely, that this is a white man's country and the white men must govern it.'"

Benton said, "Yes, losing that one eye didn't soften his demeanor. I can see why Forrest found him to be such a close confidante. They must have been like two peas in a pod."

Bowling and Jeffrey learned the itinerary and habits of Senator Tillman. He would stay in New York City with an associate, while they attempted to acquire funding for Tillman's upcoming presidential campaign. Deacon Reid would arrive with Tillman on October 18, and they would head back to Montgomery on October 30.

Ratliff focused on the timing and location to apprehend Tillman. Ratliff had become intimately familiar with the streets of Washington, but he knew little about New York. His Pinkerton training focused on the need for local talent and knowledge, which often led to the criminal element. David Trent had used D.C. criminals as associates as far back as 40 years ago, but New York required an entirely different group of talent.

A little research led Ratliff and Bowling to Dan the Dude Mulcahy's Stage Café on West 28th Street. Gang members from all over New York frequented this dark bar in the neighborhood known as Satan's Circus.

After locating Dan the Dude at the bar, Ratliff began asking questions about the waterfront and the various gang territories. After a few beers, he leaned in close across the dirty bar. "I need some help pulling off a job."

About forty years old with a compact body, Dan the Dude stared ahead silently with an expressionless face that the Pinkerton men surely envied.

Bowling tried another tactic, laying a twenty on the counter, "This round's on us." He gestured around the bar.

Dan the Dude's expression didn't change until after Bowling had bought a second and third round. "I appreciate your generosity. I tell you what. We get a lot of out-of-towners in this bar looking for help. Well, maybe I can help and maybe I can't."

"I want to start clean, so I'm going to level with you. My partner and I work for the Pinkerton Agency." As the room fell silent, Ratliff continued, "We don't have any interest in the New York gangs. This involves a long-standing matter with a Confederate bastard who is up here trying to get in good with some of your Wall Street dandies."

With the room calmed down now, Dan the Dude couldn't hold back his curiosity. "I got two questions. First, what do you want with him? Second, what kind of help do you need?"

This time Bowling jumped in. "We don't want to take him out for drinks. That's for sure. We'll need information and access. We want to get him off this island."

With Eastman Gang members Chick Tricker and "Big" Jack Zelig whispering in his ear, Dan the Dude responded, "We'd need a good deal of money to help."

Ratliff exchanged glances with Bowling and replied, "We have money. Your time and effort will be rewarded."

Dan the Dude nodded to Tricker, who said, "This ain't our territory. The Eastman Gang runs the Lower East Side. We should be able to take care of you on the docks and anywhere in that area where your man travels. Let's meet back here tomorrow and work out the plan."

Ratliff nodded and replied, "Nine PM tomorrow. We'll see you here, and we'll bring our boss this time. He'll fill in more of the details."

The Eastmans had arrived at a corner table before 9 PM. When the Pinkertons arrived, the Eastmans gestured Bowling, Ratliff, Jeffrey, and Benton over to their table at The Stag Café. The Eastmans showed some initial concern meeting with a Pinkerton boss, but Benton quickly put them at ease.

"Gentlemen, it has been a long time since I was last in New York. Back then, I met with a group led by Mike McGloin from the Whyos. I learned several years later that Mr. McGloin had died as a young man. May he rest in peace. But, he gave me this when we met for drinks at a place called the Dry Dollar. I doubt the bar remains in operation today, as it had already seen better days when I was last here," Benton said while showing the men his ring.

Tricker could not take his eye off of the eye-gouger ring. "Monk Eastman told me about this ring. On the street, he heard that Dandy Johnny Dolan had passed it on to someone in his gang. Monk always wanted to see it. Have you ever used it?"

Benton smiled. "You know your New York history very well, Mr. Tricker. But, no, I haven't used the ring yet, but I trust McGloin that it works. Mr. Tricker and Mr. Zelig, we need your help on this mission. It's very important to me and my partner personally, and it's highly secretive. No one but this table knows about the details, and it must remain this way. You can bring in other gang members to help on our work, but no one else can know why we are doing this. As a gesture of good faith and to get you started, please take these," as Benton laid out ten thousand dollars' worth of gold coins.

Zelig and Tricker knew a man's word was his most valuable asset whether he was a Pinkerton detective, a minister, or a crook. Any man that could speak this directly and trust them with such a secret was worthy of further conversation. Laying out ten thousand dollars of gold coins didn't hurt in building that trust either. "You have our word. Only the operations of the mission will leave this table. Everything else goes to our graves," Tricker replied.

Benton could tell his secrets would be safe, so he continued, "Twenty-six years ago, a group of Confederates kidnapped my mother and wife in Washington, D.C. Those days in chains during the kidnapping continue to haunt my mother every day, although she survived. But, my wife and our unborn baby never made it. All of the kidnappers have received justice except for their leader. Once I learned his name, we realized he had also led the group that murdered the parents of my partner, Jeffrey Coffin. But, this murderer has been very difficult to isolate."

"Bastard! Tell us more. Who is he?" Zelig asked while shaking his head.

"The name is Tillman. Confederate Senator Ben 'Pitchfork' Tillman. He's up here now with an aide or bodyguard named Deacon Reid trying to raise money on Wall Street for his campaign to be the president of the Confederacy." Benton pushed several newspaper clippings across the table.

"But, you don't want to kill him?" Tricker asked, while carefully taking mental notes without producing written evidence.

"Oh, we certainly will kill him. But we want to hear his confession first and we want him to suffer and think about his predicament for a while," Benton replied.

"That makes me feel a lot better. You can't let that bastard live. But, I think I have an idea. We will find out when Tillman will be down in our territory on the Lower East Side. Maybe we will get lucky and he will eat dinner downtown one evening. Then, we take him to our docks on South Street onto a boat. I don't care how tough that bastard is, after a few days alone with us on a boat at sea, he will confess everything," Zelig suggested.

"I like the plan. Please coordinate with Ratliff and Bowling so that we can move immediately when we have a mark on Tillman. Spare no expense. I have more coins where those came from. Then, we can look forward to a nice cruise," Benton said, as he stood up to leave the bar.

"Before you go, Mr. Steuben, can we hear a little more about your experiences with Tillman?" Zelig asked.

"I had planned to go out for a walk to clear my head. Why don't you join me and I can tell you everything you want to know. And please call me Benton," Benton replied.

"What? A Pinkerton detective walking down Broadway in the light of day with a boss of the Eastman gang. Aren't you worried about what people will think?" Zelig asked in disbelief.

Jeffrey, Bowling, and Ratliff just looked at each other and laughed. "Benton Steuben doesn't care what people think. We are his closest friends. He met us when we ran moonshine in the Kentucky hills." Bowling motioned to Ratliff. "And he basically adopted Jeffrey when he and his brother and sister ran from slave catchers and dogs. Don't get me wrong, the Eastman Gang deserves their reputation, but that won't bother Benton. He knows a good man when he sees one, and it looks like he put you and Tricker in that club as well. There aren't many better clubs in the world, so go ahead and be gracious and accept his compliment."

By now, Benton had walked outside of the bar to be joined by Zelig. "I walked these same streets during my honeymoon nearly thirty years ago. You can't quite compare to my dear Kristina, but I am glad to have you for company, Jack."

"My pleasure, Benton. Most tourists make a bee line straight to Central Park. Did you see it on your honeymoon?" Zelig asked.

Benton nodded.

Along the walk to the park, Benton provided more detail on the kidnapping. As they approached the park, Benton replied, "We saw a completed park back then, but it feels different now with all of your skyscrapers. We can even see some all of the way downtown from the middle of the park. What are their names?"

"Well, my friend, no one has ever mistaken me for a tour guide, but the Singer towers over everything in my view. That is the tallest now, but they say that other one under construction called the Metropolitan Life will be even taller. Seven hundred feet or so," Zelig answered.

"I can see that you are rightly proud of your city. These skyscrapers change the whole feel of New York. When I was a kid, I remember the daily progress of the Washington Monument and the politician speeches when it opened to the public. But, these seem more impressive with people working in the buildings hundreds of feet above the ground," Benton paused while looking around. "I seem to remember a park around here where Kristina and I sat on a green painted wood bench and saw the torch for the Statue of Liberty. She kissed my head and then we donated two quarters for the rest of Liberty's body. But, this area around that park looks very different than what I remember."

Zelig looked around and then smiled. "The park remains, but the neighborhood looks much different. The triangular Flatiron Building on that little patch of land changes the look and feel of this little park for sure. It causes such strong gusts of wind around 23rd Street that young men wait around that side of the building for women's skirts to be blown up. That is, until the police arrive and tell them to '23 skidoo.' Come, let's go onto its ground floor and you can have your choice from the United Cigar Store."

"Much obliged. This will energize me for our walk back downtown. Along the way, I want to see the Brooklyn Bridge," Benton replied.

"I know the tourists like to walk across. We can do that, and I can have us driven back into Manhattan?" Zelig asked reluctantly.

Benton teared up a bit. "When we came on our honeymoon, Kristina and I had the chance to walk to the towers and across to Brooklyn over the temporary paths they had set up back then. We agreed to wait and take a proper walk across once the bridge was completed—hopefully, along with our children. I don't feel right walking it now without Kristina. But, thank you for your offer."

Zelig nodded and chose to remain silent.

As they got downtown, Zelig pointed to the water, "She looks a little different with the rest of her body, doesn't she? I guess we New Yorkers can thank you for your donation to help complete her."

Benton spotted the Statue of Liberty and remembered his young bride dropping two quarters into the donation box many years ago, "We didn't give much, but it felt patriotic to help even that little bit. Yes, Liberty is quite beautiful."

Tricker informed Ratliff several days later that Tillman would dine with several wealthy prospects at Delmonico's restaurant on October 24. Opened in 1837, the financial crowd still favored it over many of the newer restaurants uptown. Tricker noted that his gang included chefs situated on the top floor of the eight-floor building as well as serving staff who would handle private parties on the second floor.

On the night of October 24, the Pinkertons laid in wait outside of Delmonico's. In the Wall Street business district, the neighborhood surrounding Delmonico's transformed from men in suits during the daytime to tramps, pimps, and working women in the evenings. Recent eastern European immigrants also crowded the streets on their way home from long days at work. In fact, this portion of New York was considered to be the most densely populated place on earth. But, on this night, Eastman Gang members constituted many of the people on the street. Benton's coins (he had provided another ten thousand dollars of coins two days earlier) bought a lot of loyalty and a lot of gang members.

Jeffrey watched a specific corner a few blocks from the restaurant. Soon, a tall gray-haired man with a Southern accent approached Jeffrey. "Boy, what are you doing around here? I want this street cleared of all of you New York trash!"

Jeffrey kept his calm, as he banged a street pole with his walking stick to signal a need for help. "I am going to stay right here."

The Southern man moved towards Jeffrey and warned, "Boy, it's about time these New Yorkers learned a little about a good old lynching. Do you know who I am?"

Bowling had just come up next to Jeffrey while Ratliff and two Eastmans approached behind the Southern man. "Now that I see your face in the light, I do know who you are. The bastard that stabbed my friend back in Kentucky all of those years ago."

Just then two of the Eastmans hit the Southern-accented man with brickbats to knock him out cold. "We will just call that an added bonus," Ratliff said. "We can take this one on the boat with us also."

As this group moved the man into a car, they heard voices outside of Delmonico's.

Benton drove a taxi and parked it next to Delmonico's after Tricker's colleagues signaled him from inside the restaurant on the second floor. When Tillman and his party finished their meal and left the restaurant, his hosts predictably deferred to him and offered Tillman the first taxi in line in front of the restaurant.

With Benton parked behind two other taxis, there was no need for concern. Eastman members drove the first two taxis away before Tillman could enter their cars.

Tillman called for his colleague, Deacon Reid, but let himself in Benton's cab after Reid didn't respond. "He's a big boy. He can get home on his own. Probably visiting one of your many cat houses," Tillman muttered to the cab driver.

Once Tillman closed the doors to Benton's cab, and the taxi had proceeded two blocks toward Tillman's hotel, Chick Tricker popped up from his hiding position under blankets in the front seat. Before Tillman had a chance to react to Tricker's pointed gun, Zelig had climbed into the car from the unlocked door behind the driver. With another Eastman guarding the rear passenger side door to keep Tillman in the cab, Zelig then applied a towel soaked with chloroform to Tillman, and he quickly passed out.

Benton drove the car toward the docks with Jeffrey now wedging himself into the front seat beside Tricker. At the docks, they loaded Tillman onto a large boat owned by the Eastmans. Soon, the party of six Eastmans and four Pinkertons had joined the two unconscious Confederates in the boat.

The Eastmans motored the boat away from Manhattan as they stayed close to the New Jersey coastline. Once the sun rose the next morning, Duncan Reid remained alone chained below deck, while the Pinkertons and Eastmans got their first good looks at Tillman—awake and agitated.

Bowling could not resist. "You must be the ugliest senator in the Confederacy. How the hell did you think you could be elected president?"

Tillman lunged at Bowling, but to no avail. Tillman would remain heavily chained during the duration of the voyage. His one eye bulged and then narrowed. He demanded, "Do you know who I am? You can't just kidnap the next president of the greatest country on earth!"

The Eastmans were starting to scream back at Tillman, but Benton politely gestured them away. He looked Tillman over carefully. Still full of strength and fire, Tillman's posture and his attitude clearly showed he expected to always get his way.

Benton had no interest in arguing with or screaming at Tillman. He only wanted one thing from Tillman before he died—a full confession. Benton knew Tillman's experience and ruthlessness would make this a difficult objective to achieve. But, as doubt entered his mind, Benton remembered the words Jonas told him many times, "A Steuben never says I can't."

Benton reasoned that a less direct and more patient line of attack would stand the best chance of success. "Sir, can you tell me what the temperature was in Washington, DC on September 7 of the year 1881?"

Bowling and Ratliff just looked at Benton, while Zelig and Tricker chuckled softly in confusion. None of them understood the reason for this particular question, but Benton had their full attention.

"You're wasting my time with this silly game. I'm no history teacher or weatherman, boy. Find your own almanac!" Tillman screamed, fully believing that the extra decibels in his voice would frighten Benton.

Benton focused his eyes directly on Tillman. "Sir, we live in a free country and you may certainly scream your responses as you wish. It may be that such screaming has scared people in the past to your benefit. I can assure you this will not be one of those times. We are grown men here. Let's not waste each other's time with childish intimidation and idle threats."

Tillman stared back at Benton, while the others on the boat whispered to each other and nodded.

Benton continued, "By midday, the temperature had reached 104. The oppressive heat made the streets deserted."

Jeffrey watched intently, and Benton's latest line of questioning gave him no further understanding of where he was headed.

If this meant anything to Tillman, he did not let on. His poker face remained immobile. "I don't live in that Yankee town! Can't see why I care if a bunch of nigger-loving Americans are too yellow to go outside in the sun!" he replied sternly as he lunged at Benton.

Benton remained in his current position, as the chains pulled Tillman back. "Well, you probably remember who served as president at that time?"

"Yeah, my good friend, Nathan Forrest," Tillman replied with a smile.

"I should have been clearer," Benton replied. "Not your dead friend whose assassins you never found. I meant the president of the United States."

"I think you had elected that Jew bastard, Benjamin," Tillman answered.

With that, Tillman received a hard right to the jaw from another Jew bastard standing next to him on the boat, Jack Zelig.

Benton smiled. "Sir, I am afraid you will become more and more acquainted with my friends with further comments like that. But, yes, Judah Benjamin had been elected in 1880 after he moved up from the Confederacy. I suppose your parents named you Benjamin in his honor?"

Tillman's face turned red. "Thems fighting words, boy. My parents hated Jews as much as I did. Unlock me and give me a chance to defend myself."

This time, Zelig's uppercut landed right in Tillman's gut.

"I think we are done for the day. Please take him back down in the hole," Benton said, as Bowling and Ratliff reapplied Tillman's gag and took Tillman below deck again to his holding room. Unbeknownst to Tillman, Duncan Reid also remained isolated below deck without food and water in a different room.

Benton and his colleagues continued this process for four more days. Each day, Benton would hint at various parts of the kidnapping without tying the clues together. One day, he asked about a Delaware telegraph station, while another he asked about Rafer Allison. To each of these inquiries, Tillman offered no information.

On the fifth day, the team dragged Tillman up on deck with the sun shining brightly. Tillman squinted his one eye while being forced to face directly into the sun. Benton then focused his eyes directly on Tillman and asked, "Today, it's barely 50 degrees outside. Imagine what people felt like on September 7, 1881, in Washington DC? Scientists say the only one thing hotter for man to experience than a 100-degree day out in the sun is to be struck by lightning."

Tillman's eye and mouth revealed that he knew, as he remembered burying his favorite daughter, Addie, a dozen years ago after lightning struck her. Starved, dehydrated, chained, and forced to think about the worst days in his life, Tillman was truly a sore sight to see.

Benton left Tillman alone. Jeffrey then took his turn with Tillman. "Red Shirts. Does that mean anything to you?"

"I'm not talking to no nigger!" Tillman screamed.

Jeffrey nodded and Zelig was happy to slam an oar up against Tillman's head.

"You may want to change your mind on that. I can guarantee you that I will be the last person that speaks to you in this world," Jeffrey continued.

"Tell me who my friend and I are," Jeffrey said pointing to Benton.

"I've never met your friend, but his obsession with September 7, 1881, leads to only one conclusion—Benton Steuben, Washington Chief of the Pinkerton Agency. Kidnappers took his mother and wife that day, and his wife passed away," Tillman said.

"Along with his unborn baby. But, go on," prodded Jeffrey.

Some of the blood drained from Tillman's face, as he heard this last response. "You got another thing coming, though, if you think I had anything to do with that or you want me to confess!" Tillman screamed, as he got some of his strength back.

"A great man named David Trent who trained me emphasized the importance to focus not just on the content of a person's words, but in their mannerisms when they speak. Sir, your mannerisms give away your lies here. Like most common people, you cannot hold your stare in a lie. That being said, it looks different coming from a one-eyed man," Jeffrey said.

"Fancy words for a detective. I never had you pegged for a dandy. Where I come from, son, fine words butter no parsnips," Tillman continued to rant.

Not having heard that Confederate expression before, Jeffrey and Benton could not contain a quick smile, as Jeffrey continued, "Well, maybe we can move to another topic. Your daughter. Why don't you tell me a little about when the lighting was striking her skin and hair. Did her hair set on fire? Was her skin sizzling? Or, did she burn to death immediately?"

"Bastard. You will pay for those questions. A Southern gentleman would never engage in such conversation even during an interrogation," Tillman stated, trying to look defiant with a tear in his eye.

"Perhaps. But, none of us on this boat wish to be the type of men you call gentlemen that made my family slaves, killed innocent people, impoverished an entire country, and stole elections. You will note that this boat does not travel through the halls of the Confederate Congress or out on one of your plantations with your sharecroppers. It only moves up and down the Atlantic coast of the United States while being steered by a bunch of Jews and Negroes," Jeffrey continued.

"You look like you have done this before. My only advice would be to take it a little easy on that stealing elections thing. You can meet a nice class of people stealing elections," Tricker whispered to Jeffrey with a chuckle.

Jeffrey sat down to make himself comfortable. "The simple fact is that you're my prisoner and too far out of range for anyone to rescue you. Maybe, you find it easier to think of yourself as my slave. You eat when I say and drink when I say. And like the slaves whose trade made you rich, at my will and discretion, I may choose to beat and torture you as I see fit."

Jeffrey simply motioned Benton, Bowling, Ratliff, Tricker, and Zelig to join him on the other side of the ship, where they ate a slow lunch as Tillman fought the glare of the sun.

A few more hours in the sun had weakened Tillman's resolve considerably. Days without food or water had taken their toll.

The Pinkertons thought Tillman had died, but then they noticed him breathing with his one eye open barely open. He now offered his confession in exchange for water. Bowling and Ratliff took down his confession:

Forrest was a great man, but he hadn't thought through all of his ideas. He wanted to go to the nigger communities in Washington, Philadelphia, New York, and Boston and just bomb a couple of apartment buildings. I told him Americans didn't care anymore for the niggers than we do, so try something else. Kidnapping rich white ladies would scare the tar out of most Americans. We found the perfect target in Katia Steuben, with her support for Republicans and the central location of the Steuben stores. The boys kept us updated on their progress by telegram—at least until the Pinkertons caught them. But, they both died when the authorities raided them. We were glad the Pinkertons didn't get a chance to torture them to give away our names.

"That wasn't the way I heard the last part. It turns out that the Pinkertons did get the name of your colleague before they let the kidnappers die. Rafer Allison," Jeffrey continued while looking at Benton.

Tillman shook his head in disbelief, as he continued his confession.

We continued the kidnapping sprees around the country for a few months, but then it stopped as soon as Forrest was murdered. My family and friends wore black in mourning for a whole year. The country was in chaos.

If I ever see one of the men that murdered Forrest, I swear I'll kill him with my bare hands.

"I don't think so. I first met Benton when I was a little boy in North Carolina on his way back to Virginia from the Forrest assassination," Jeffrey replied with a knowing smile.

"You? It can't be!" Tillman cried, as he looked at Benton.

Zelig and Tricker gasped as well, but remained silent, as their admiration for Benton Steuben only grew.

Jeffrey looked at the first page of the confession written by Tillman. "Next is the Red Shirts."

Tillman remained too much in shock to do anything else. Without food or water, he could not remember everything, but he gave away the names of more than two dozen Confederates involved in the kidnappings and the terror of the Red Shirts. There would be plenty of Pinkerton work ahead to track down these men—those that were still alive more than a quarter century after the kidnapping.

As he finished signing the document, however, Tillman made a noticeable twitch and soon his body tensed up. He was still breathing, but his arms, legs, and head, were all in a locked position. Tillman had suffered a serious and debilitating stroke.

Benton looked carefully at Tillman before addressing Zelig and Tricker. "Gentlemen, I doubt he can survive, but I don't think we'll get anything more out of him. I rely on your expertise to find a place to dump him. Perhaps somewhere that his body will not be discovered? I understand that is well within your areas of expertise."

By now, the Eastmans had brought Duncan Reid on deck, and he overheard this conversation while watching his long-time boss suffer a stroke. "You can't throw the Senator overboard. The sharks will cut him up something fierce."

Benton took off his shirt to reveal his scar. "Cut him up like you did to me back in Kentucky, Mr. Reid?"

Reid's face revealed the truth. He remembered the night in Kentucky and the stabbing. "I only stabbed you to support my boss and be as loyal as possible."

"You chose the wrong boss, Mr. Reid," Tricker replied. "But, I have the perfect way for you to perform one last honor for your boss. We will even move you over within his view so Tillman can witness your sacrifice in his catatonic state."

The rest of the team remained confused until Tricker whispered something to Benton who then passed Tricker the eye-gouger ring.

"For years, Tillman has been a hideous beast without his left eye. By losing your left eye as well, you can honor him. Maybe in some way, he might think that you two are the normal ones and the rest of us are the hideous beasts with two eyes. Wouldn't that be something?" Tricker continued.

"You must be crazy if you want me to pull out my own eyeball!" Reid snarled at Tricker.

"You're right. I wasn't asking and I am happy to oblige," Tricker replied, as Dandy Johnny Dolan's eye-gouger resurfaced after being underground and tucked away for thirty years. Tricker marveled when he took a simple tug and pulled Reid's eye out in one motion.

"You're crazy!" Reid screamed, "I have blood all over me."

"Don't worry, we will get you off the boat quickly, so we have less blood to clean. I hear blood can be detected for miles around by sharks." Tricker motioned and the Eastmans threw the two Confederates into the shark-infested waters.

It took no more than five minutes for the first sharks to arrive. After the sharks had taken a few cautious bites from his body, Tillman regained full consciousness. Then, the sharks began to attack from all sides. Within minutes, the Pinkertons and the Eastmans could see no more of Tillman's or Reid's body.

Ratliff stood in amazement and looked at Tricker with a mix of caution and respect. "Remind me to stay on your good side, Chick."

Benton looked in the direction of the sharks, as he spoke to his friends. "For most of my adult life, I have chased this man, and now it's all over. I don't feel a need to celebrate with the death of any man, but this does offer me a certain calmness."

Benton slept better that night than he had for many years.

When they got back to shore the next morning, the men all shook hands before parting. At last, Zelig whispered to Benton, "About that Forrest assassination …"

Benton turned around. "We will discuss it over a beer. But, that's another story that goes to the grave …"

CHAPTER 17

JANUARY 1, 1916: CONFEDERACY DECLARES WAR ON MEXICO

Benton, Nathan, and Sandra formed a somber circle around the ailing Katia. Wearing his Nationals baseball cap, Nathan tried to cheer Katia up and hold her interest, as he summarized the headline in the *Daily Times-Herald* from Dallas, Texas, Confederate States of America. "Apparently, too many Confederates have been moving to Mexico. I guess President Wilson thinks the Mexicans encourage them to leave. The paper reports that border skirmishes have continued there for twenty years."

Sandra added. "Yes, the newspaper says Wilson declared war in order to help his reelection campaign this year."

"I don't know about that. Remember this is Wilson we are talking about. He came to this job from being President of Clemson University, the school Ben Tillman co-founded. Wilson just thinks white, English-speaking men should rule everyone else due to their superior intelligence. He wouldn't even consider giving women the voting rights that Laura White and her friends just secured here. Ultimately, I think he just believes the Mexican people are beneath him and the Confederacy. He views this as a short war to teach them a lesson. But, I wouldn't bet against Mexico in this one," Benton countered.

"Well, now that you are sounding like Dad with your political and history lessons, I think Sandra and I will take a break to get us some lunch," Nathan said, and he and Sandra walked outside.

As his siblings left, Benton sat near the small bed where Katia propped herself up with four soft pillows. Finally, alone with his mother, Benton knew the time had arrived.

Benton took a deep breath and said, "Mom, I've kept this secret from you for more than thirty years. For many years, I couldn't tell you, and then I could never find the right time. But, I must tell you now."

Katia was very weak, but she perked up a little and turned to him. "It has to do with the kidnapping, doesn't it?"

Benton smiled. "Mom, you can fool everyone else with your lethargy, but I know you're still one sharp cookie. Yes, your kidnappers didn't really die at the scene. They told us the name of their supervisor, Rafer Allison. They said he reported to another man who himself reported to President Forrest," Benton replied.

Katia lay back on the cushion, pensive. "Us? You mean you and David?" Katia asked.

"Yes, David. I miss him every day. Well, we vowed to exact justice upon each of these other three men. First, President Benjamin called upon David, General Jeb Stuart, and me to assassinate President Forrest," Benton said.

Katia nodded. "David never told me before he passed away, but I always suspected that he had a role in that," Katia replied.

"Yes, for our safety, we tried to hide this from everyone for many years and we still don't share that information with many people. Only a few Pinkertons and some associates. You probably remember both of us had an out of town assignment for several months just around the time of the assassination. Well, a number of good men and women assisted us, but David's bullets killed Forrest in Greensboro, North Carolina," Benton continued.

"Justice," Katia said excitedly.

"On our way back across the border that night, we stumbled upon three runaway slave children. An older man running the Underground Railroad—the late Addison Coffin—asked my help to take these three across the border and to look out for their safety. The Red Shirts in South Carolina had just murdered their parents. The children took on the Coffin last name and the two younger ones became my family."

"Oh my. You experienced so much, and you were only twenty-one-years-old," Katia replied.

"Yes. Well, it took us another few years to find the next man involved in the kidnapping, Rafer Allison. His boss struck fear into him, but he gave away his boss's name before we allowed Allison to take his own life," Benton added.

"Wow. You still have one man left in your story?" Katia asked with her eyes fixated on Benton.

"Yes, former Confederate Senator Ben Tillman," Benton continued.

"Pitchfork Tillman? Why, they never found his body after that dinner in New York a few years ago …" Katia spoke aloud as she thought to herself.

Benton held his mother's hand. "Yes, one and the same."

Katia's pulse beat faintly, but she managed to gently squeeze Benton's hand. "I remember your trip to New York coincided with the mysterious disappearance of Pitchfork Tillman," Katia said with a knowing smile.

"Mom, the Pinkertons missed out on a great detective by not hiring you," Benton joked.

"Maybe in my next life," Katia laughed, but Benton noticed her face had gone very pale.

Benton knew he had to speak quickly, but he wanted Katia to know everything. "Jeffrey, Bowling, Ratliff, and I captured Tillman with the help of a local gang. Tillman eventually couldn't handle the interrogation pressure, starvation, and dehydration anymore, and he provided details and names on all of the Confederate kidnappings from that time. Right after he confessed, he suffered a stroke that required medical attention. We found a group of sharks in the Atlantic offering such medical services. They quickly relieved Tillman's suffering."

"Justice for our dear Kristina," were the last words that Katia uttered.

CHAPTER 18

OCTOBER 16, 1925: SENATORS FALL IN NINTH IN BID TO REPEAT AS WORLD SERIES CHAMPIONS

"Well, look here, Benton. A story about the World Series and they quote Nathan," fifty-one-year-old Jeffrey Coffin said, as he adjusted his reading glasses to *The Washington Star* article.

"You are lucky your wife packs your reading glasses for you, Jeffrey. I forget my glasses a lot these days," sixty-four-year-old Benton replied.

As Terri Coffin Grant entered Steuben & Trent, she joined in. "I can read this amazing story to you old men:

Washingtonians had celebrated a year ago in a game seven against Pittsburgh. The fireworks, champagne, and beer came out in full force just as they did back in November 1918 when the armistice ended the Great War and we celebrated with President Charles Evans Hughes. Last year's World Series celebration had begun even before the final game began, as long-time Washington player and manager, Nathan Steuben, willed his ailing body to the pitching mound to make a strong opening pitch that none other than President Herbert Hoover caught at home plate.

Thousands waited with bated breath for the same outcome in game seven this year. Pittsburgh had the home field advantage, but the Senators could send the ageless Walter Johnson out on the mound. Four errors prevented another heroic walk-off for the great pitcher. Leaving Pittsburgh on the late train, the celebration starting there reminded this reporter of the Mexicans in New Orleans in 1919 after gaining the Texas and Louisiana territory from the defeated Confederacy."

"That truly is some remarkable writing. I wonder what talented reporter could take credit for it?" Jeffrey joked.

"Well, I don't like to pat myself on the back too much, but you can believe your big sister put that one together, Jeffrey Coffin. But, I still can't believe those four errors that cost the Senators the series." Terri smiled.

"Congratulations again my dear. But, I think it is about time, that your brother and I started our workday. After all, we are Pinkertons. We never sleep. Please pass this on to your grandkids for me," Benton replied, as he gave Terri a hug.

By 1927, Nathan's health had declined significantly. He looked more like a ninety-year-old, but he had not yet reached seventy. He was optimistic that his health was only "going through a slump," just like he experienced from time to time in baseball. His doctors, however, presented the truth to his family. "We don't really know the source of his health problem, but the speed of his decline doesn't give him too much time."

In those last few months, baseball seemed to keep him alive, especially hearing about Babe Ruth hit sixty home runs with Lou Gehrig taking the league's most valuable player award. Just after that great Yankees team won the World Series in October, Nathan passed away peacefully in his sleep.

Benton retired at the age of sixty-eight in 1929. By then, he had out-lived most of his friends and family. He found himself visiting their graves often in Rock Creek Cemetery. These visits also allowed Benton to go back in time to visit with Washington's most famous and infamous local charac-ters of the nineteenth century. Friends that joined him on such walks found Benton's descriptions of the exploits of writer Henry Adams, Postmaster General Montgomery Blair, Supreme Court Justice John Marshall Harlan, and city political boss Alex Shepherd to be more entertaining than reading a best-selling book or watching one of the new talking movies.

Benton also started to spend a good deal of his time in this same part of Washington visiting old friends living at the Old Soldiers' Home. As he spent more time here and found less need for the downtown and Georgetown business districts, Benton decided to move out into this resi-dential area. Finding the neighborhood just west of the Old Soldiers' Home comfortable and convenient to the streetcar turnaround, Benton moved into his townhouse on 2nd Street NW in 1930.

Benton grew to love the usual quiet on 2nd Street, but this Friday, October 6, 1933, was not a usual day. Game four of the World Series with the New York Giants would soon begin at Griffith Stadium and Washington was abuzz with October baseball for the first time in eight years.

Bowling started the discussion at Benton's home, as he finished a cold beer. "I always feel a lot better after a beer. You know, I missed my call-ing. I could have just moved south and become a rich moonshiner. Hell, that whole country has been dry for near twenty-five years now."

"More likely, you could have moved south and wound up in one of their prisons—or dead. As you know, even rich moonshiners get their comeuppance," Ratliff replied with a knowing smile.

"I tell you that country produces a whole lot of baseball players, but not a whole lot else," Benton said.

"I hear people talk about our countries' shared ancestry, but it has been seventy years that the Confederacy has been on its own. That is a lifetime. Most of the states were apart longer than they were together. Since then, we have gained lots of territory while they lost much of theirs," Bowling replied.

"Alright. I know we live in Washington with a team called the Senators, but enough politics for now. It's baseball time now. Who knows when Washington will next host a World Series game? Terri arranged for press passes and good seats right on the first-base line. Jeffrey picked them up and he'll meet us in front of the stadium," Benton said, as the three old friends slowly raised themselves up to leave the house.

Eighty-year-old Sandra Trent had hoped to join the crowd for game 4, but she still felt a bit tired after having gone to game 3 the day before and staying for the celebration after the Senators shut out the Giants. So, as game 4 began, Sandra made herself comfortable on the couch where she fidgeted with her newest Monroe adding - calculator LA model. Soon, she could hear Walter Johnson announcing for NBC radio, "And Gibson catches Paige's fastball right down the middle. The Senator pitcher has fanned the side in the first inning."

EPILOGUE

FEBRUARY 22, 1938: MOTHER GIVES BIRTH TO FOURTH BOY ON NATIONAL HOLIDAY

It turned out that the story of Benton Steuben's life required more than a few bottles of wine over more than one Friday night dinner with the Peckertskis during the 1937-1938 winter. Benton found himself serving as the unofficial referee for the boys' boxing matches and ball games outside the Peckertski apartment. As the days turned shorter and colder, the outdoor sports transitioned to listening to radio shows like The Lone Ranger or Fibber McGee and Molly. But for the boys, nothing could match Benton's stories.

By the time the Peckertski boys finished the cake that Gussie had baked to celebrate Benton's seventy-seventh birthday in early January, the Peckertskis understood Benton as few ever had. Hearing the last chapter would be a special treat.

When the boys saw Benton sitting at his typical vantage point in front of Scott Hall at the Old Soldiers' Home on Wednesday, February 16, Stanley said, "Mr. Steuben, our mother doesn't get around very well these days. She's going to have the baby very soon. I'm not sure whether she can help cook much on Friday night."

Benton had been reading that day's *Washington Post* and an advertisement caught his eye, "Boys, I have an idea. Take a look at this."

They read the ad for a downtown restaurant named LIDO, which invited people to "COME DOWN TRY LA PIZZA." Pizza had never been advertised before in a Washington newspaper, and the boys had no idea what it meant.

"What's pizza?" Wally asked.

"Trust me—you will love it. Tell your mother we will bring in dinner on Friday to your apartment, so that she doesn't have to walk out in the cold or cook a big meal. The three of us can go downtown on the streetcar to LIDO and bring back pizza for dinner. Make sure to clear it with your parents first," Benton said.

That Friday, Benton picked the boys up in front of the apartment building with their brother, Melvin, and Adam Johnson, the Negro son of the building's superintendent.

"We told Adam about pizza, and he never heard of it either," Wally said.

"Yes, Mr. Steuben. What's it like?" Adam asked Benton.

"Well, Adam, I wanted to make it a surprise for the boys, so I haven't told them about it yet. If your parents will let you, I can bring you down with us on the streetcar to see and taste it yourself. We can bring back dinner for your family too," Benton said.

It took Adam less than thirty seconds to drag his parents outside to talk with "Mr. Steuben." They both knew Benton from his many evenings at the Peckertskis and from around the neighborhood. They also knew he had essentially adopted two Negro children escaping slavery while he was a young man, and that established a high level of trust in him. But the Johnsons did not want to impose.

"Are you sure you can handle Adam along with Wally and Stanley? They can be wild boys, Mr. Steuben," Mrs. Johnson asked.

Benton laughed and responded, "You are right, Mrs. Johnson. I'm not as young as I used to be, so it may be a challenge. But, they're all good boys. And, Melvin will help as well. But, I'll make sure to keep an eye on them. We'll bring back pizza for your family as well. It's my treat."

"That's mighty kind of you, Mr. Steuben. We're much obliged," Mr. Johnson said.

The boys couldn't sit still on the streetcar the whole ride downtown with the anticipation of this new food. They got to LIDO early to watch the pizzas being made by hand. Luigi Calvi flipped the dough up in the air before placing it into the large brick oven. A friendly man that everyone called Loui, Calvi let the boys each toss a ball of dough also.

Benton ordered five pizzas, and the boys helped him carry them back on the streetcar on an unseasonably warm Friday night in February. Walking back toward Webster Street, Benton and Melvin took the pizzas and asked the three younger boys to run ahead to alert their parents. Not wanting to miss any time with the pizzas, the boys sprinted towards Webster Street.

Benton smiled as the residents of Webster Street took to pizza like Sandra had taken to math—or Nathan had taken to baseball. While the boys polished off the final pizza slices in the last box, Benton finally finished the last chapter of his story. As he finished, he pulled out the framed, ancient photograph of the Steuben family in 1861 at the Lincoln inauguration. As the Peckertskis crowded around to put a face to the names from the story they had heard, Benton pointed to himself in the picture. "That baby Benton had no idea of all of the adventure and heartache that would follow. And maybe that's the whole point ..."

The following Tuesday was President Washington's birthday, and *The Washington Journal* interviewed Gussie Peckertski with her new baby boy at George Washington Hospital. Her fourth straight boy born on a national holiday was cause for celebration, and the newspaper carried that unique story in the evening addition with a picture of the mother and new baby.

"My husband and I hoped for a little girl this time, but we fell in love with our baby boy at first sight. We hope he grows up and gives honor to his name—Benton Peckertski."

When Benton saw the story and picture of the Peckertski baby in the newspaper the next day, he grasped the matching wedding rings on his necklace and whispered, "My dear Kristina, there is a new baby Benton!"

USE OF HISTORY

Unpardonable follows an alternative history from 1845 through 1938 as seen through the life of a fictional character, Benton Steuben. Steuben serves as the narrator of his life story as an old man speaking to a young family during the winter of 1937-38 with each chapter of the story being introduced chronologically by a newspaper headline from a particular day in history.

Whenever possible, names, dates, and places reflect actual history or history that would have potentially occurred in this alternative history without the Civil War. All but the main characters in the book actually existed at the addresses and dates specified in the story.

Of course, this alternative history changes some lifespans and careers. For example, Virginians Jeb Stuart and John Mosby occupy significant positions in this U.S. government, while Ulysses Grant makes no appearance in the newspapers of the time. Similarly, James Blaine and Judah Benjamin become U.S. Presidents, while Ulysses Grant, Benjamin Harrison, Rutherford Hayes, Chester Arthur, and Woodrow Wilson never do.

Certain events known to history either occur at different times or do not occur at all. In addition to the Civil War, Reconstruction and (U.S.) Prohibition never occur. These removals allow resources to be deployed elsewhere and cause, for example, early completions of the Transcontinental Railroad and the Washington Monument. Germany's failed attempt to divert the United States into a war with Mexico during World War I becomes partially successful in this alternative history where the Confederacy must spend those years fighting a (losing) war with Mexico.

The Peckertski family to whom Benton tells his story lived as they did in the book. The author's late father, Benton, was born in February 1938 in Washington, DC, after the family's last name had been changed to Becker. In 1974, Benton Becker would become a part of history himself as the young lawyer who wrote, delivered, and negotiated Richard Nixon's pardon on behalf of President Gerald Ford.

SOURCES

BOOKS

Alexiou, Alice Sparberg. *The Flatiron: The New York Landmark and the Incomparable City that Arose With It.* Thomas Dunne/St. Martin's, New York, 2010.

Anbinder, Tyler. *Five Points.* Free Press, A Division of Simon & Schuster, New York, 2011.

Asbury, Herbert. *The Gangs of New York.* New York: Alfred A. Knopf, 1928. ISBN 1-56025-275-8

Bartlett, Bruce, *Wrong on Race: The Democratic Party's Buried Past,* St. Martins Griffin, New York, 2008.

Carrier, Thomas, *Images of America: Washington, D.C. A Historical Walking Tour,* Arcadia Publishing, Charleston, 2014.

De Ferrari, John, *Historic Restaurants of Washington DC,* History Press, Charleston, 1999.

De Ferrari, John, *Capital Streetcars: Early Mass Transit in Washington, D.C.,* History Press, Charleston, 2015.

Dickey, J.D., *Empire of Mud: The Secret History of Washington, D.C.*, Lyons Press, Guilford, CN, 2014.

Hines, Christian, *Early Recollections of Washington City,* From the Collections of The Columbia Historical Society Reprinted with Illustrations and Notes by the Junior League of Washington, Washington, D.C., [1981] 1866.

Kantrowitz, Stephen, *Ben Tillman and the Reconstruction of White Supremacy*, Chapel Hill, the University of North Carolina Press, 2000.

Kelly, Charles Suddarth, *Washington, D.C. Then and Now: 69 Sites Photographed in the Past and Present*, Dover Publications, Inc., New York, 1984.

Kendi, Ibram X., *Stamped from the Beginning: The Definitive History of Racist Ideas in America*, New York, Nation Books, 2016.

Kennedy, John Fitzgerald, *Profiles in Courage*, Harper & Brothers, New York, 1955.

Lisicky, Michael, *Woodward & Lothrop: A Store Worthy of the Nation's Capital*, History Press, Charleston, 2013.

McCullough, David Mark, *The Great Bridge*, Simon & Schuster, New York, 1972.

Muller, John, *Mark Twain in Washington, D.C.: The Adventures of a Capital Correspondent*, History Press, Charleston, 2013.

Schwantes, Canden, *Images of America: Georgetown*, Arcadia Publishing, Charleston, 2014.

Simkins, Francis Butler, *Pitchfork Ben Tillman, South Carolinian*, Columbia, SC, University of South Carolina Press [2002] 1944.

LIBRARIES, JOURNALS, NEWSPAPERS, & WEBSITES

1880 Telegraph Map, Washington, DC:

https://www.amazon.com/
Poster-Telegraph-Washington-Antique-Reprint/dp/B00DKBZOAC

about Education site:

http://history1800s.about.com/od/railroadbuilding/fl/Why-We-
Have-Time-Zones.htm

alphaDictionary language resource site:

http://www.alphadictionary.com/slang/?term=&beginEra=1900&en-
dEra=1915&clean=false&submitsend=Search

Ancestry Magazine:

http://www.istrianet.org/istria/history/1800-present/immigration/
castle-garden1.htm

Art Now and Then:

http://art-now-and-then.blogspot.com/2012/11/octagon-house.html

Atlas of U.S. Presidential Elections:

http://uselectionatlas.org/RESULTS/state.php?year=1860&fips=51&off=0
&elect=0&f=0

Ancestry.com:

http://www.ancestry.com/genealogy/records/
addison-coffin_34934823

Baseball Almanac:

http://www.baseball-almanac.com/teamstats/schedule.php?y=1881&t=BS4

http://www.baseball-almanac.com/teamstats/roster.php?y=1881&t=BS4

Baseball-Reference:

http://www.baseball-reference.com/bullpen/1878_National_League

http://www.baseball-reference.com/bullpen/1881_National_League

http://www.baseball-reference.com/bullpen/1882_NL

http://www.baseball-reference.com/bullpen/1887_National_League

http://www.baseball-reference.com/bullpen/1888_NL

Boyd's Washington and Georgetown directory: containing a business directory of Washington, Georgetown, and Alexandria 1860:

https://archive.org/stream/boydswashingtong1860wash/boydswashingtong1860wash_djvu.txt

Boyd's Directory of the District of Columbia 1881:

https://archive.org/stream/boydsdirectoryof1881wash/boydsdirectoryof1881wash_djvu.txt

Boyd's Directory of Washington, Georgetown, and Alexandria 1903:

https://babel.hathitrust.org/cgi/pt?id=njp.32101077270567

Boyd's Directory of Washington, Georgetown, and Alexandria 1906:

https://babel.hathitrust.org/cgi/pt?id=njp.32101077270575

Boyd's Directory of Washington, Georgetown, and Alexandria 1908:

https://babel.hathitrust.org/cgi/pt?id=njp.32101077270583

Civil War Academy:

http://www.civilwaracademy.com/springfield-model-1861.html

Civil War Richmond:

http://www.mdgorman.com/Events/death_of_john_tyler.htm

Civil War Trust:

http://www.civilwar.org/education/history/biographies/john-single-ton-mosby.html?referrer=https://en.wikipedia.org/

Clay County Kentucky Land of Swinging Bridges:

https://sites.google.com/site/claycountykentuckyusa/a-wild-history

Congressional Cemetery Records:

http://www.congressionalcemetery.org/pdf/obit-surname-w.pdf

Connecticut Copperthite Pie Baking Company of Georgetown

www.cocopieco.com

Council on Tall Buildings and Urban Habitat:

http://www.ctbuh.org/AboutCTBUH/History/MeasuringTall/tabid/1320/language/en-GB/Default.aspx

D.C. Crime Stories:

http://dccrimestories.com/crime-history-dec-31-1860-d-c-police-nab-congressmen-shortly-pistol-duel/

Digital Library of Appalachia:

http://dla.acaweb.org/cdm/singleitem/collection/Pikeville/id/123/
rec/3

Directory of Greensboro, Salem and Winston 1884:

http://libcdm1.uncg.edu/cdm/singleitem/collection/GSOCityDir/
id/58/rec/1

Encyclopedia Virginia:

http://www.encyclopediavirginia.org/
Stuart_Henry_Carter_1855-1933

Fading Magic:

https://fadingmagic.wordpress.com/

Field and Stream Magazine:

http://www.fieldandstream.com/articles/guns/rifles/2003/12/
rifle-won-west

Find a Grave Website:

http://www.findagrave.com/cgi-bin/fg.cgi?page=gr&GRid=80693693

http://www.findagrave.com/cgi-bin/fg.cgi?page=gr&GRid=14497272

http://www.findagrave.com/cgi-bin/
fg.cgi?page=gr&GRid=113782679

http://www.findagrave.com/cgi-bin/fg.cgi?page=gr&GRid=48883370

http://www.findagrave.com/cgi-bin/fg.cgi?page=gr&GRid=9509202

https://www.findagrave.com/memorial/116981012

https://www.findagrave.com/memorial/19040713

Fishing Works:

http://www.fishingworks.com/arkansas/little-river-ar/lake/pleasant-lake/

Genealogy Bank:

http://www.genealogybank.com/newspapers/sourcelist/dc

http://www.genealogytrails.com/main/lastveteranobits.html#owenedgar

Ghosts of DC:

http://ghostsofdc.org/2012/11/26/history-of-the-telephone-in-d-c/

http://ghostsofdc.org/2012/09/19/washington-pizza-history/

http://ghostsofdc.org/image/zoom/awesome-1880-map-of-washington-streetcars/13709/view.jpg

Google Weather:

https://www.google.com/webhp?sourceid=chrome-instant&rlz=-1C1LENP_enUS578US578&ion=1&espv=2&ie=UTF-8#q=sunset%20time%20september%202012%201881

Greater Greater Washington:

http://greatergreater.com/images/201302/281019.jpg

Guilford College Hege Library:

http://library.guilford.edu/c.php?g=142981&p=1036364

http://library.guilford.edu/ld.php?content_id=8565070

http://library.guilford.edu/c.php?g=142981&p=1419135

Humanities Kentucky:

https://networks.h-net.org/node/2289/discussions/171682/
john-daugherty-white-clay-county-and-louisville-advocate-woman

Internet Archive Wayback Machine:

http://web.archive.org/web/20100208205253/http://www.endex.com/
gf/buildings/bbridge/bbridgefacts.htm

Laurel County (Kentucky) History:

http://laurelcokyhistorymuseum.org/2016/02/11/
laura-r-white-teacher-scholar-architect/

Laurel Hill Home of Jeb Stuart Website:

http://www.jebstuart.org/

Library of Congress:

http://chroniclingamerica.loc.gov/lccn/sn82014760/

National Governors Association:

https://www.nga.org/cms/home/governors/past-governors-bios/
page_alabama/col2-content/main-content-list/title_cobb_rufus.
default.html

National Park Service:

https://www.nps.gov/parkhistory/online_books/wamo/wash_hsr1.
pdf

https://www.nps.gov/nr/travel/indianapolis/unionstation.htm

https://www.nps.gov/stli/index.htm

National Weather Service:

http://www.weather.gov/lwx/winter_DC-Winters

NCpedia:

http://ncpedia.org/biography/rondthaler-edward

NY.com:

https://www.ny.com/articles/centralpark.html

Office Machines America:

http://officemachinemanuals.com/catalog/monroe.htm

Pike County Health Department:

http://www.pikecountyhealth.com/v3/index.php?page=history

Radio History:

https://www.old-time.com/halper/halper37.html

Steak Perfection:

http://www.steakperfection.com/delmonico/History.html

Streets of Washington, Stories and images of historic Washington, D.C.

http://www.streetsofwashington.com/2011/08/scott-hall-at-soldiers-home-damaged-in.html

http://www.streetsofwashington.com/2014/08/the-heyday-of-german-restaurants-in.html

Texas State Historical Association:

https://tshaonline.org/handbook/online/articles/eed13

The American Presidency Project:

http://www.presidency.ucsb.edu/showelection.php?year=1860

The Bowery Boys: New York City History:

http://www.boweryboyshistory.com/2016/05/podcast-rewind-wrath-whyos-vicious-gang-new-york.html

the Calculator site:

http://www.thecalculatorsite.com/articles/units/history-of-the-calculator.php

The Cooper Union site:

http://cooper.edu/about/history/foundation-building-great-hall

The Georgetown Metropolitan:

https://georgetownmetropolitan.com/2009/01/03/is-it-dumbarton-st-or-avenue/

The History Channel:

http://www.history.com/this-day-in-history/herbert-hoover-has-telephone-installed-in-oval-office

http://www.history.com/news/history-lists/7-infamous-gangs-of-new-york

The Portal to Texas History:

https://texashistory.unt.edu/ark:/67531/metapth547728/m1/1/

The Railroad System of Texas Map, Chicago: Rand McNally & Co., 1883 for *The Galveston News:*

http://alabamamaps.ua.edu/historicalmaps/us_states/texas/index2_1876-1885.htm

The USGenWeb Sites:

http://www.theusgenweb.org/dcgenweb/history/school/school_list.shtml

The Washington Post:

https://www.washingtonpost.com/lifestyle/food/resurrecting-a-slice-of-history-easy-as-pie/2012/01/31/gIQAYb5ywQ_story.html

The Washington Post Magazine:

November 15, 2015 The White House Museum Website:

http://www.whitehousemuseum.org/floor2/lincoln-bedroom.htm

The White House Website:

https://www.whitehouse.gov/1600/eeob

United States Senate:

http://www.senate.gov/artandhistory/history/minute/The_Caning_of_Senator_Charles_Sumner.htm

University of North Carolina, Documenting the American South:

http://docsouth.unc.edu/nc/coffin/menu.html

Vintage Calculators Web Museum:

http://www.vintagecalculators.com/html/addometer.html

Washington Kaleidoscope:

https://dckaleidoscope.wordpress.com/category/art-architecture/buildings-by-type/hotels/

Welcome to Bernkastel-Kues:

http://en.bernkastel.de/holiday-region/bernkastel-kues/what-to-see/ruins-of-landshut-castle-burg-landshut-express-landshut-castle-express.html

Welcome to Leaksville, North Carolina:

http://www.leaksville.com/leaksville_covered_bridge_1937.htm

West Virginia Division of Culture and History:

http://www.wvculture.org/history/statehood/statehood03.html

Wikipedia:

https://en.wikipedia.org/wiki/Josiah_Dent

https://en.wikipedia.org/wiki/Chick_Tricker

https://en.wikipedia.org/wiki/Dan_the_Dude

https://en.wikipedia.org/wiki/Ida_Burger

https://en.wikipedia.org/wiki/List_of_mayors_of_Washington,_D.C.#1802.E2.80.931871:_Mayors_of_the_City_of_Washington

https://en.wikipedia.org/wiki/The_Buffalo_News

https://en.wikipedia.org/wiki/List_of_the_oldest_newspapers#Europe

https://en.wikipedia.org/wiki/Streetcars_in_Washington,_D.C

https://upload.wikimedia.org/wikipedia/commons/5/57/1850_Mitchell_Map_of_Washington_D.C._%5E_Georgetown_-_Geographicus_-_WashingtonDC-m-1850.jpg

https://en.wikipedia.org/wiki/Whyos

YesterYear Once More:

https://yesteryearsnews.wordpress.com/2009/07/20/
baker-howard-feud/